Secrets of St. Joe

Charles Farley

Pineapple Press, Inc.

Sarasota, Florida

Inquiries should be addressed to:
Pineapple Press, Inc.
P.O. Box 3889
Sarasota, Florida 34230

www.pineapplepress.com

Library of Congress Cataloging-in-Publication Data

Farley, Charles, 1945–
    Secrets of St. Joe / Charles Farley.
        p. cm.
    ISBN 978-1-56164-727-9 (pbk. : alk. paper)
1. Murderers—Fiction. 2. Physicians—Crimes against—Fiction. 3. Port Saint Joe (Fla.)—Fiction. I. Title.

PS3606.A695S435 2014
813'.6—dc23

                                                              2014016375

First Edition
10 9 8 7 6 5 4 3 2 1

Design by She' Hicks

Printed in the United States

Author's Note

Although parts of the following story are based on actual events that occurred in and around Port St. Joe, Florida, in 1939, the rest is fiction.

Three may keep a secret if two of them are dead.
—*Benjamin Franklin*

Now was the time. He would make them pay, to suffer, to bleed like the tears from his bitter eyes. He would no longer be afraid, no longer cower, no longer be at their mercy. Instead he would watch them face the whirling saw, watch them cry out for mercy, watch their red blood splatter against the walls, so that he at long last could be free.

And liberty plucks justice by the nose;
The baby beats the nurse, and quite athwart
Goes all decorum.
—Shakespeare, *Measure for Measure,* I.iii.23

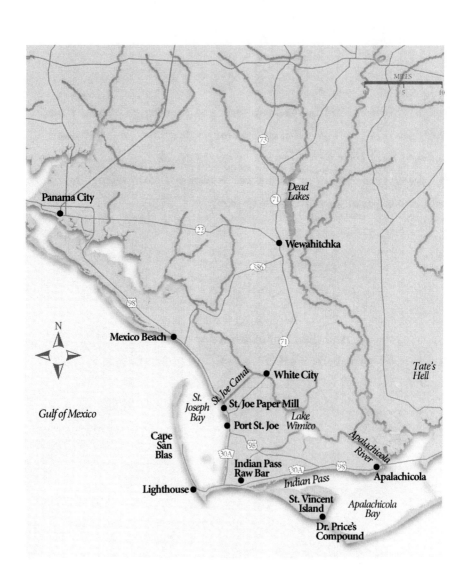

MILES
0   5   10

73

Dead
Lakes

71

Panama City ●

22

Wewahitchka ●

386

98

N

Mexico Beach ●

71

White City ●

St. Joe Canal

St.
Joseph
Bay

St. Joe Paper Mill ●

Tate's
Hell

Gulf of Mexico

Lake
Wimico

Port St. Joe ●

Apalachicola
River

Cape
San
Blas

98

30A

Indian Pass
Raw Bar ●

30A

98

Lighthouse ●

Indian Pass

Apalachicola ●

St. Vincent
Island ●

Apalachicola
Bay

Dr. Price's
Compound ●

Chapter 1

The doctor was dying. Of that there was no doubt. It was just a matter of time. And the way that he was feeling of late, that final moment couldn't come any too soon. The stiffening in his neck kept him from seeing anything behind him without turning his entire body around. All of his muscles tightened whenever he was idle for any length of time, making every new movement an exercise in agony. The outside of his right calf was permanently numb. Despite his diminished hearing, he could still clearly hear his bones protest as he descended the stairs from his bedroom to the kitchen below—quick snapping pops like brittle branches being broken abruptly in half. His stomach and throat burned from breakfast to bedtime, no matter what he ate or what he drank. His sinuses were constantly clogged, so that he couldn't smell much of anything, good or bad. And worse than all that, his heart continued to ache as it had every day since his housekeeper and best friend, Jewel Jackson, had abandoned him—now more than a year ago—to follow her blues-belting boyfriend, Gabriel White, to New York City.

So here he was, alone—or almost so—on this sunny, summer morning, down in swampy, sorry Port St. Joe, on the Gulf side of Florida's provincial Panhandle where, if it hadn't been for the opening of the town's new paper mill just over a year ago, there would not have been much more

than a few fishermen and lumberjacks, bugs as big as buzzards, oysters and
scallops as sweet as tupelo honey, which was collected each spring just a
few miles north along the Chipola and Apalachicola River bottoms, and,
nearby on Cape San Blas, the most beautiful, wide, white-sand beaches in
the world. Thankfully, he still had the occasional company of his fishing
and hunting buddy, Gator Mica, a half-breed Seminole Indian who had
taken up residence on nearby St. Vincent Island as the caretaker of the
notorious Dr. Price's livestock and oyster harvesting operations.

And he had Vivian Jackson, the young Negro girl, somehow
distantly related to Jewel, whom Jewel had found to take her place as
the doctor's housekeeper and cook. The shy, slight teenager, having been
just graduated from North Port St. Joe's shabby, three-room school for
colored students, was as introverted as Jewel was outgoing. But she was
quick and efficient—he had to give her that—much more so than Jewel,
if truth be told. She could accomplish in an hour what it used to take
Jewel all day to plow through, since Jewel spent a lot of her time chatting
and gossiping with whomever she came in contact with, whereas Vivian
conducted her business like a stealthy spy, inconspicuously infiltrating
her surroundings unseen and unheard by most everyone around her.
She couldn't cook as well as Jewel—few could—but she did okay. So
the doctor wasn't complaining, but he did wish the girl would speak up
more, because he did terribly miss talking and laughing and just being
with Jewel. And at times he was still angry at his former housekeeper
and companion for taking off with Gabriel and their eight-year-old son,
Marcus, and leaving him here alone, lonely, and dying in this forgotten
little village by the bay.

Dr. Van Berber's only solace in this mounting misery was contained
in the brown bottle that sat like a siren on his bedside table. He poured
the magic liquid into a waiting glass of lukewarm water and swirled it
around a bit before slowly drinking it all and reclining on his pillows as the

morphine took effect—a soft, comfortable, fuzzy feeling that somehow took the edge off of everything that ailed him. He was drifting back to sleep when he heard the telephone ring on the kitchen wall downstairs. Vivian answered it on the third ring and he heard her exclaim about something, but with his fading hearing he couldn't quite make out what she was saying. She did sound excited though, so the doctor guessed some emergency or another had arisen and he had better get up, shower, and get dressed so he could attend to whatever fresh, new tragedy had now beset their usually quiet little town down here in the swampy backwaters of Florida's languid coast.

"Who was that on the phone?" the doctor asked Vivian as he sat down at the kitchen table.

"You'll never guess . . ."

"You're right, Vivian. I never will. So why don't you just tell me?"

"Jewel," she answered, as she placed a plate of grits, bacon, and a slice of watermelon before him.

"Jewel? Really? Why, we haven't heard from her for a long time. What'd she say?"

"Says her and Gabriel and Marcus are comin' back for a visit in a couple of weeks. Says for you to call her back when you got up."

"That all?"

"Yes, sir, that's all she said."

"I'll call her back when I get to the office," the doctor said. The grits were good—nice and creamy and buttery, like he liked them. The bacon was a bit too crispy but still tasty. The watermelon was cold and juicy and sweet.

"Good watermelon. Where'd you get it?"

"On the back porch this morning. The note said it was from Claude Ramsey. I put it in the icebox when I came in."

"Yeah, he owed me for sewing up his son's cut hand last week."

Vivian poured the doctor a cup of coffee and watched him eat. She was a tall girl, "thin as a rail," as Jewel would say, with brown skin the color of a Pullman railway car, a pretty face with a funny, crooked smile, which she hoarded, and a starched white dress with a perfect blue apron that never seemed to retain a single stain. The only problem with the child, aside from her consummate shyness, was an occasional, unaccounted-for lapse in memory.

"Juice," the doctor reminded her. He drank a small glass of orange juice each morning, but she had forgotten it this morning for some reason. "Something on your mind today?" he asked her.

"Not really," she answered as she scurried toward the icebox.

"You sure?"

"Well . . ." she hesitated.

"Spit it out."

"Well, what . . . what if Jewel comes back," she whimpered, "and she decides to stay? I know you miss her and like her better than me. So then what happens to me?"

"Oh, Jesus, Vivian. I thought you said she was just coming back for a visit."

"That's what she said, but I have this feelin' that maybe there's more to it than that."

"Well, let me talk to her, and I'll let you know what she says. But I wouldn't worry if I were you. Jewel put up with me for three years, and my guess is that stretched the limit of her patience about as far as it could reach."

"Okay, if y'all say so. I just got this funny feelin' . . ."

"Don't worry about it. Your job's safe with me. No one could ever replace you, not even Jewel."

The doctor meant it too. After a year with Vivian, he now realized that she was a better housekeeper than Jewel, almost as good a cook, and, most importantly, someone he could count on to take care of him as he stumbled awkwardly into old age. In her absence, he had come to realize that Jewel had become much more than a housekeeper and cook to him. She had, in fact, become over the years a surrogate wife, even though they had never consummated the marriage, either formally or sexually. Miscegenation was, after all, against the law in Florida in 1939, as it had been since 1832, except for a brief period during Reconstruction, and it was a statute not to be taken lightly. Folks around this part of north Florida still talked about the 1923 Rosewood Massacre just south of here in Levy County where six Negroes and two white people were killed when a white woman falsely claimed a colored man assaulted her. And it was only five years before that Claude Neal, a young Negro man who was accused of raping and murdering a white woman in nearby Marianna, had been publicly lynched by an angry white mob and left hanging from a tree outside the Jackson County Courthouse. Indeed, Port St. Joe's chief of police, John Herman Lane, had told the doctor recently that Florida ranked at the top of the most racially violent states in the nation as measured by the number of lynchings that continued to occur there regularly. The doctor had to wonder if Billie Holiday had Florida in mind when she sang her new hit record, "Strange Fruit." In his case, the racial and sexual stereotypes were reversed—he was white and Jewel was black—but still . . .

If all this weren't enough, the doctor's own marital history posted another strident warning sign against any additional assignations, since he had already been married three times. His first wife, Annie, had been his first true adult love but had mysteriously disappeared in the spring of 1927 on a train trip to visit her sister in Washington, D.C., and he still missed her. His second, Carrie Jo, had died of lung cancer six years earlier after four years of marriage. And his third, Jennie, had divorced him back in '35, only a year into their volatile marriage. So even if the law and stringent societal standards allowed Jewel and him to be together, the doctor would still not have been any too eager to enter into such an arrangement once again.

Yet there was no doubt that his and Jewel's bond had gone beyond the usual employer/employee relationship and could never exist again in that simple workaday way. If Jewel were to return for more than a visit, the doctor and she would have to forge some new, different kind of kinship. Not that it made any difference at this point. Jewel was with Gabriel whom she seemed to love and who was the father of her son. And Gabriel's career as a singer and performer would never permit them to stay tethered to tiny Port St. Joe for very long anyway.

"Not to worry," the doctor told Vivian as he gathered his dirty dishes and deposited them in the kitchen sink. "Not to worry."

That was enough to coax that curt, cockeyed smile from the girl, and that in turn was sufficient to content the doctor at the start of what would have otherwise been just another dreary day in their quiet corner of paradise.

"Okay, Doc," she said. "It's like one of them Proverbs says: 'Heaviness in the heart of man maketh it stoop; but a good word maketh it glad.' So, thanks. I won't worry. Go to work."

And so he did.

Chapter 2

July, the hottest month of the year for them, could be sweltering in the Florida Panhandle. And if it weren't for the sea breezes wafting across the deep waters of St. Joseph Bay, it would have been unbearable. As it was, the temperature was already creeping through the upper reaches of the eighties at 8:30 in the morning as the doctor walked from his house on Seventh Street to his office on Reid Avenue in downtown Port St. Joe.

He had begun walking the seven blocks to work each weekday morning in a largely unsuccessful attempt to stay trim enough to fit into his summer suits. So the seersucker slacks he was wearing today were too tight around his waist and he had already doffed the constricting jacket, which he held over his shoulder in one sweating hand while clutching his black bag in the other. To protect his balding head from the rising sun, he wore a straw fedora, which he tilted a bit to the right to give what he hoped was a slightly rakish look, if in fact a somewhat portly, sixty-six-year-old, perspiring white man in an ill-fitting seersucker suit with red suspenders could appear anything approaching rakish. Rumpled was the more apt descriptor.

The walk each morning did, however, give him a chance to stretch his aching muscles and clear his agitated brain in the absence of people, patients, phones, and pain. All of which he was becoming increasingly impatient with, with each passing year. If there had been another doctor in town, he would've thought about retiring, but there wasn't and he hadn't saved enough to get by without working anyway. Roosevelt's new Social Security Act wouldn't allow him to collect benefits for another three years, so he was trapped. He needed to continue, even as his workload increased as more people moved into town to work at the new paper mill that was now operating at full capacity and employing nearly a thousand workers at its bustling plant just north of town.

The doctor realized he was walking faster than usual this morning, the sweat soaking the back of his undershirt and seeping through to his starched white dress shirt. He was in a hurry to talk to Jewel. He didn't want to call her back with Vivian hovering about in the kitchen. The girl was fearful enough without her having to hear one side of a telephone conversation and her active imagination filling in the other half with God knows what kind of paranoid nonsense.

He had talked to Jewel no more than a dozen times since she had left more than a year earlier. He had not wanted to disturb her in her new life with Gabriel, and long-distance telephone calls were expensive and seemed strangely antiseptic with her so far away and him so wishing she wasn't. They were able to keep each other up to date on the facts of their lives but were unable to address all those other things that continued to be left unsaid in the desolate long-distance lurch. But the news that she was returning for a visit was exciting, and he wanted to hear about it directly from Jewel's mouth with no one else around.

Nadyne Wakefield was at her desk in the reception room as the doctor, slightly out of breath and sweating profusely, entered his office. She looked up over her wire-rimmed glasses at him and gave him something between a smile and a scowl because she disapproved of his morning walks, especially in this heat. She had hinted that she thought his walking to work, when he owned a perfectly good car, was somehow beneath him and his professional status in town, and, although she had not stated as much, this reflected poorly on him and, of course, indirectly on her as his receptionist, nurse, and office manager.

The doctor would have dismissed anyone else who was so concerned with such superficial appearances, but not Nadyne. Unlike the doctor, she was a native of Port St. Joe, the only daughter of a struggling shrimp fisherman and his sturdy wife. Now somewhere in the middle of middle age, Nadyne possessed an inherit understanding of the culture and unwritten mores of this insulated little village that was so deeply entangled in such a fine web of Southern gentility, pioneer pride, and fisherman fortitude that the doctor would never decipher it. So he deferred to her insight in these matters and tried to conform to the town's parochial deportment as best he could. Besides, Nadyne knew the medical history of everyone in town, whom to call when the roof leaked, and how and when to extract a payment from a deadbeat debtor. In other words, she ran the place and without her the doctor would have long since given up hope and launched himself off the Bay Road Bridge into the murky waters of the new St. Joe Paper Mill Canal.

"What do we have this morning?" the doctor asked her.

"Let's see," she answered as she peered at her open appointment book. "Annie Power with some sort of gastrointestinal problem. Mildred Henricks for her second trimester checkup. Her husband still has her working like a dog out on that pitiful farm of theirs. Bobbie Mitchell is having a hard time breathing. Sounds like Mike Jansen may have some sort of venereal disease. That Lollar boy caught his hand in a machine out at the new mill. And Gail Stinson is coughing up blood. Then house calls in the afternoon, after you traipse back home to get your car in the noonday sun. So if you haven't had a heat stroke by then, there's the usual: a bunch of old people too lazy or too sick to get out of bed. A.J.

Brimley's ulcers. Maggie Morgan, Mary's little girl, fell out of a tree again. Sounds like she may have broke her ankle this time. Jim Hurley cut his foot on something, to the bone, according to his wife."

"Okay, Nadyne, must be Monday morning. Hold 'em off until I can make a quick telephone call, will you?"

"Will do."

The doctor dialed Edna, the town's day telephone operator, and asked her to connect him to Jewel's number in New York City. He listened to the echo of the phone ringing many miles away somewhere up in exotic Harlem. Jewel answered on the second ring. "Hello?" she said.

"Hello, Jewel. It's Van. How are you?"

"Oh, Doc, I'm fine as frog's hair split three ways. It's been a coon's age. How 'bout you? Vivian been takin' good care of you?"

"Yeah, we're doing all right. But I was thinking maybe you'd fallen off the face of the earth, like Amelia Earhart. I haven't heard from you in so long. Vivian said y'all are finally coming home for a visit though?"

"Yeah, we are. Gabriel's got some time off comin' and we heard from Mama that Daddy's s'pose to get outta Raiford on July thirty-first. Mama says he done served most of his time and has been sick, so they gonna let him come home . . . probably to die, Mama says."

"What's wrong with him?"

"Mama says he got TB, but I don't know. I guess we'll find out soon enough."

"When exactly?"

"Well, in a couple of weeks. Gabriel gets off on the twenty-eighth, so we plan on drivin' down that weekend so I can pick up Daddy on Monday."

"Then what?"

"That's a good question. You know Gabriel ain't none too eager to face Daddy after all these years, and I can't blame him. Why, he's about as nervous as an upright, grown-up person. And I ain't any too eager myself after what happened back then. But I guess we gotta face the music."

What happened back then was that Gabriel had gotten Jewel pregnant, and when her father found out he had gone after Gabriel with a shotgun. Gabriel happened to be performing at a white nightclub in Mexico Beach when Jewel's daddy, crazy mad and liquored up lush, busted into the club with the intent of blowing Gabriel's brains out. The white clientele of the club had other ideas, however. They weren't ready for Gabriel's music to stop quite yet, so they stepped in to save him, which resulted in a struggle that left several white folks seriously injured and ultimately a ten-year prison sentence for Jewel's daddy. Both Jewel and Gabriel weren't expecting Jewel's father to be suddenly forgiving after all that. So the music they would face didn't portend to be pleasing.

"Listen, Jewel," the doctor said, wiping the sweat off his forehead with his handkerchief. "If you think it'll make it any easier, I could request your father's medical records from the prison and then check him out before y'all face him."

"Hmm," Jewel said. "That ain't a bad idea. I don't know if it'll make a tad of difference or not. Might just prolong the inevitable, which is both me and Gabriel wakin' up with a spade in our faces."

"Well, give it some thought and then come and see me first thing when you get back down here so we can talk about it some more. Meanwhile, I'll call the prison and ask them to send your daddy's medical file to me. I'll give them your phone number if they need permission from a family member. What's his full name?"

"John Jefferson Jackson. 'Cept everybody calls him Django."

"Django?"

"Yeah, Django. Mama says a band of gypsies come through the turpentine camp when he was a little boy and Daddy liked to stay up late and sing with 'em. Anyway, they took him under their wing and started callin' him Django and it stuck."

"Hmm, okay. I'll see what I can find out."

"Okay, Doc. Sounds good. We should be rollin' in there sometime on Sunday afternoon, the thirtieth, I think, if all goes well. We'll see you then."

"All right. I'll be looking for you. Oh, how long are y'all planning to stay?"

"Gabriel has to be back to work on August fourteenth, so for a couple of weeks, I guess. We ain't got it all figured out quite yet. We been so worried about seein' Daddy."

"You okay, Jewel?"

"Yeah, I'll be fine, once we git this business with Daddy all taken care of. How 'bout you?"

"I miss you."

"I miss you too."

"See you soon."

"See you, Doc. Good-bye."

My God, he did miss her—a lot. But at least she was returning, even if it was just for a visit. The doctor had something to look forward to for the first time in a long time.

The doctor drove out toward Cape San Blas that afternoon to check on Mary and Eli Morgan's daughter. This wasn't the first time. The Morgans operated one of the biggest, most successful orchards in Gulf County. As the doctor drove down the narrow dirt road to their house, he passed through groves of Satsuma orange, Meyer lemon, kumquat, nectarine, apple, pear, and pecan, many of which were heavily laden with fruit, maturing at one stage or another. When the doctor arrived at Eli Morgan's house, a sprawling, ramshackle cabin behind a row of tall pecan trees, he was led by Mary Morgan to a cramped bedroom where he found the couple's little girl, no more than ten years old, in bed with a badly swollen right ankle. The doctor examined it and asked the girl to turn it, but she couldn't as she winced in pain.

"What happened?" he asked her.

"I fell out of a pear tree," she whimpered.

"What were you doing up there?"

"Pickin' pears."

"Who told you to do that?"

"Daddy."

The doctor turned to the girl's mother and raised his eyebrows, then led her out of the bedroom and closed the door.

"Mrs. Morgan," the doctor began, "we've talked about this before. You know you can't have these kids, especially the young ones, up in those trees. The last time I was out here, Maggie just had a sprain. But now I'm afraid she's broken her ankle."

The woman, who was still pretty but weary and worn after bearing six children, bowed her head and began to weep. "I'm so sorry," she cried. "I told Eli that he can't send the younguns up in them trees, but he don't never listen to me. Most of 'em do okay, but Maggie, she ain't got as good a balance as the others. She's always fallin' out."

"Well, then," the doctor said, "you're going to have to pack her up and get her to the hospital in Panama City. They'll do an X-ray and then probably put her in a cast. Then you have to keep her out of the trees. Do you understand me?"

"Yeah, but Eli's just too cheap to pay for help. Says why should he do that when he's got six able-bodied kids to do the work."

"Well, this one's not so able bodied anymore. You tell Eli—or I will, if you want me to—that it's going to cost him a pretty penny to get that ankle set in Panama City, unless y'all have insurance, and that I'm going to report him to the sheriff for breaking child labor laws. And I'm not kidding."

"Okay, Doc," she said. "I'll tell him, but I don't know if it'll do any good. The man's as stubborn as an ol' mule."

"Well, maybe he'll listen to the sheriff then, because I'm about at the end of my rope on this thing. If I'm called out here again for some child falling out of a tree, I'm going to press charges and have your husband arrested. You tell him that. If he has a problem with it, have him come and see me. You understand?"

"Yes, sir," she sighed.

"Okay. Keep that ankle iced, and get her to the hospital in Panama City as soon as you can."

The doctor was disgusted. He saw it almost every week: one child or another forced to work under hazardous conditions because his family couldn't afford to hire workers. And, despite his threat, there was not much to be done about it. The child labor laws exempted farm work, and that was where most of the abuse occurred. If worse came to worse and Eli Morgan didn't get those children out of the trees, the doctor swore he would get them out himself by shooting the son of a bitch if he had to.

Chapter 3

When the doctor walked to work a few days later, he found Gator Mica's rusty old Chevy Capitol pickup parked in front of his office on Reid Avenue.. Gator was slumped behind the steering wheel, his ragged, straw cowboy hat pulled down over his eyes, his loud snoring groaning through the truck's open window.

"Gator," the doctor said, nudging the big Indian's shoulder, "time to get up. Your snoring's disturbing the whole town."

"Oh, mornin', partner," Gator said, as he tipped back his hat and pulled himself upright. "Just catchin' a little shut-eye. How y'all doin'?"

"I'm okay for an old man. How about you? I haven't seen you for weeks now. Dr. Price keeping you busy out there?"

"Yep, seems like I git one thing done, then there's somethin' else croppin' up. I ain't got time to tie my own shoes half the time. What about you? You doin' okay?"

"I guess I can't complain. I'm still alive and more or less kicking. What brings you into town this fine morning?"

"Good question. For one thing, I ain't seen you for a while and we ain't been huntin' or fishin' since I don't know when, so I was gonna ask you to go fishin' with me out on one of the lakes on St. Vincent. Them little ponds are filled with perch, bream, and big ol' black bass that'll pull you in if you ain't careful. And for another, Dr. Price is laid up sick in bed with some kind of ailment so I'd like you to take a look at him, if you don't mind."

"No, I don't mind at all. What's wrong with the doctor?"

"Not sure. He's got himself a fever, muscle pains all over, and a bad headache. He's been treating himself with some of them patent medicines his company makes, but he don't seem to be gettin' any better."

"Surprise, surprise. How long has this been going on?"

"Oh, just a couple of days, but I'm kind of worried about him since he ain't never sick, even though he is an old man. And he just don't look right."

"Okay, sounds like I better take a look at him soon."

"Yeah, I think so. He just seems to be gittin' worse."

"Well, I was planning on staying home and reading, since it's Saturday, but how 'bout tomorrow?"

"That sounds good. We could go over there in the morning, you could check on the doctor, and then we could go fishin' the rest of the day."

"All right. Let's do it. What if I meet you at Indian Pass at, say, nine o'clock?"

"I'll see you there," Gator said, as he tried to start his truck. As it sputtered and finally rattled to a shaky idle, the doctor remembered Jewel. "Gator, wait. Guess who's coming back for a visit?"

"Don't tell me."

"Yep, Jewel. In a couple of weeks. I'll fill you in on the details tomorrow. We definitely have to have a get-together for old time's sake."

"Oh, yeah, for sure. Damn! Jewel. I was beginnin' to wonder if we'd ever see that ol' gal again."

Frankly, so was the doctor. Even though Jewel's mother still lived in her little shotgun shack in North Port St. Joe, the doctor had seen more than enough young people abandon their elders during this terrible Depression to find work elsewhere, never to return. When the doctor had done all that he could to save them, he had seen too many of these poor old people buried in paupers' graves, alone and beaten down by malnutrition, dementia, and the miserable lives they had been left to live. But it looked like Jewel was going to be different.

However, it was one thing to return to check on her mother but still another to face her father after all that had happened so many years earlier. Now that was courageous, or maybe crazy—the doctor wasn't sure which—but it sure did set her apart from all those deserters who had turned their backs on their families and friends and had forsaken forever this impoverished little town by the bay.

The next morning, the doctor parked his old Ford near the landing at Indian Pass, a natural waterway about a quarter of a mile wide between the mainland and St. Vincent Island, joining Apalachicola Bay to the east and the Gulf of Mexico to the southwest. The sun, as usual, was strong and bright and the wind, unusually calm. As the doctor peered into the dark water, hoping to catch a glimpse of the sandbar sharks, bottle-nosed dolphins, or West Indian manatees that frequented the area, he heard the distant roar of a big speedboat entering the pass. As the launch approached, the doctor soon recognized, there at the helm of the polished twenty-five-foot, triple-cockpit Chris-Craft Runabout, none other than a beaming, sunburned Gator Mica, carefully guiding the craft to shore.

"Ahoy, matey," Gator hollered, offering his left hand to the doctor. "Permission for the landlubber to come aboard is hereby granted. But only if you take off your shoes. We don't allow no scratches on the deck of this baby."

"My, my, this is a thing of beauty, Gator," the doctor said as he removed his shoes and socks, rolled up his pant legs, and waded into the surf. "Quite a step up from that old glade skiff of yours, if you don't mind me saying."

"No shit. But don't worry. We'll be usin' that ol' skiff to get into the lakes later this afternoon. Here, give me that bag and your shoes."

The doctor waded the remaining few feet to the boat, handed Gator his black bag and his shoes, and grabbed the rope ladder that Gator had dropped over the side of the boat. But before he could pull himself up over the gunwale, Gator had snatched him under his right armpit and heaved him up into the elegant front cockpit, outfitted in plush black leather and a shiny chrome instrument panel that housed five round, shining gauges.

"Now this is living."

"Ain't it, though?" Gator replied as he gunned the rumbling engine and steered the big beast of a boat eastward up through the middle of St. Vincent Sound toward St. Vincent Point, about nine miles away at the northeast corner of the eighteen-square-mile island. It was like gliding on silk as they sailed effortlessly across the placid waters. The doctor was not an admirer of how Dr. Price and his father had amassed their fortune—by selling useless patent medicines to poor, gullible, sick people—but he had to admit that some of the luxuries they were able to afford with these ill-gained dollars, like this stunning boat and this beautiful island that they were now speeding past, argued for the merits of these deceptive dealings.

St. Vincent Island was indeed a wild and wonderful retreat from the encroaching commercialism that was ravaging the rest of their state. Beyond the broad, white-sand beaches that they were now sailing past stood a high forest of slash pine, live oak, and mixed hardwoods, one of the few remaining virgin timber stands left anywhere in the eastern United States. Bald eagles, brown pelicans, and laughing gulls soared above, almost as thick against the azure sky as were the stars against the expansive heavens of the ebony sky at night. The waters surrounding the primeval island were as bountiful as any food source on the planet, with the most delicious varieties of oysters, shrimp, scallop, tarpon, sunfish, flounder, and mullet to be found anywhere in the world. To his credit,

Dr. Price had protected these natural resources with an unflagging vigor from the encroaching development that continued to threaten his island paradise with increasing intensity.

At St. Vincent Point, Gator swung the boat east around a shallow sand bar and then continued south across Apalachicola Bay for about three and half miles to West Pass, the waterway separating St. George Island and the southeastern tip of St. Vincent Island. When they sighted a long, whitewashed dock extending out into the pass, Gator backed down the engine and steered the Chris-Craft alongside the pier. As the big boat rocked to a stop, Gator switched off the engine, crawled up onto the top of the shiny, mahogany bow, unfurled a hemp rope from its forward stanchion, and jumped in his stocking feet onto the dock, where he tied the motorboat up and helped the doctor ashore.

At the land end of the dock and beyond a low dune was a narrow sand road that led about a quarter mile to the Price compound. Sweating and swatting mosquitoes and deer flies, the two men trudged up the sandy path that ended in front of a large, two-story, pine-log cabin with a wide plank porch encircling it on three sides. A narrow creek that flowed at the edge of the clearing had been damned to form a swimming hole near the tall pines that towered all around. Behind it were three smaller, cypress clapboard cottages, and nearby a red horse barn and a long cedar-shingled tool shed that formerly housed Dr. Price's moonshine distillery.

With the increasing scrutiny of the patent drug industry by the Food and Drug Administration, Price had diversified his business by producing and selling moonshine when Prohibition was instituted. But when Prohibition ended in 1933, the market for the doctor's moonshine gradually dried up. With Gator's help and the bounty of the oyster beds around St. Vincent Island, Dr. Price had abandoned his moonshine business the previous year and started harvesting the plentiful beds of oysters in Oyster Pond, Sheepshead Bayou, Indian Lagoon, Flag Island Cove, and St. Vincent Sound.

The doctor remembered the two dogs that had greeted them on their last visit, but there was no evidence of them or of any other life today. The dogs must have belonged to Jed Washington, whom Gator had replaced as the manager of the island's livestock. The only sounds this morning were a slight breeze that rustled through the trees and seagulls squabbling on the beach behind them. It was a little eerie, the doctor thought, all this muted wilderness so far from civilization. For some reason, he thought of how easy it would be for someone to pick them off with a rifle from the top of the windmill that rose sixty or so feet above the compound. He looked up and saw only the long wooden blades spinning innocently.

They climbed the big cabin's front stairs and walked across the porch, their steps echoing through the clearing. The doctor's heart was beating rapidly, more rapidly than it should have been for such a brief walk and climb up the stairs, but it was pounding nonetheless as he had hurried to keep up with Gator. The big Indian knocked twice on the door, and they waited . . . and waited, not a sound coming from within the house. Now what? The doctor looked at Gator, and Gator shrugged. He raised his fist to knock again, but before his knuckles hit the door, a horrific, high-pitched screech blared across the compound. They jumped in unison as the heavy front door swung open and a tall, stately Negro dressed in a formal black suit and a regimental, striped tie stood grimly before them.

"What the hell was that?" the doctor asked the man.

The man tipped his head to the yard next to the house. And there, strutting through the sand from behind the house, was a bird as big as a turkey but with a long, iridescent blue-green plumage bouncing behind it.

"Peacock," Gator said.

As the serious man led them down a long hall, the doctor remembered his name. Tom Black was Dr. Price's butler of many years, according to Jewel who seemed to know, one way or another, every colored person and who they were kin to in and around Port St. Joe and the surrounding county. The house smelled of some sort of cleaning fluid and rubbing alcohol. Black led them up the narrow stairs to the second floor, then down a long, dark hallway into Dr. Price's bedroom.

He did not look well. He was in a large brass bed, his skeletal head propped up on a pile of pillows and the rest of his body covered by a thick, faded quilt. It had been more than a year now since Dr. Berber had last seen Dr. Price, and it appeared that the year had not been a good one for the old man. He was much thinner now, his white hair a wiry tangle, and his red face wrinkled and wet. His forehead was covered with a damp cloth, his eyes closed. His butler nudged his bony shoulder until he opened his eyes and saw Gator and the younger doctor standing before him.

"Welcome," he said in a weak voice that the doctor could barely hear. "It's been a while. Forgive me if I don't get up and shake your hand. I'm afraid I'm ill, and I don't want to pass anything on to you. How have you been?"

"Well," Dr. Berber answered. "And you, sir?"

"Up until a few days ago I was doing fine, but I seem to have come down with some sort of ailment that I can't, for the life of me, shake. Normally a few doses of Dr. Price's Potent Prescription would have fixed me right up, but not this time. I seem to be getting worse."

"Tell me what hurts."

"Well," the old man muttered, "about everything. I was having a swim earlier this week and got pretty eaten up by mosquitoes. They're particularly bad this year with all the rain we've had. Anyway, a few days later I suddenly struck a fever, well over a hundred. I took some aspirin and a dose of Dr. Price's Select Smartweed. That brought the fever down briefly, but then it went back up again. Then my muscles began to ache all over, and, despite the aspirin and Dr. Price's Golden Medical Discovery, I developed a headache that just keeps getting worse and worse."

Dr. Berber opened his black bag and examined the old doctor. By the time he had taken his temperature and his blood pressure and looked him over carefully, he was confident of his diagnosis. A similar case nearby had been reported in one of his medical journals a few months earlier.

"Dr. Price," Dr. Berber began, "last year a mosquito-borne alphavirus was discovered in humans not far from here. The virus is normally found only in wild songbirds and certain mosquitoes that live in and around wooded, freshwater swamps, like those on St. Vincent Island. The mosquito is called *Culiseta melanura,* if I remember correctly, and it's common in this area, as, of course, are many varieties of wild songbirds. Strangely enough, these mosquitoes don't bite people, but they do bite birds. And if another type of mosquito that bites both birds and people bites an infected bird and then bites a horse or a human, it can pass along this virus. Most of this activity occurs between May and August, or right about now."

"What are they calling this virus?" Dr. Price asked in a shaky voice.

"Eastern equine encephalitis."

"And the treatment?"

"None that has so far been discovered."

"The prognosis then?"

Dr. Berber stared at the old doctor and tried to measure his words carefully. "Your symptoms may become worse over the next two weeks," Dr. Berber told him, "and show the onset of encephalitis, with seizures, vomiting, and focal neurological deficits. A coma or death could occur. Or—and this is the important part—you may recover."

"And the chances either way?"

"At this point, there's not a lot of data to know how humans react to the virus. But based on how it affects horses, your chances of recovering are two out of three."

"Damn! So what you're saying is I have a one-in-three chance of dying?"

"Yes, that seems to be the case. So all we can do at this point is to make you as comfortable as possible. Take whatever Dr. Price's potions make you feel better, and I'll leave some morphine and instructions with Mr. Black on how to administer it. Questions?"

Dr. Price stared at the doctor in disbelief, his black, beady eyes boring into this bearer of such bad news. Finally, he said, "Thank you, Doctor, for telling me the truth, as painful as it is to hear. I now have my work cut out for me. I've been putting it off, but I now need to change my will immediately. Black, call that lawyer Huggins in Port St. Joe and get him out here right away. Those people from the new mill in town want the timber rights to my island, and they aren't going to get them. If I die now, this place goes to my three children, and they don't give a whit about it, so I'm going to make sure it goes to someone who cares."

"Who?" the butler asked.

"Just get the damn lawyer!"

And so he did.

Chapter 4

Dr. Berber showed Tom Black how to prepare the morphine. He gave him a small brown bottle of the concentrated drug and extracted the prescribed amount with a glass dropper. He then placed the open end of the dropper into Dr. Price's dry mouth and pinched the rubber bulb. Dr. Price coughed, and the younger doctor handed him a glass of water to chase the opiate's bitterness. The pain would ease in about fifteen minutes, the doctor told him. He had administered the drug to himself so many times that he no longer needed a dropper to measure the correct dosage, and he preferred to cut the bitterness by mixing the morphine with water before he drank it, but the dropper would ensure that the butler measured the right amount.

Dr. Berber, the butler, and the Indian wordlessly watched the old doctor drift off to sleep. *He'll die someday soon,* the doctor thought to himself, *if not from the encephalitis, then from some other untreatable ailment or old-age affliction, of which there were plenty.*

Then Gator and the doctor walked downstairs and sat side by side in two of the rocking chairs on Dr. Price' front porch, peering out at the dark waters of West Pass. A bald eagle circled high above them, and a few chickens and peafowl quietly roamed the sandy clearing.

"Now what?" Gator asked as he produced a pair of Partagas cigars and lit one for himself and the other for the doctor.

"Don't know," the doctor answered, shaking his head and exhaling the rich, gray cigar smoke. "Don't know. I know I hate this job sometimes and would give it up in a heartbeat if I had a choice."

"So you think the old doctor will die?"

"Probably. He's old, probably not strong enough to fight off the virus. But then again, you never know. He's survived this long. What age do you peg him at?"

"Oh, I'd say at least seventy-five. I can't recall he ever mentioned a number, but look at him. He's old."

"Too bad his children aren't around," the doctor said, "even though he doesn't seem to think much of them."

"Yeah, the three of 'em live up north somewhere. New York, I think. The doctor says they hardly ever visit, that they think this place is too wild and uncivilized."

"Maybe they're right. Look what it's done to their old man."

"Well, that's true," Gator agreed, "but still he's enjoyed many a good year down here. And I'd have to agree with him that this has got to be one of the prettiest, unspoiled spots on earth."

"Yes, and it would be a pity to see the paper mill take all its timber. Too bad his children don't like the place. So who do you think he's going to will it all to now?"

"Beats me," Gator answered.

They sat in silence, rocking gently in unison, smoking their cigars. The two had hunted and fished together long enough that they didn't have to say too much to know what the other was thinking. Mortality was the subject of the moment. Old Dr. Price, in truth, was not that much older than Dr. Berber, maybe ten years at the most, and Gator was more than ten years younger than Dr. Berber. The younger doctor knew only too well that he had already passed the life expectancy of an

American man in 1939. So, at this point, it was all gravy. He wasn't about to suffer through some long and painful illness either. He had long ago determined that he would end it all rather swiftly if he were ever faced with that eventuality.

Gator, on the other hand, had a few more good years left in him. And the man was as strong and healthy as the proverbial horse. The doctor had treated him a couple of years earlier for some cuts and bruises suffered in a brawl at the Indian Pass Raw Bar, a clash that had resulted in another man's death and the doctor's hiring Bob Huggins, the best lawyer in Gulf County, to defend him and get him off on grounds of self-defense. Other than that, Gator had not seen a sick day as long as the doctor had known him.

Gator didn't talk much about his past, but the doctor had been able to piece together some of his history from the snippets that Gator had now and then revealed as they sat sipping Spearman beer and waiting for a fish to bite or a deer to appear within range of their loaded rifles. From what the doctor was able to glean from these occasional utterances, Gator was the only son of Holata Mica, the last Seminole chief to surrender to the United States Army, and a white woman named Eliza Clinton. He was born around the time of Geronimo's final surrender in Indian Territory in Oklahoma, to which his parents had been removed. On the reservation, Gator had been schooled by the strict nuns who operated the Catholic mission school there. After school, he had had the rare good fortune to have been trained to box by a retired professional boxer who believed the Indian boys on the reservation needed some sort of athletic outlet to channel their natural speed and energy. Nicknamed the "Pottawattamie Giant," Jess Willard had been a great heavyweight boxer and also a good teacher. He was tough and knew how to hit and be hit. He had knocked out the legendary Jack Johnson in 1915 and, for his effort, had been given his other nickname, "The Great White Hope." In

1919 he had received one of the worst beatings in boxing history when he was knocked out by Jack Dempsey.

Willard took a liking to Gator, who possessed both the size and speed of Willard himself. Gator was a good student. He learned quickly and was able to win every amateur fight he fought on the reservation before he ran away from home at sixteen and returned to the Everglades, where his father had been raised. There he learned to fend for himself and live off the land, fishing, hunting, gardening, and killing an alligator now and again for its meat and valuable hide, which he sold to buy the provisions he could not grow or kill himself. Then, in 1934, he had beaten a man to death in a Florida City bar in a dispute over a woman and fled north. Gator's predilection for getting drunk and getting into bar fights concerned the doctor, but, regardless of Gator's violent past, the doctor and Gator became fast friends, and the former was willing to overlook these infrequent lapses, as he would have those of an errant son, in favor of his friend's candor, loyalty, and simple unaffectedness. Aside from a Bohemian-American contractor named Karl Rossmann, with whom he had hunted and fished in Lynn Haven City, the doctor was as close to Gator as he had been to any man, including his father, who had existed in an isolated state of deep depression most of his life.

Gator got as far north as Port St. Joe, where he bought an old houseboat and propped it up on stilts in the dunes near Indian Pass. He survived there, as he had in the Everglades, through his skills as an outdoorsman. He had become so adept at oyster fishing that Dr. Price had hired him to manage his oyster business and later, when his senior hired hand moved on, to tend to the island's livestock: the chickens, peafowl, goats, and cattle that Dr. Price had acquired to feed his household. The meat supplemented what his gardener and his wife grew to feed themselves, Dr. Price, Tom Black, his wife (who did the cooking), their three children, and now Gator, who had moved there the previous year.

It was quite a little community, and now it seemed it might all be coming to an end as their patron lay dying in the bedroom upstairs.

"Now what?" Gator asked again. The doctor did not know whether Gator was referring to his and the others' fate there on the island or what he and the doctor were going to do next.

"I guess we either go home or go fishing," he said, since he did not have an answer to the question of their destiny. "But I have to tell you I'm not as excited as I once was about going out there in those swamps, which, if my diagnosis is correct, are teeming with encephalitis-infected mosquitoes."

"Yeah," Gator agreed. "It does sort of put a damper on it, don't it?"

"On the other hand, if Dr. Price is in fact suffering from Eastern equine encephalitis, it is rather a rare occurrence. After all, you and the others who work out here every day haven't shown any symptoms, as far as I know."

"Yeah, but we ain't silly enough to go skinny-dippin' with the mosquitoes in that pond over yonder like Dr. Price likes to do. We pretty much stay covered up like any sensible person would."

"That's true. But still . . ."

Gator thought for a moment and finally said, "You're right, partner. Those fish over there in them lakes ain't goin' nowhere. They'll still be there and even bigger in the winter when the mosquitoes ain't around, and we'll be a lot cooler too. 'Course then hunting season will be on, and I wanna git you over there to Tate's Hell to go bear huntin' this year. But we can do both, I guess."

"To where?"

"Tate's Hell, over toward Carrabelle. Ain't you ever heard about it?"

"Sounds vaguely familiar. But I'm not sure I'm too crazy about going to a place that's got the name 'hell' in it. Doesn't sound real inviting, to tell you the truth."

"Oh, you'll love it. It's really wild and beautiful, almost as good as St. Vincent, except they got big ol' black bears there that we can try to shoot."

"I don't know, Gator. Let me think a little bit about that one, but coming back here in the winter to fish sounds good to me."

"You know, since we do have the rest of the day and I guess there's no more we can do for Dr. Price, we could take that Chris-Craft out in Apalachicola Bay and see what we can catch. There's still plenty of gas in it, and I got some beer in the icebox we could bring along. Who knows? Maybe we'll git lucky and catch us some sea trout, pompano, tripletail, or tarpon."

"Let's do it," the doctor said.

As Gator headed for his cottage for the beer and fishing gear, the doctor tapped on Dr. Price's front door. Tom Black soon appeared and told him that Dr. Price was still sleeping soundly and sweating less, so the doctor said good-bye to the solemn butler, grabbed his black bag, descended the porch stairs, and waited for Gator on the sandy path to the pier.

Gator soon returned, carrying two five-gallon lard cans, one in each hand, and two cane fishing poles tucked under his right arm. The doctor took the poles from him, and they plodded slowly through the sand to the sea.

They loaded the boat, and when the doctor and Gator were settled on the leather-covered bench behind the chrome-rimmed windshield, Gator, at the mahogany wheel, inserted and turned the key on the dashboard ignition and pressed the starter button on the floor with his right foot.

Then the boom blasted them up and out of the boat, a shock that echoed across the pass and shattered the serenity of the morning like a brick through a plate-glass window. The doctor first felt the shock to his ears, and he was sure his eardrums were being ruptured. He instinctively raised his hands to his head, but before they arrived there he found himself flying swiftly through the air. He saw what must have been Gator zooming upward alongside him. And then, just as suddenly, he was falling into the sea, sinking in the water, kicking with legs he could not feel in an attempt to surface for air. Finally, when he was ready to gasp a lung full of salt water, he saw the sun and his head bobbed above the waves. He was alive, but his head and his heart were pounding furiously. He tried to move his legs to stay afloat, and he tried to gasp for more air in case he went back under, and he tried to fathom what the hell had just happened to him. All he could see were waves and scraps of wood and thick black smoke, which he breathed in hungrily, scorching his throat and lungs with each gasp. His legs were not working, despite what his head was demanding of them. He took one last breath and descended into the depths.

Chapter 5

And then the light blended from green to gray to black and finally to a broad expanse of white. He followed the light, floating peacefully as a fetus in his mother's womb. It was warm and white and strangely silent. And it was not his mother's womb but that of his first wife, Annie. He somehow saw, from his watery compartment, her lying, pretty and pregnant, in a blanched room on a wide bed with stiff, white sheets. He tried to speak to her but he could make no sound. He wanted to tell her how much he loved her, how much he missed her, and how happy he was that she was finally pregnant, but all there was was soundless serenity and sempiternal space. He was drifting into an elegant abyss.

Then something pulled him back, and he was suddenly blinded by the sun and saw a huge, blurry, familiar red face hovering above him. It was not God, as he had expected, but Gator, kneeling and huffing behind his head with a hand grasping each of the doctor's wrists and repeatedly pulling up his arms and folding them across the doctor's chest and then extending them open and back out and down to the sand. The doctor was spitting up salty water and stomach bile and breathing again, as Gator continued this exercise.

"Okay, enough, Gator," the doctor gasped, as the wet Indian pounded his arms back into the sand one more time.

"You okay, partner?"

"What?" the doctor asked, as the water and the ringing in his ears all but muffled the sound of Gator's voice.

"You okay?" Gator shouted.

"Yeah, thanks to you. Thanks, Gator. I thought I was a goner for sure this time."

"Me too."

"What?"

"Me too. I thought you was a goner too."

"What happened?"

"The boat blew up when I turned it on. The blast blew us into the ocean. The boat's in a million pieces, floating around out there like dead fish. We was damn lucky, let me tell you that. If the explosion hadn't blown us sky high, we would've been blown to bits too."

"How'd I get here?" the doctor asked, still lying soaked on his back on the beach.

"I swum around 'til I found you, down about seven feet at the bottom of the pass. Pulled you out and gave you artificial respiration. Didn't figure it would work. You was awful purple, but it looks like you're gonna pull through."

"What?"

"You're gonna live."

"Oh, good. Thanks, Gator."

"No problem, partner. Let's see if we can git you up now."

Gator reached under the doctor's armpits and pulled him to a sitting position. The doctor spit out more water and looked around. There were still thin wisps of black smoke in the air, but a steady eastern breeze was blowing them and the acrid gasoline stench out to sea. Gator jerked him up again, this time to a standing position. The doctor's legs were shaky, but at least he could feel them again and, when Gator let go of him, he could stand and even walk, if somewhat unsteadily. That was a relief. There was no way he was going to spend the rest of his life in a wheelchair. He'd throw himself back into the pass before he'd stand or, more precisely, sit for that. He still had that damn ringing in his ears but it wasn't nearly as loud now.

"Listen, you okay here for a little bit?" Gator asked. "If you're all right, I'm gonna hike over to the creek and git my ol' skiff and take you home."

"What?"

"I'll be right back with my boat," Gator shouted and turned back toward the sandy road that led to Dr. Price's compound just as Tom Black and a white man who the doctor assumed was the gardener came running toward them. Gator met them about halfway down the path, and the doctor saw but couldn't hear him explaining to them what had happened. Gator suddenly raised his arms to the sky; if the doctor had been closer and not so deafened, he knew he would have heard Gator yelling, "Boom!"

While Gator was gone, Dr. Berber walked slowly to the pier, which was now in two almost equal pieces, with a huge gap in the middle that was filled with flowing sea water and a shiny, rainbow slick of gasoline and oil. Scraps of the Chris-Craft floated all around as Gator had described, but that was about it. That was all that remained of that beautiful boat. He couldn't quite comprehend what had happened and how miraculously Gator and he had survived. If he had been a religious man, he would have credited it to divine intervention, but since he wasn't, he simply chalked it up to dumb luck, which Gator and he seemed to have gained more than their fair share of lately.

So the doctor stood on the beach, soaked and shaken, and reveled in the sun and the sea and his good fortune, until finally he saw Gator and his glade skiff bouncing across the waves and through West Pass to what was left of the dock. Gator's boat was something he had built to navigate the narrow, shallow channels of the Everglades, not the Gulf of Mexico. But here it came anyway, about fifteen feet long, a yard wide, and no more than a foot deep. Attached to the cypress stern was a little one-and-a-half-horsepower Briggs and Stratton engine that Gator called a "hothead" and that the doctor now heard faintly sputtering at idle as he hurried to climb onto the narrow bench in the bow.

Then they were off—a far cry from the speed and ease and fluency of the Chris-Craft. There they sat, damp and bedraggled, like two deposed kings cast suddenly into the ranks of retainers. The hothead labored gallantly against the current and the wind, but they were buffeting the waves haltingly and had no choice but to wait as the boat slowly plowed its way ahead, parallel to the island's long southwest beach toward Indian Pass and the mainland. The doctor was too exhausted to talk. He just wanted to be home in his own bed. Gator concentrated on keeping the boat away from the shoals and out beyond the incoming tide, but they were still close enough to shore that they could plainly see the snowy plovers and American oystercatchers feeding on the beaches. Wood storks and the ever-present laughing gulls flew by overhead. Alongside they spotted redfish, sea trout, and cobia scattering erratically as the noisy skiff bounced by. The engine strained gravely as it pushed them along against the building wind as they entered Indian Pass.

A dusty white Franklin County patrol car waited for them at the landing. As the doctor pulled the skiff out of the water and Gator pushed from the stern, a tall, dark-haired policeman in a crisp khaki uniform and green-lensed aviator sunglasses got out of the patrol car and walked toward them. The doctor couldn't see the sheriff's eyes because of the tinted glasses, but the man's frowning, tight-lipped mouth told him the sheriff was not there for a social call. The doctor thought he looked like the news photographs of that recently retired, hotshot general in the Philippines. What was his name? McArthur. Yes, Douglas McArthur. If it weren't for that wad of chewing tobacco bulging from the inside of his right jaw, he might have been the spitting image.

"Cliff Duffield, Franklin County sheriff," he announced as he extended his right hand to them. "Dr. Van Berber and Gator Mica, I presume?"

"One and the same, or is it two and the same?" the doctor said, shaking the sheriff's hand. "At any rate, we're them, or is it they? Oh, well, nice to meet you, Sheriff. To what do we owe the pleasure?"

"Heard you fellows had some trouble over there on St. Vincent. Got a radio/phone call from a Mr. Black over there. Said Dr. Price's boat blew up."

"What?" the doctor said.

"Sure did," Gator said. "Blew all to hell."

"What happened?" the sheriff inquired and then sent a stream of sticky brown tobacco juice from his mouth onto the sand not too far from the doctor's left foot.

"Good question," Gator answered. "Don't know for sure. I just turned the key and pushed the starter button and caplooie! Damn thing blew into a million pieces. Like a bomb went off."

"Hmm," the sheriff said, tipping back the visor of his hat. "Don't often hear about something like that happening to a Chris-Craft, if I ain't mistakin'. It was a Chris-Craft, wasn't it?"

"What?" the doctor said.

"Yeah, it was a Chris-Craft," Gator barked to the doctor.

"Yeah, *was* a Chris-Craft," the doctor added.

"Any idea what could have caused an explosion like that?" the General McArthur sheriff asked, his eyes still masked by his sunglasses.

"No. Wish I did," Gator answered.

"You think there's any chance that it wasn't an accident?"

"What?"

"That maybe someone was trying to blow you up?" the sheriff said loudly.

"Why?" asked the doctor.

"Don't know," the sheriff said. "You tell me. Got any enemies?"

"Got any what?"

"Enemies?"

"Enemies."

"Like Lucky Lucilla," the sheriff shouted at the doctor.

"Lucky Lucilla?"

"Wasn't he the guy who was trying to kill you and a bunch of other people last year?"

"What?" the doctor asked. "Lucky Lucilla? What are you saying?"

"He's escaped," the sheriff said matter-of-factly. "Escaped from the state insane asylum in Chattahoochee yesterday. No one's seen a trace of him since."

"What?"

"Lucky Lucilla has escaped," Gator shouted.

"Ah, shit," the doctor sighed.

Chapter 6

Anthony Lorenzo "Lucky" Lucilla had first been committed to the Florida State Hospital in the fall of 1933 after he had brutally axed to death his entire family—his mother, father, sister, and two brothers—in the Ybor City section of the booming port town of Tampa, Florida. The following year he had escaped from the insane asylum after he had killed another man there. Then four years later, in 1938, he had resurfaced in Port St. Joe as a moonshine distributor for none other than the now-dying Dr. Price. He had then proceeded to terrorize the town, attacking a number of innocent people, including the doctor himself. Finally, Lucilla had been captured not too far from Indian Pass by Port St. Joe police chief John Herman Lane, Doc Berber, Gator, and an amateur posse of colored people hastily assembled by Jewel Jackson.

After Lucilla had recuperated from the gunshot wounds delivered by Lane and the doctor during the capture, he had been sent again to the state hospital in Chattahoochee, where a panel of psychiatrists had determined once again that he was mentally unfit to stand trial. Their diagnosis this time was dementia praecox and constitutional psychopathic inferiority, two types of mental diseases that were apparently hereditary. Harry Jacob Anslinger, commissioner of the U.S. Treasury Department's Federal Bureau of Narcotics, had blamed Lucilla's crime wave on the murderer's use of marijuana, against which Anslinger was waging a fiery campaign. But the insane asylum doctors had found no such connection.

Unfortunately, as the doctor had become more embroiled in the search for this psychopath during the previous year, he had fallen in love with Sally Martin, the widow of the assistant lighthouse keeper at the Cape San Blas Lighthouse whom Lucky Lucilla had hacked to death. She was beautiful and half the doctor's age, and he, against all rationality and advice, had plunged into an absurd, amorous relationship with her. As anyone except the doctor could have foreseen, their romance had been short lived. When they had finally captured Lucilla, the madman admitted that he too was in love with the widow.

Since Sally had moved from the lighthouse into Port St. Joe, and since the doctor, Gator, and Jewel had orchestrated Lucky's last capture, Dr. Berber didn't have to think very hard to guess where Lucky Lucilla would turn up next. And it wasn't far away. He was out there somewhere, and the doctor had the frightening feeling that he was heading their way, unless, of course, the sheriff was right: Lucilla had already arrived and had just attempted to blow him and Gator to smithereens.

So the doctor wasn't at all embarrassed to ask Sheriff Duffield if he wouldn't mind checking under the hood of the doctor's old Ford before the doctor attempted to start it. All three—the doctor, the sheriff, and Gator—peered cautiously into the car's engine compartment, but they didn't see anything unusual there. Still, the doctor's heart was racing when he clicked the ignition and turned on the gas valve, disengaged the spark lever, pulled the choke, and—holding his breath—stepped on the floorboard starter button. The engine rumbled to life as always, and the doctor put it in gear and waved good-bye to the sheriff and Gator.

Despite his exhaustion, the doctor tried to stay alert on his way back to town. There seemed to be a car lurking behind every dune and down every side road waiting to pursue him. When he saw in his rearview mirror a speeding car approaching, he almost drove off the road and into the marsh. But he soon saw the red light on the car's roof and realized that Sheriff Duffield had apparently decided to escort him along Indian Pass Road. At that moment, he gave a sigh of relief but realized that this was not going to be a pleasant way to live, with a killer waiting to pounce at any moment.

When the doctor stopped at the corner of Sand Bar Road, the sheriff pulled up next to him and told him he was going to turn right and head back to Apalachicola. The doctor thanked him for his brief escort and then looked straight ahead at the Indian Pass Raw Bar. He had no idea what time it was because the crystal of his pocket watch had fogged over, but there were about a dozen cars in the roadhouse's oyster shell parking lot. And he now realized he was starving. So he decided to cross the road to the Raw Bar, despite his memory of Lucky Lucilla whacking him with an oyster rake in the back parking lot not so long ago. He still had scars from that one. But that was at night, and now it was bright and sunny, and he easily found a parking space near the front of the white clapboard building. He doubted that Lucilla would try to kill him here, on a main road in broad daylight with people all around. Besides, he was hungry.

The Indian Pass Raw Bar was half filled with working men—turpentiners, fishermen, farmers, laborers—most of them eating lunch, with a couple of groups in the back playing dominoes. They stared at the doctor in his damp dungarees and soaked shoes. Bob Wills and His Texas Playboys sang "San Antonio Rose" on the jukebox, and smoke hung heavy over it all. The bar's owner, Sadie McIntire, a withered old woman with a cigarette hanging from the corner of her mouth, sat behind a worn cash register near the entrance.

"How are you?" the doctor asked her.

"Not complainin'," she said. "How 'bout yo'self?"

"I've felt better, to tell you the truth."

"Yeah, you don't look your usual spiffy self. What happened? Looks like you've been swimmin' in the bay."

"More or less," the doctor said.

"Been a while since I seen you. Last time was when y'all caught that moonshiner, if I'm not mistaken. What was his name?"

"Lucilla. Lucky Lucilla."

"Whatever happened to him? Did they 'lectrocute him?"

"No, unfortunately not. They sent him away to the insane asylum in Chattahoochee. And I've just now found out that he's escaped."

"You're kiddin'!"

"Wish I were. You haven't seen him around by any chance?"

"Heavens, no. I'da called the sheriff if I'd even got a whiff of him. Man's crazier than a mad hound dog on a hot day."

"Can't argue with that," the doctor said.

He took a stool at the bar and ordered a Spearman beer, a dozen raw oysters, and bowl of gumbo. The Pabst Blue Ribbon Clock on the wall behind the bar read 1:15. *Time flies when somebody's trying to blow you up,* the doctor thought. Roy Acuff launched into "Freight Train Blues" on the jukebox. Apparently, the doctor's hearing was beginning to return because the song sounded pretty loud even though the jukebox was on the other side of the room.

As the doctor ordered another Spearman and ate his dinner, he thought about what to do about Lucky Lucilla. He figured Gator could take care of himself, but he was worried about Jewel. It might be hard for Lucilla to find her in New York City, but he'd have ample opportunity to do whatever he had in mind if she returned to tiny Port St. Joe. The doctor decided that he had better call and warn her when he got home.

It was only about ten miles from the Raw Bar to his house, but he almost fell asleep on the way there, even though he knew he should have been extra vigilant with this crazy ax murderer on the loose. He parked as usual in the crushed-shell driveway behind his compact Victorian cottage and plodded up the back porch stairs. Before he inserted his key, he listened. All he heard were the birds singing and a car honking somewhere off in the distance. If there was someone inside, the doctor probably couldn't have heard him anyway, since, even before this morning's explosion, his sense of hearing had been fading steadily with each passing year. Maybe now, with this additional damage, he would be motivated enough to look into getting a hearing aid, though he still hated how big and ugly they were.

He turned the key and entered. The house was dark and quiet. He switched on the kitchen light and listened some more. He thought he heard something, like a creaking floor, upstairs. He crept into the parlor and turned on the lights, then the dining room. He opened the front door and looked on the porch and out across the front lawn. Nothing. He tiptoed back down the hall, found the switch in the stairwell, and started up to the second floor. He pushed the door open to his bedroom and thought he saw an unfamiliar shadow in the corner. He turned on the light and saw the empty chair where the shadow had been. He checked the bathroom, whipping back the shower curtain to find the white porcelain tub stark and empty. He returned to his bedroom and flung the closet door open. There was nothing there but his clothes and his shotgun. He took the red box of shotgun shells from the top shelf of the closet, laid the gun on his bed, and carefully loaded it. As he slammed the barrel back into shooting position, he heard footsteps coming up the front porch stairs and across the porch to his front door. Had he locked it? He couldn't remember. With his heart racing, he then heard the banging on his front door. *Lucky Lucilla would probably not knock first,* he thought. He went to the front bedroom window and looked out onto the street below. There, parked in front of his house, was a black-and-white Port St. Joe police car.

"Coming," he yelled.

Chief John Herman Lane, in his usual tan uniform and Panama hat, stood before the doctor at the front door. He was middle aged, slim, blue eyed and, as always, unsmiling. The doctor opened the screen door and invited the chief in. He declined, so the doctor joined him on the front porch.

"Duffield called me and told me what happened out there on St. Vincent," the chief began. "You okay?"

"I've been better. But I'll live. Or, at least, I hope I will."

"We just found out late last night that Lucilla had escaped. I tried to call you this morning, but you weren't here. Now I know why."

"What happened? How'd he get loose again?"

"Apparently he was in the dispensary where they treat physically sick patients. The Florida state highway patrolman I spoke to on the phone said that Lucilla was complaining of severe stomach cramps. So they sent him there for observation. Sometime in the middle of the night, the nurse on duty was stabbed and Lucilla got away. That's about all I know. The guy said they had everybody out looking for him, but so far, nothing."

"Jesus!"

"I know, after all we've been through with this nut and all the warnings we gave them, and he gets away again. It's unbelievable."

"Yeah," the doctor said. "What do we do now?"

"Do our best to find him. That's about all we can do at this point. I expect it's you and me that he's after, since we're the ones who shot him, but who knows with a nut like this. So keep your doors locked and your shotgun loaded. I'll send around a patrol car as often as I can. Hopefully we'll catch him soon. Meanwhile, get some rest."

And so he did.

Chapter 7

Bul it was a fitful rest, with all that had happened that day dancing
around in his head like Nijinsky and his fear of being surprised
rising like the moon as the sun silently set in the west, even with
his loaded shotgun propped against the wall next to him. He had
nightmares about being chased down empty country roads and across
deserted, desolate beaches. He woke up entangled in a sweaty ball of
sheets as the sun peeked through his bedroom window.

It was Sunday morning, and Port St. Joe was as hushed and hollow
as a whore's heart. All he heard was a cardinal chirping merrily outside in
the old live oak and church bells clanging somewhere off in the distance,
but he *did* hear them and the ringing from yesterday's explosion was no
longer banging against his brain. Nevertheless, he reached for the bottle
of morphine on his bedside table and wondered where Lucky Lucilla was
on this new day and what he might be plotting and how he, the doctor,
was going to stay sane while this lunatic was out there on the loose.

The doctor gave Vivian each weekend off. There were always plenty
of leftovers in the icebox, and he just piled his dirty dishes in the kitchen
sink for her to wash when she returned on Monday morning. He found
some bacon and eggs and fried them up in a black, cast-iron skillet while
the coffee was brewing in the old, blue graniteware coffee pot that he had

somehow inherited from his mother.

After breakfast, he poured himself another cup of coffee and sat out on the screened-in back porch and read the Port St. Joe *Star* and the Sunday edition of the Panama City *News Herald*. The *Star* reported on the front page that three hunters in Nile had shot a three-hundred-pound black honey bear and then loaded it on a truck and brought it into Port St. Joe, "where it was viewed by many." The *News Herald* wrote that Florida Governor Fred P. Cone had given a speech in Lake City where he had declared that the people of Florida were "now eating high on the hog," because of better economic conditions in the state. You could have fooled the doctor. All he observed were poor and sick people who could barely afford to eat—high, low, or anyplace else on the hog. If they were lucky enough to afford any section of the animal, it would have more likely been the more lowly cuts like jowls, chitlins, hocks, and heals.

Most of the folks he treated were like the Joads and other poor Okies in John Steinbeck's new novel, *The Grapes of Wrath*, which he was about ready to read, but he made the mistake of turning on the radio in the parlor first. There was nothing but bad news from Europe, with another war apparently looming in the not-too-distant future. The reporter said that Churchill was anticipating this second major war of the young century to begin sometime this year. In preparation, he was now urging the British government to form a military alliance with the Soviet Union. Hitler had taken over Austria and invaded Czechoslovakia and had already formed his own alliances with Mussolini in Italy and Franco in Spain. A few months before, the Fuhrer had issued a directive to his Army High Command to prepare for an attack on Poland in September.

The newscaster reported that Adolf Eichmann, Hitler's henchman, had a few days earlier been appointed director of the Prague Office of Jewish Emigration. This was in the wake of a nationwide pogrom that had been organized the previous November by Nazi authorities against the Jews in Germany and Austria. On the night of November ninth, which was now being called *Kristallnacht,* or Night of Broken Glass, Jewish homes, businesses, and synagogues had been looted and burned. Ninety-one Jews had been killed, and twenty thousand had been sent to concentration camps. As early as 1933, Hitler had begun to systematically strip Jews of their civil rights, purging them from civil service jobs and restricting their participation in the nation's universities and professions. By 1935 Hitler's Nuremburg Laws had institutionalized anti-Semitism in German law by making Jews ineligible for citizenship, removing their right to vote, and making it illegal for them to marry or have sexual relations with non-Jewish Germans. In 1937 the Nazis had imposed a so-called Aryanization program that had confiscated Jewish businesses and placed Jews in special ghettos segregated from the "Aryan zones" of cities and towns. Now, the newscaster said, Jews were being forced to wear yellow Stars of David on their clothing when they were in public so that they could be easily identified for mistreatment.

One story reported on the radio struck the doctor as particularly poignant since a part of it occurred so close to home. With this escalating environment of discrimination and hate led by Hitler and his government, Jews were, not surprisingly, attempting to escape by any means possible. But apparently this was becoming increasingly difficult because of Germany's restrictive emigration policies and the strict visa requirements and immigration quotas of other nations, including the United States. Nevertheless, 937 Jewish refugees obtained what they believed were the necessary documents and had saved enough money to book passage on the ocean liner SS *St. Louis,* which sailed out of Hamburg harbor on May 13, 1939, bound for Havana, Cuba. The plan was that once the refugees arrived in Cuba, they would wait there until they were allowed to enter the United States under its quota regulations.

The ship arrived at Havana harbor on May 27 but was denied entry by the Cuban government. It seemed, according to the reporter, that just before the *St. Louis*'s departure from Germany, Cuban authorities had changed the island's immigration policies, effectively closing the loophole by which the passengers had hoped to enter the country: under tourist visas purchased from the ship's owner, the Hamburg-Amerika Line. Negotiations ensued to no avail. Under threat of removal by the Cuban navy, the *St. Louis*'s captain, Gustav Schroeder, weighed anchor on the morning of June 2. But instead of returning to Germany, the captain set sail for the coast of Florida in hopes of finding refuge for his passengers in America. When the liner was only a few miles from Miami, however, U.S. authorities refused to allow its docking under strict U.S. immigration quota laws.

Finally, on June 7, with diminishing food supplies and no legal means of docking in Florida, Captain Schroeder ordered the ship to change heading and return to Europe. As the ship turned away from Florida, a group of academics and clergy in Canada tried to persuade Prime Minister William Lyon Mackenzie King to provide sanctuary to the ship, which was only two days away from Halifax, Nova Scotia. However, Canadian immigration officials and cabinet ministers hostile to Jewish immigration convinced the prime minister not to intervene.

So the *St. Louis* headed back across the Atlantic, even as Captain Schroeder refused to return the ship to Germany until all of the passengers had been given entry into some other country. Finally, a number of countries, namely France, Belgium, the Netherlands, and Great Britain, accepted groups of the refugees after the ship docked at Antwerp, Belgium, on June 16. From there, other ships transported the passengers to their new homes.

The doctor shuddered to think what would happen to these refugees if Hitler were to have his way and bring the entire European continent under Nazi control. He turned the radio off and returned to the back porch and to the plight, closer to home, of the poor Joads, who were not escaping Nazi persecution but a more familiar form of torment, that of poverty and destitution, not unlike what he saw in the patients he treated every day.

The doctor figured Jewel would be home from church by now so he placed a call to her. Gabriel answered on the third ring. "Hello?" he said.

"Hi, Gabriel, this is Dr. Berber in Port St. Joe. Is Jewel around?"

"No, she's still at work. You okay?"

"Yeah, I'm fine. How about y'all?"

"We're good. Workin' hard. Marcus and me was just fixin' to walk over to Aunt Dinah's Kitchen where Jewel's cookin' and have dinner."

"Well, I'll let you go then. I just wanted to call and let y'all know that that crazy man we caught last spring out at Indian Pass has escaped from the nuthouse in Chattahoochee."

"You're kiddin'."

"Wish I were. I doubt he'd ever come looking for Jewel in New York City, but I thought I would warn y'all before you got back down here. Somebody tried to kill Gator and me yesterday, and I'm guessing it was this escaped lunatic Lucilla."

"Jesus!"

"Yeah, well, I don't know what to expect next, but I wanted to warn y'all to be careful once you got back into town."

"Okay, Doc, thanks. We'll keep an eye out. You think he'd really come after Jewel?"

"I don't know. I hope not. But there's no doubt he's crazy as hell so you can't be too careful."

"All right, I'll talk to Jewel. You know she ain't afraid of nothin' so it probably won't make no nevermind to her anyway. But I'll take care of her."

"Thanks, Gabriel. Have a good trip and, again, just be careful."

"We will, and you too, Doc. Sounds like you're the one who needs to watch out more than us."

The doctor hung the receiver back on the kitchen wall and returned to the *The Grapes of Wrath* on the back porch. Just as he was drifting off, he heard a car rolling up the crushed-shell driveway. He had left his shotgun inside and here was an old black Chevy bearing down on him. But before he could heave himself up and get inside, he recognized the bashed rear fender and the familiar face of Vivian in the car's open window.

"What are you doing here on Sunday?" he asked as she strutted up the porch stairs with a round reed basket in her hands, fresh and faultless in her Sunday best, straight from the Zion Fair Baptist Church on Avenue C, the doctor guessed.

"Deliverin' dinner. Heard you had a little trouble out at St. Vincent yesterday. Thought you may not be feelin' too good. Maybe some of Mama's good home cookin' will cheer y'all up some."

"Well, I'll be damned," the doctor said as he opened the kitchen door for her. "That's mighty nice of you and your mama. Y'all didn't have to do that."

"I know, but Mama says it weren't no trouble to just throw a couple more pieces of chicken in the fryin' pan, and she's always got leftover tater salad, and we got tomatoes from the garden comin' out our ears, purty near. And there's a piece of rhubarb pie in here too, if I ain't mistakin'."

Vivian unloaded the basket as she spoke, carefully setting the table for the doctor.

"Vivian, how many brothers and sisters did you say you have?"

"Six, at last count."

"And y'all still got somethin' to share with an old white man?"

"Sho 'nuff. Ain't no big deal, Doc. Y'all pay me regular like and let me take home any leftovers I want. Only seems fair, if we got a little extra, we share it with somebody that almost got hisself blown up. Why, the preacher was sayin' just this mornin', 'he that hath two coats, let him impart to him that hath none; and he that hath meat, let him do likewise.' "

"Okay, Vivian, I'm not exactly destitute here, but if you say so," the doctor said, sitting down in front of the loaded plate that she had set before him. "Sure looks good, and I am kind of hungry now that you mention it. Why don't you join me?"

"Naw, I done et. I'll see you in the mornin', though, if there ain't nothin' else I can git for you now."

"No, Vivian, nothing else. Tell your mama thank you and have her bring all your brothers and sisters in for a checkup before school starts. On me."

"Thanks, Doc. Enjoy your dinner."

And so he did.

Chapter 8

It was dark and the doctor was running as fast as he could. He was chasing Lucky Lucilla, who was racing down the middle of a long railroad track with a bloody butcher knife in his hand. Ahead of Lucilla was the caboose of a train and on its platform stood his first wife, Annie, and a little girl, both in long white dresses, holding hands, and waving to Lucilla or the doctor, he couldn't tell which. They were smiling even as Lucilla gained on them and the doctor dropped further and further behind. Just as the train entered a tunnel, Lucilla lunged forward and the doctor fell onto the gravel trail between the rails. As his head hit a black creosote tie, he heard the train's whistle blowing a long, lingering, lonesome note.

Until he woke up on the floor of his bedroom with the telephone ringing repeatedly in the kitchen downstairs. He stood up, blood trickling down his nose from what he felt to be a gash in the middle of his forehead. The phone continued to ring as the doctor descended the stairs and turned on the kitchen light. He picked up the receiver and held it to his ear.

"Hello?"

"Morning, Doc. I got Nelly Waiters on the line for y'all. She says it's an emergency."

"Okay, Marie, put her on."

There was a clicking noise on the line and then a shrill, breathless voice came on. "Howdy, Doctor," it said. "This is Nelly Waiters. I hate to wake you up this early in the mornin', but I got a problem out here. This woman's been in labor for two days now, and now everything's come to a dead standstill and I'm afraid for her and her baby. Could you come out and give me a hand?"

"Sure, Nelly," the doctor answered. "Where are you?"

"Out in the country, on Butlers Bay Road. I'm callin' from a neighbor's house that's got a phone. But the woman in labor's at the second house on the left, after you turn left off of Parker Avenue."

"See you there soon. What time is it anyway?"

"Three forty-five. I'll meet you there."

Nelly Waiters was one of three Negro midwives who lived and worked in Gulf County. She was a pretty good one in the doctor's estimation. She had more experience in delivering babies than he had, in fact. She had delivered most of the colored babies in North Port St. Joe during the past twenty years. The white babies were now routinely born in the hospital in Panama City, so the doctor handled only emergency situations. Nellie took the proper sanitary measures and gave good prenatal advice, although it wasn't always followed. But, most importantly, she knew when to call for help. The other midwives sometimes waited too long, resulting in the death of the baby or the mother or both, usually by excessive bleeding caused by a retained placenta.

The doctor dressed hurriedly, grabbed the new black bag that had replaced the one he had lost in West Pass, and trotted through the steady rain to his car. There wasn't time this morning to check under the hood. If there was a bomb there, he was just going to have to blow up. Fortunately, the old Ford started right up without mishap, and he pushed it as fast as he dared north on a slick Parker Avenue toward Mexico Beach. After about

ten minutes, he located Butlers Bay Road, or at least what he thought to
be Butlers Bay Road. It was raining hard now, and there was no sign that
he could see. The rutted road was slippery and muddy, but his car stayed
on it until he saw a shirtless colored man in faded bib overalls standing
alongside it, waving the doctor over.

"You Dr. Berber?" he asked.

"Yes, sir, I sure am. Where's the mama to be?"

"Over yonder. In that house back there." He pointed down a muddy
trail into the woods. "But I don't think your car'll make it back there
without gittin' stuck. So I'll go git my tractor or you can walk."

"We don't have time for you to get your tractor, and I'm not walking
in this rain, so get in and let's go."

"Yes, sir."

Miraculously, the doctor's car did not get stuck in the muddy tracks
that led to a rundown cabin about a hundred yards back in the woods.
The colored man led the doctor through a messy room that seemed to be
serving as a combination living room, dining room, and kitchen. In the
cramped bedroom on an iron bed lay the woman, with Nelly Waiters at
her side, mopping her brow with a wet washcloth.

"Where are we now, Nellie?" the doctor asked.

"I can feel the head, but I can't hear a heartbeat. What happened to
your head?"

"I fell out of bed. Let me take a look at her."

The doctor examined the overweight woman. She was only slightly
dilated, and he could not hear a heartbeat either.

"Give her some water. She looks to be dehydrated. And then get that
husband back in here. We're going to get her into the backseat of my car
somehow, and I'm going to take her to my office in town. You come on
with me, Nellie. I'll call Nadyne to come and help us when we get there."

"Yes, sir."

The pregnant woman was so overweight that the three of them couldn't lift her, so they eased her off the bed and led her through the messy room and pouring rain to the doctor's car. The doctor told her husband to go get his tractor in case the doctor's car got stuck. It was rough going, with his car sliding around from one side of the trail to the other, but they somehow made it out to the main road without getting stuck.

The rain was letting up a bit when they pulled onto Reid Avenue. The doctor was not optimistic about the baby's chances, but he knew they would be better here in his antiseptic emergency room that contained all the supplies, medicines, and instruments he might need. Nadyne arrived a few minutes after the doctor called her, and he, Nadyne, and Nelly Waiters began working with the woman. When she was comfortable and hydrated, the doctor carefully inserted a Foley catheter, a balloon-type device, into the woman's womb. Then he slowly pumped a saline solution into it, and in a few minutes the woman finally recommenced labor.

By noon, the doctor had delivered a healthy baby boy. He was taking off his gown and getting ready to leave and let Nadyne and Nelly finish up when Nadyne called him back. There was a foot sticking out. Another baby was coming, and it was coming out the wrong way. The doctor put his gown back on and found all the instruments that he needed for a breech delivery. Then the real work began for all of them but especially the mother. Finally, around 1:00, they had the other baby boy out, wriggling and screaming. The doctor stayed this time to watch Nellie deliver the placenta and cut the cord, and Nadyne to clean and swaddle the younger twin.

No matter how many times he went through the delivery process, he always got a thrill from it. There was something very gratifying about helping a new life come into the world, even if the world was not always such a pleasant place to come into. He wished at times that he could deliver more babies. But with all the white mothers going to the hospital in Panama City and all the colored mothers relying on the cheaper, more traditional midwives, he didn't often have the pleasure.

But when he did, it made him wish again that he had been able to have children of his own. He had tried valiantly with all three of his wives, with no success. The doctors were not sure why he was afflicted with this condition, but their tests proved it was truly *his* problem and not his partners'. He had explained his sterility to Carrie Jo, his second wife, and Jennie, his third, before they were married, so they were not that disappointed. But he was unaware when he married his first wife, Annie, bless her, and she was heartbroken when their doctor told them they would never bear children of their own. And while he would have liked to have had a family, he was sadder for Annie than he was for himself. They had discussed adopting but had never seemed to be able to focus on the issue long enough to see it through. It was as if the disappointment of not having their own children hung in front of them like a never-rising stage curtain that kept them from ever actually acting. To the doctor, Annie's pain was palpable. He would have given her anything to make her happy, but the thing she wanted most he was unable to grant. So they had been as happy as they could make one another, under the circumstances, up until the day she had vanished, seemingly into thin air, somewhere near Charleston, South Carolina, on a train trip to visit her sister, Alexandria, in Washington, D.C. That was a dozen years ago now, and there wasn't a day that went by that he didn't miss her. Her absence had prompted his morphine addiction, which had soon proved to be only a slight solace to the desperate loneliness. So delivering babies was a bittersweet venture because of all the mixed feelings it brought forth for him, feelings he wished again he could share with Annie.

Chapter 9

Two days later, when the doctor had just returned to his office after making his afternoon house calls, he received a phone call from Sheriff Duffield in Apalachicola.

"What's up?" the doctor asked, wondering if the sheriff was still wearing those green-tinted, aviator sunglasses.

"There's been a death out on St. Vincent Island."

"A death? Who?"

The doctor had been calling Tom Black every day since he had visited the island to treat Dr. Price, and the butler had told him yesterday that the old doctor's fever had broken and he was feeling better.

"Apparently, Price. I got a call from Tom Black just now saying that he was dead—apparently murdered."

"Murdered?"

"Yeah, Black says he heard a pop so he went up to Price's room and found the doctor dead, his throat slit and a bullet through his chest. Blood all over the place."

"Holy shit!"

"I don't know what's going on out there, Doc, what with that boat blowin' up and now this, but I intend to find out. But, look, here's the thing. Doc Phillips is in Tallahassee for some reason, and I need a doctor to take a look at the body and to help if anyone else has been hurt. So is there any way you could meet me at the Oyster House dock on Thirteen Mile Road? I'm gonna take our boat from here and then if we could meet up there, we can go on over together."

"All right, Sheriff. I'll leave right now and get there as soon as I can."

"See you there."

It was another hot, muggy afternoon. Dark clouds that might or might not deliver an afternoon thunderstorm were moving in from the west. The doctor's joints ached, and it smelled like rain. He drove out on Constitution Drive, took a right on Sand Bar Road and then a left at Dead Man's Curve, past the Indian Pass Raw Bar and Indian Lagoon, on east to Thirteen Mile Road. There he turned right and followed the shell trail until it ended at the Thirteen Mile Oyster House on St. Vincent Sound. The Oyster House was more like an oyster shack than an oyster house; nevertheless it gleamed white and pristine in what remained of the afternoon sun. Dr. Price owned the oyster fishing business and Gator Mica managed it. Dewey Miller, the operation's main packer, was out on the narrow dock in dungarees, a torn work shirt, and rubber boots, stacking oyster crates as the seagulls squawked above and the waves lapped the barnacle-enveloped support posts below.

"Seen Sheriff Duffield?" the doctor asked the squat, weathered man.

"Nope. He s'posed to be here?"

"Yeah, I'm supposed to meet him here. There's apparently some kind of trouble out on St. Vincent. Have you seen Gator today?"

"Nope," Dewey answered. "He said yesterday he wasn't comin' today. Said instead he was gonna chase strays on the island. What kinda trouble?"

"Well, the sheriff said Tom Black called him and said that Dr. Price was hurt. That's why I'm here."

"Here he comes now," Dewey said, pointing across the water toward

Apalachicola. Off in the distance the doctor could see the long boat skimming across the gray waves like a fast, sleek missile. When it slowed to approach the dock, the doctor could see that it was an eighteen-foot Gar Wood Runabout with forward and aft cockpits and a large inboard engine compartment.

"You ready to go?" the sheriff shouted above the deep rumble of the idling engine.

"As I'll ever be," the doctor said as he stepped into the forward cockpit next to the sheriff, who adjusted his aviator sunglasses, pulled down his cap, spit into the sea, and steered the craft out across the choppy waters of St. Vincent Sound. The boat buffeted out over the gray waves like a well-skipped stone as the dark clouds swelled above them.

The sheriff steered the boat into what was left of Dr. Price's dock, Gator's glade skiff tied at its end, bobbing like a cork in the wake of the sheriff's big runabout. After they had tied up the boat, they trudged up the sandy path to the old doctor's cabin. In a few minutes, they were at the front door, where they were met by Tom Black, standing before them, frowning, as formal as ever in his dark suit and striped tie. He led them up the dim stairs and down the hall. This time the house smelled like death—a dusty, damp, rotting scent that the doctor was all too familiar with. As the butler opened the bedroom door, the smell became almost overpowering. The old doctor was still in the bed where the doctor had left him only a few days before. But now his sheet and blankets were soaked in rust-colored blood. Dr. Price's head had been nearly severed. A deep cut almost halfway through his neck went from ear to ear and was filled with oozing, clotting blood. Dr. Berber pulled back Price's blood-soaked pajamas and found a round, red bullet hole on the left side of the man's chest.

"Okay, Tom, let's hear it," the sheriff told the colored butler, who was standing straight and stiff and solemn next to the bedroom door.

"I brought him up dinner at around noon. He was doing much better. The fever was gone. His color was back. He was hungry and was talking about getting up and taking a shower. Then I went downstairs to the kitchen, and I heard a pop, so I came back up and this is what I found," the butler said, nodding at Dr. Price's bed.

"Did you hear anything? See anybody?"

"No, nothing. Just that pop. Sounded like a firecracker."

"Whatta you think, Doc?" the sheriff asked.

"Well, it is what it is. He's obviously had his throat slit by something really sharp and been shot in the heart at close range. There's not much more to say."

"Were the doors locked?" the sheriff asked the butler.

"No. We don't generally lock them."

"Who else is on the island today?"

"As far as I know, just me and the missus and Gator. The rest are out oyster fishing."

"And where exactly were y'all when he was killed?"

"Well," Tom Black said. "The missus and I were downstairs in the kitchen eating our dinner and then cleaning up afterwards. Gator was out someplace hunting stray cattle. I haven't seen him since breakfast."

"Okay, Tom, I want you to leave this room exactly like it is now. Don't touch a thing. I'm gonna have some crime scene cops from Tallahassee come down here and dust for prints and go over the place with a fine-tooth comb. When they've gone, I want you to contact the undertaker, either the one in Port St. Joe or the one in Apalachicola, and arrange for them to do their thing. Did the man have any family around here?"

"No," Black answered. "They're all up North, but I know how to contact them."

"Okay, I'm gonna ask you to do that and then figure out when to bury him."

"Yes, sir."

"Does he have a will, do you know?"

"Yes, sir," the butler answered. "When he got sick, he had the lawyer come out and bring it up to date."

"Who's the lawyer?"

"Bob Huggins in Port St. Joe."

"You got a copy here?"

"Yes, sir. It's downstairs in Dr. Price's office. In his desk drawer, just where he told me to put it."

"All right, Tom, I'll need that, and tell me where I can find Gator."

"Yes, sir, I'll get it for you. As far as Gator goes, I don't know exactly where he is. Could be almost anyplace if he's chasing a stray. But one thing for sure is he'll be back by suppertime. If I was you, I'd wait until then. Be a lot easier than running around through the woods after him."

"Okay," the sheriff said. "That makes a lot of sense. When's suppertime around here?"

"Seven sharp."

"Where's Gator's house then? Dr. Berber and I'll wait there for him."

"Just yonder," the butler answered. "You know where it is, don't you, Dr. Berber?"

"I do. Follow me, Sheriff."

"I'll get you the will on your way out," Black said, leading them out of the room and down to Dr. Price's office.

After the butler had handed the sheriff a thick white envelope, Dr. Berber and Sheriff Duffield walked over to Gator's cottage, which sat silently at the back of the compound. It was like the other two cottages: white clapboard, green trim, cypress shingle roof, tall brick chimney, with a wide front porch, all sitting on stilts about five feet above the sandy clearing.

"You don't think Gator would mind if we took a look around inside, do you?" the sheriff asked as they ascended the front porch stairs.

"I guess not," the doctor answered, "but let's knock in case he's decided to take a nap instead of chasing strays."

The sheriff pounded on the door, but there was no reply so he opened the screen door and pushed the heavy inside door open. They first entered a living room or parlor, which was sparsely furnished—just an old couch and a wooden rocking chair, nothing else. Then there was a kitchen behind the parlor that had a round, wooden table and two chairs in the center and a sink full of dirty dishes. The doctor felt uneasy about nosing around in Gator's house without his being there, but the sheriff seemed intent on investigating. Next there was a bedroom with an unmade iron bed and a dresser and another room at the back of the house, probably used as another bedroom by former tenants but apparently used by Gator as some sort of workshop. There was a long table on one side and stacks of orange crates lining the other three walls. The crates were filled with all manner of things: scraps of rope; coffee cans filled with nuts, bolts, and nails; sacks of sugar and flour; boxes of shotgun shells and rifle bullets; tools of all kinds. There were two doors on the back wall, one leading to the back porch, the other closed and latched. The sheriff played with the padlock on the latch and when it didn't open, he casually reached over to the long table and picked up a crowbar, which he used to quickly pop the latch from the wooden doorframe. The steel latch, padlock and all, clattered to the dusty floor. The sheriff opened the door and pulled a string hanging from a bare bulb on the ceiling of what turned out to be a small closet.

"Look what we have here," he said, peering through his sunglasses into the corner of the closet.

The doctor walked over next to him and followed his gaze to the dim corner. There, leaning against the wall, were a rifle and a bloody machete.

"Whatta you think?" the sheriff asked.

"I have no idea," the doctor said, staring in disbelief.

"I was planning to sit out on the front porch and wait for Gator, but I think maybe we should wait for him in that shed over there, where he can't see us and we can see him when he comes back."

The doctor followed the sheriff to the shed. Inside, one end of the building was filled with various farm implements—a Ford tractor, a lawn mower, an old wagon. At the other end stood what was left of the old moonshine distillery—three large copper tanks with round gauges and connected with shiny copper tubing. The sheriff found a window near the tractor that gave him a good view of Gator's cottage. He removed his pistol from its holster, placed it on the windowsill, and peered out through the weathered window pane.

"Now what?" the doctor asked.

"We wait," the sheriff answered, placing a wad of tobacco in his cheek.

"For what?"

"The murderer," Sheriff Duffield answered.

Chapter 10

As the red summer sun began to descend behind the clouds beyond the tops of the surrounding slash pine forest, it became increasingly difficult to see Gator's cottage through the dirty windows of the shadowed shed. The sheriff removed his sunglasses and propped them on the bill of his hat. It was the first time that the doctor had actually seen his eyes. They were squinting and narrow and dark and made him looking vaguely Asian, but their most striking detail was their total lack of life. The sheriff's eyes were two barren orbs that showed nothing.

The doctor couldn't imagine why Gator would lock up a rifle and a bloody machete in a closet in his workshop, but it was obvious that Sheriff Duffield believed Gator had used them to kill Dr. Price. Dr. Berber didn't, however. That just wasn't Gator's style. If Gator had wanted the old doctor dead, all he had to do was sneak up to his bedroom and smoother him in his sleep. Everyone, including Dr. Berber, would have chalked it up to the encephalitis. There was no reason to slit his throat and shoot him. That was the work of a madman, not a loyal employee, not Gator Mica. But if this particular madman happened to be Lucky Lucilla, why would he want to murder Dr. Price? Lucilla had indirectly worked for Price, selling his moonshine out of a panel truck behind the Indian Pass Raw Bar, but, according to Price, they had met face to face only once, when Price had hired him a few years before.

The doctor did have to consider Gator's violent past, however. There was that bar fight over a woman in Florida City a few years back when he had beaten a man to death, and the other beating death at Gator's hand when someone had foolishly called him a half-breed son of a bitch at the Indian Pass Raw Bar. It seemed that when Gator had too much to drink and someone crossed him, he didn't know how really powerful his punches could be. But killing a man the way Dr. Price had been killed was not something the doctor believed Gator could have or would have done. Lucky Lucilla, yes, but Gator Mica, no. He was about to explain all this to the sheriff when they saw a weary Gator shuffling across the clearing and up the front steps of his house.

The sheriff took his pistol from the windowsill and motioned the doctor to follow him. They walked across the sandy clearing and up the steps. The sheriff banged on Gator's front door. Presently Gator appeared behind the screen door.

"What are y'all doin' here?" he asked.

"You're under arrest," the sheriff said, raising his pistol and pointing it at Gator.

"What?"

"You heard me. You're under arrest for the murder of Dr. Elmer Price."

"Murder?" Gator looked pleadingly at the doctor.

"Price was shot and had his throat slit," the doctor explained. "Tom Black called the sheriff just a little while ago. The sheriff asked me to come out here with him."

"Oh, no. He was doin' so well too. I believed he was gonna make it."

"He didn't," the sheriff said.

"But why me? I was out chasin' strays all day."

"We found your rifle and your machete covered with blood locked in your closet."

"What?"

"I'm gonna bet that they'll be covered with your fingerprints too."

"What closet?"

"You know, back in the workshop. The one you padlocked."

"Padlocked? I ain't never padlocked nothin' in my life. Why would I?"

"'Cause you didn't want no one to find them," the sheriff said. "You might as well 'fess up, Gator. Why'd you do it?"

"Do what? I didn't kill nobody."

"The judge and jury will be the judge of that. Now come on, let's go. I gotta take you in," the sheriff said, his pistol still pointed at Gator's stomach.

"No," Gator said, shaking his head.

The rest happened fast. The sheriff pulled the screen door open with his gunless hand. Gator stepped back. The sheriff reached for the silver handcuffs in a leather packet on his belt. Gator's left hand suddenly swiped toward the sheriff, knocking the pistol from his hand as it fired. At the same time, Gator's right clinched fist landed with a sickening thud against the sheriff's left temple. A stream of tobacco juice flew from the sheriff's mouth as he collapsed to the floor in a crumble. Gator and the doctor stared at him, seemingly lifeless on the dusty floor of Gator's cottage. Apparently no one had been hit by the pistol's discharge. There was no blood on the sheriff or on Gator.

"Ah, shit, Gator," the doctor said, shaking his head. "I wish you hadn't done that."

"I'm sorry, partner. I just couldn't help myself. No way I'm goin' to jail."

"But you didn't do anything. Huggins will get you off just like he did before."

"I ain't so sure. I think it's time for me to be movin' on. All this killin' and cold-cocking the sheriff is bound to catch up with me. What am I gonna do anyway with Dr. Price gone?"

"Hell, I don't know, Gator, but we'll figure it out. There's no use running. Stay here and let's deal with this."

"No, partner, I don't think so. I ain't gonna take the chance. I ain't gonna be locked up. Even for just a little while."

"Gator?"

"You tend to the sheriff. I'm gonna pack some stuff, get my ol' glade skiff, and head on up the coast. I'm thinkin' Tate's Hell might just turn out to be Gator's heaven after all this. But don't tell nobody."

"Gator, don't!"

"Time to go, partner."

And, with that, the big Indian began throwing things into a burlap bag, including the sheriff's pistol, as well as the rifle and bloody machete from his closet. The doctor knelt over the sheriff, who was still out cold but breathing evenly.

"See you later," Gator said, as he reached the door.

"Gator, please."

But he was gone into the dusk, like the setting sun descending silently into the sea around them.

In the gathering twilight, the doctor stared down at the sheriff. The man was laid out like a napping dog. His police hat and aviator sunglasses had been knocked off, either by Gator's single blow or during his fall. It all happened so fast, the doctor wasn't sure. The doctor had some smelling salts in his black bag, but since the sheriff continued to breathe regularly and his pulse was strong, he decided to let the man rest a little longer and give Gator a chance to put some distance between himself and the fallen officer.

When the sheriff finally did come around, he was mad. "Goddamn it," he said, sitting up and trying to get his bearings. "I can't believe I let this happen. Your Injun friend is fast; I'll give him that. And now he's gone. I don't suppose he told you where he was going, did he?"

"No," the doctor lied. "Not a word."

"I figured as much. How long have I been out?"

"Oh, not that long, maybe ten minutes."

"Hmm," the sheriff muttered as he felt the bump growing on his forehead. "And now it's gettin' dark. Does he have any way of gettin' off this island?"

The doctor had to think on this one. If he lied, the butler would undoubtedly know about Gator's boat and would tell the sheriff when he was questioned. Finally, he said, "He does have that little glade skiff we saw tied to the dock, so he could use that, I guess."

"Okay, listen," the sheriff said, as he stood up and then unsteadily leaned over to retrieve his hat and sunglasses. "Wait a minute. Where's my pistol? Goddamn it, he stole my pistol, that bastard!" And then he stomped back to the workshop, and the doctor heard him curse again when he saw that the rifle and machete had been taken as well. He returned to the doctor, shaking his head.

"All right, as I was saying," the sheriff said, "I'm gonna use Price's radio/phone to call all this into my office. I'll get all my men out looking for him and in the morning we'll get Pop Albertson's bloodhounds to start searching. Meanwhile, don't touch anything here. Head back to the boat while there's still a little light, and I'll meet you there in a few minutes."

As the doctor walked back toward the sheriff's motorboat and thunder rumbled in the distance, he wondered about his friend Gator. The little one-and-a-half-horsepower motor on his glade skiff wouldn't propel him up the coast very fast. So there was a chance that the sheriff's boat, with its superior speed, could overtake him somewhere along the way. But it was still a big ocean out there, and the thickening clouds were blocking the light from the moon and the stars. The roar of the Gar Wood's big engine would drown out the putter of Gator's puny motor so the sheriff would actually have to sight him if he had any chance of capturing him. But, of course, there were no running lights on Gator's simple skiff.

Despite the sheriff's intent scouring of the shoreline, all they saw on their return trip to the mainland were the wine-dark sea, black clouds, an occasional star, and the slim sliver of a crescent moon occasionally peeking into view. But no Gator Mica.

When the sheriff helped the doctor out of the boat and up onto the dock at the Thirteen Mile Oyster House, he ordered him to keep an eye out for Lucky Lucilla and to let him know if Gator tried to contact him. The doctor said okay, but they both knew he would heed only the former command and not the latter.

So here he was again, approaching the Indian Pass Raw Bar at mealtime. This time it was dark outside and beginning to sprinkle, but the doctor was awfully hungry. It was well past 8:00 when he located a parking spot in front of the roadhouse, dragged himself in, and greeted Sadie McIntire at her usual perch behind the ancient cash register.

"How you doin', Mrs. McIntire?" he asked.

"Ain't complainin'. How about y'all?"

"Been better, but I'll live."

"You found that Eye-talian guy yet?"

"Not yet. You seen anything of him?"

"Nope, not a trace."

The doctor took a seat at the bar. As usual, the place was filled with cigar and cigarette smoke, and music was blaring from the jukebox. This time it was Cliff Bruner wailing "Truck Driver's Blues." The doctor felt like the despondent lyrics of the song: "feelin' tired and weary from my head down to my shoes." So he ordered his usual: a Spearman beer, some steamed shrimp, and a bowl of gumbo. He thought about Dr. Price and Gator Mica. Price was an odd fellow but who would want to kill him?

Gator had been the doctor's best friend, except maybe for Jewel, for the past three years. Now they were both gone.

It then occurred to him that he really didn't care that much anymore if Lucky Lucilla did kill him. At this point, what difference would it make? Jewel was gone. Gator was gone. He was old, tired, and alone. "I've got nothin' much to lose," Cliff Bruner whined. This realization gave him a sudden sense of relief. With this new-found fatalism, he no longer had to worry about when the madman would strike. The sooner the better, as far as he was concerned. But, then again, he would like to see Jewel one more time, and she would be back in a few days now. He hoped Lucky Lucilla would hold off just a little bit longer.

The next morning, the doctor called Bob Huggins' secretary and made an appointment to see the lawyer that afternoon. Huggins was widely considered to be the best lawyer in Gulf County, especially if you were facing jail time. He was on a first-name basis with Judge Arthur Denton, who heard most of the cases in and around the county, and he could wrap a jury around his little finger like the diamond pinkie ring that he always wore with his homespun, down-home approach to uncovering the truth and fashioning the facts. He had recently won the release of Michael Madison Mitchell, who, before being charged with the murder of Sheriff Byrd "Dog" Batson and the assault of three union organizers, had been the manager of the St. Joe Paper Company. Fortunately for Mitchell, who bore a striking resemblance to W.C. Fields, he had Huggins as his attorney and only one witness against him, the lunatic Lucky Lucilla, who was locked away in the loony bin and not considered by anyone to be the most credible observer around.

Huggins was a slight man with round, wire-rim spectacles and an unruly head of graying hair that he unsuccessfully tried to control by what looked and smelled to be a fistful of Brylcreem. When the doctor sat down across the oak desk from him later that day, the lawyer was thoroughly polishing his glasses with his handkerchief and leaning back in his padded leather chair. "What brings you here?" he asked. "As if I didn't know. I heard through the grapevine that your friend Gator Mica has got himself into some trouble again. So why don't you tell me what's going on?"

The doctor explained Gator's predicament. Huggins listened attentively, not saying much as the doctor described what had happened the day before out on St. Vincent Island.

"So," the doctor asked when he had finished telling the lawyer the entire story, "what do you think?"

"I think your friend Gator Mica is—let me see, forgive me for putting this in legal terms—in a shitload of trouble."

"Yeah, I figured as much."

"At best, he assaulted an officer of the law. He stole evidence in a murder case, not to mention the sheriff's pistol. He left the scene of a crime. And, at worst, he may have committed a murder."

"But why would Gator kill Price? What could his motive possibly be?"

"You really wanna know?" Huggins said, lightly tapping a manila folder on his desk.

"Of course. Why?"

"Well," the lawyer said. "This is all supposed to be confidential, but it's all gonna come out in the next few days anyway, so you might as well know now. When Dr. Price had me change his will, which I just happen to have right here on my desk, he eliminated his children as the heirs to St. Vincent Island and he replaced them with . . . guess who."

"You're kidding," the doctor said.

"Nope, Gator Mica, wherever he is, now owns St. Vincent Island."

"Oh, no! But I don't think Gator even knew. What do we do now?"

"Well, Doc, there's your motive, if he did know. I think the only thing that will save him now is that we somehow find him and get him to turn himself in. Then we sort this whole thing out and try to show a jury how little sense it makes that Gator slit the doctor's throat and then shot him when he could have staged an accident or failing health so much more convincingly. But it would help us even more if we could find the real murderer."

"Lucky Lucilla," the doctor said.

"If you say so," Huggins said.

"Damn, will I ever get this man out of my life?"

Huggins didn't answer. He just leaned back again in his chair, frowned, and shook his head.

Chapter 11

The next Sunday morning, the doctor again listened to the radio and heard a report about British Prime Minister Neville Chamberlain's reaffirming England's support for Poland and stating that it would intervene on Poland's behalf if hostilities between Germany and Poland broke out. Chamberlain had also written that very day, according to the reporter, that "no doubt the Jews aren't a loveable people. I don't care about them myself. But that is not sufficient to explain the pogroms." Meanwhile, the United States had just announced its withdrawal from its commercial treaty with Japan.

The doctor switched off this continuing news of impending war and turned again to *The Grapes of Wrath*. The Joads were making their way west on Route 66. As they were setting up camp west of Amarillo—their dog run over, Granpa dead from a stroke, Granma going into convulsions from the heat, and nothing more to eat than cold pan biscuits leftover from breakfast—the annoying telephone on the doctor's kitchen wall tolled like a bell buoy in a summer storm. He heaved himself up, hobbled stiffly to the kitchen, and answered the disrupting nuisance of a machine.

"Hi, Doc. It's Jewel," the voice said.

"Jewel! Where are you?"

"We're here, in town, at Mama's house."

"Oh, thank goodness. When can you come over?"

"How 'bout tonight after church? Mama wants to spoil Marcus at little bit longer, and Gabriel and me could both use us a little nap this afternoon. We're 'bout as tired as a pig layin' in the sun."

"That tired, huh? Well, okay, I'll be looking for you."

"'Round six then."

At five o'clock, the doctor showered, put on his loosest black gabardine slacks and starched white shirt, and waited, with Steinbeck, on his screened-in back porch. There was so much to say to Jewel that he was momentarily speechless when she, Gabriel, and Marcus pulled up in his driveway in Gabriel's new red Cadillac convertible. Jewel looked stylish, dressed in a form-fitting, flowered dress, her hair pulled back, her brown skin shining in the late afternoon sun. Gabriel was almost as glamorous in silk, sharkskin slacks and a white linen shirt, his hair slicked back like Cab Calloway's. And Marcus had grown several inches and looked so mature in his pressed dungarees and spotless white T-shirt that the doctor hardly recognized him. The doctor hugged them all, breathing in Jewel's special scent, a heady confection of starch, laundry soap, and lye, and led them onto the back porch.

"Everybody, sit down and relax," the doctor ordered. "I'll bring drinks."

He had prepared a big pitcher of lemonade and still had a quart of moonshine that Gator had brought by not too long before. He carried them both out to the porch, where Gabriel and Jewel were now sitting on the white wicker love seat and Marcus was rocking furiously in the rocking chair.

"Marcus, get up and help me with the glasses, will you?" the doctor said to him.

When they were in the kitchen and out of earshot of the boy's parents, the doctor quizzed him about his new life in the big city. "So, how is it up there? You doin' okay?"

"It's all right," Marcus answered. "At first I was homesick and it gits awful cold in the winter. I even saw some snow right after Christmas. We went sledding in Central Park."

"You're kidding. What about school?"

"It's big, really big. But I've got some friends now, and my teacher is real nice, so it's okay."

"How are your grades?"

"As and Bs so far."

"Good. What about your mama and daddy? They doing okay?"

"I guess. Mama works while I'm at school and daddy works at night mostly. They're tired a lot."

"Y'all happy then, up there with all those Yankees?"

"Yeah, it's different than here, but it's all right."

"Okay," the doctor said. "I guess we better get these glasses out there before they get too thirsty."

The doctor poured the moonshine for the adults and the lemonade for Marcus. "So how was your trip?" the doctor asked.

"It was long," Gabriel answered, "but the Caddie is fast and smooth, so we didn't have no trouble."

"'Cept in North Carolina," Jewel said, "where some Cracker sheriff thought a colored family shouldn't be out drivin' in such a fancy car, puttin' on airs. Held us up for nearly an hour, checking Gabriel's license and registration and title and insurance papers. He even searched the trunk, the dumb yahoo."

"Tell Dr. Berber what we got for him," Marcus interrupted.

"Oh, yeah, Mama's church ladies put on a real feast for us down in the church basement, a homecomin' potluck dinner after church, and they give us all the leftovers to bring to you. We got 'em out in the car. So whenever you git hungry, just holler. We'll spread 'em out and have a picnic."

"That was mighty nice of those ladies," the doctor said.

"Well, you know they all love you, Doc. You've treated most of 'em, even when they couldn't afford to pay you, when most white doctors won't even give 'em the time of day."

"Tell them thanks for me."

"I will. Ain't Vivian feedin' you enough?"

"She's doing fine. Do I look like I'm starving?"

"No," Jewel answered. "In fact, y'all lookin' as healthy as an ox."

"Thanks, Jewel, I think. By the way, where's Reggie? He didn't come along with y'all?"

"No," Gabriel said. "Are you kidding? We dropped him off in Eatonville, where he's got family. I don't think we'll ever git Reggie back in this town again after what happened to him the last time he was here. In fact, I doubt you'll see that boy anywhere in Gulf County again for the rest of his life."

Reggie Robinson was Gabriel's musical partner. He played a variety of instruments as he accompanied Gabriel, who sang and played guitar. Gabriel was referring to Reggie's mistaken arrest for the murder of Sheriff Byrd "Dog" Batson. Until they had found the real murderer, Reggie had spent several unpleasant weeks awaiting trial, first in the Port St. Joe jail and then in the county lockup in Wewahitchka.

"What about Gator?" Jewel asked. "I was hopin' you'd have him over this evening too. How's he and Dr. Price gittin' on?"

"Not too well," the doctor answered, and then he told them the entire story of their blown-up boat, Dr. Price's murder, Gator's assault of Sheriff Duffield, and finally his escape, apparently to Tate's Hell.

"You and Gator," Jewel said. "I see nothin's changed since I left. Y'all like two peas in a pod. Y'all git together and there's trouble, sure as shootin'. Well, what are we gonna do? Just let him rot out there all by hisself in that jungle?"

"I don't know," the doctor answered honestly. "I talked to Bob Huggins about it, and he said that as long as Gator slugged the sheriff and took the evidence, it would appear to most people that he was guilty, especially since he was named the new owner of St. Vincent Island in the doctor's will. He said that if we can find him and convince him to turn himself in, maybe we could sort through it all and try to get him off. Or better yet, find the real murderer. But as it stands, Gator's in a lot of trouble."

"But he didn't do it," Jewel protested.

"You know that and I know that, but it appears nobody else knows anything except that Gator assaulted the sheriff and absconded with the evidence so he looks like the murderer. When the will gets read in the next few days, people will be even more convinced. So nobody is looking for the real murderer since everyone believes Gator did it."

"So who do you figure the real murderer is then?" Gabriel asked.

"I'm not sure," the doctor answered. "It has all the earmarks of Lucky Lucilla to me. The slit throat and all. But I don't have a clue to why the nut would want to kill Dr. Price. I believe he blew up the boat to get back at Gator and me for capturing him, but Dr. Price had nothing to do with that. So I don't know."

"Well, we're here for a couple of weeks," Jewel said. "And once we git this business with my daddy done, I'll be as bored as a blind man at the beach. I intend to find out just who the real murderer is so we can git Gator back."

"Jewel," the doctor said. "That may be easier said than done. Maybe you're forgetting that Lucky Lucilla is on the loose again, and Chief Lane told him about your little colored-folks posse so he knows you had a part in his capture."

"Well, it seems to me," Jewel said, "that we don't have a choice, one way or the other. If Lucky Lucilla is out to kill us all, then we better find him first and get to the bottom of this before it's too late."

"But ain't that the police's job?" Gabriel asked.

"Greasy gravy, who you kiddin'?" Jewel said. "The law don't care about us or any of this stuff. They're glad that Price got killed 'cause they were all taking bribes from him when he was runnin' that moonshine business. Now he can't tell no one about that. Gator is just another dumb Injun in their minds so it's easier to convict him than to chase after some escaped lunatic."

"Even if the lunatic is probably out to kill me, you, and Gator," the doctor said, "not to mention Chief Lane, who also shot the nut."

"Well," Jewel said, "you can put your lot in the hands of Chief Lane if you want, but I ain't that trusting my ownself. I'm gonna do something—I ain't quite sure what yet—to find this nut and git him locked away for good."

"Okay, Jewel, I guess you're right. We really don't have much of a choice, but we're going to have to be careful."

"Well, don't worry about me, Doc. You should know by now that I know how to take care of myself. But I catch your drift. This Lucilla man is crazier than a pet coon."

"Can we eat now?" Marcus asked.

The church ladies had outdone themselves. There was fried chicken, potato salad, some sort of squash casserole, homemade pickles, cornbread, and pecan pie. As Gabriel and the doctor spread the food out on the wicker coffee table on the back porch, Jewel and Marcus brought out the plates and utensils from the kitchen.

"This sure is good," the doctor said as he chewed a bite of chicken. "Now tell me about your plans for your daddy. I got the medical report from the state prison and it doesn't look good. It says he has an advanced form of tuberculosis, and the X-rays they sent confirm that."

"What does that mean?" Jewel asked.

"Well, I hate to tell you, but at his age," the doctor said, "it means that he probably doesn't have long to live. There is no known cure for the disease. He really should be in a sanitarium where he can't infect other people, especially his family. There's only one around here that accepts colored people, and that's at Florida A&M College in Tallahassee. It's a small place and usually has a waiting list to get in. Plus it costs a lot of money."

"So what do we do?" Jewel asked.

"Well," the doctor said, "here's what I suggest. After you pick him up tomorrow in Raiford, bring him back to my office. You planning to make it there in one day?"

"I'm drivin' over in Mama's old Ford. I'm leavin' Gabriel and Marcus here. I wanna see how Daddy's feelin' about Gabriel before he meets him. I figure it's gonna take me most of the day to git there. Then we'll stay with a cousin in Lake City and drive back here the next day."

"Okay, bring him back to me when you get to town. Let me examine him to make sure the prison's diagnosis is correct. You and Marcus don't get too close to him. Let your mama feed him and take care of him. She can do pretty much everything they would do at a sanitarium. She can put him out on the front porch every day so he can get plenty of fresh air. He needs to rest, and he needs to eat right—plenty of protein—to build up his immune system. With any luck, he'll live for a few more years and your mama won't become infected. After I examine him, I'll talk to him about all this and also talk to him about you and Gabriel, see how he's thinking about that. Then let's figure out what to do from there."

"Okay, Doc," Jewel said. "If you say so."

"Now, tell me about your lives in New York City. Do you love it or hate it?"

"Love it," Gabriel said.

"Love it and hate it," Jewel said.

"Marcus?"

"Like I said," Marcus answered, "it's okay most of the time. But I like it better here."

"Tell me everything," the doctor said as he refilled everyone's glass.

"Harlem is a fascinatin' place," Jewel began. "It's filled with colored people that treat each other like real human beings. All the businesses are owned and run by Negroes. People talk all the time about the New Negro and how Jim Crow and racism gotta go. I'm workin' as a cook in a little place called Aunt Dinah's Kitchen up on One Hundred Thirty-Fifth Street. I cook Southern food like I cooked down here and people seem to like it."

"So why do you hate it then?" the doctor asked.

"It's cold. People ain't as friendly. They's always in a hurry. Sometimes they look down on us cause we're from the South. And once you git outta Harlem, white people are pretty near as ugly as they can be down here. So . . . it can be excitin' livin' with all them colored folks, but you still gotta go downtown every now and again."

"Gabriel?"

"Jewel's right," Gabriel said. "It's an excitin' place. There's music and plays and radio and books all made by colored folks. Even some white folks like all the energy. There's one place up on Lenox Avenue called the Cotton Club that's just for whites, where all the great Negro big bands play: Ellington, Basie, Henderson, Calloway, all of 'em. Our radio show with an all-colored cast, the *Sheep and Goats Club*, is goin' great guns, and I'm hopin' to git a part in a new play called *St. Louis Woman* by a couple of colored fellows named Arna Bontemps and Countee Cullen. It's a great place and time for a musician like me. It's jumpin' every night. You can walk down the streets in Harlem and hear the music everywhere."

"What about the World's Fair? Y'all been to that yet?"

"Oh, yeah," Marcus exclaimed. "We been there. It's amazing. They've got all this future stuff, like cars and something they're calling a television. It's this box where the pictures actually move, like at the movies."

"Yeah," Gabriel said. "And pictures you can take with a camera that when you git them developed they come out in color, like the real colors, and something called a fluorescent light that's this long tube that lights up really bright."

"And get this," Jewel added. "This DuPont Company, the same one that owns the paper mill here in Port St. Joe, it's made this new material they's callin' nylon that's really strong and made all from chemicals of some sort."

"Oh, my," said the doctor. "All that's hard to believe. Do you think any of that will actually happen someday?"

"Naw," Jewel said. "It's just all a bunch of fakery to git people to come and see it. Ain't none of that gonna happen in real life."

"I bet it all happens," Marcus said.

The doctor tried to talk Gabriel into bringing in his guitar and singing some songs, but he said he was too tired. Jewel wanted to go home and get a good night's sleep before driving all the way to Raiford in the morning. Marcus wanted to stay up and play records on the doctor's Gramophone. It was good to see Jewel again, but the doctor was tired so he said good night to them all and watched the big red Cadillac back slowly out of his driveway and into the night. Now all he wanted was to have a morphine nightcap and go to bed.

And so he did.

Chapter 12

Now that the doctor had become resigned to his own death at the hands of Lucky Lucilla, he didn't mind offering himself up as a target by walking to work each morning. But as long as he was alive, he figured he might as well do what he could to save Gator, Jewel, and even Chief Lane from this violent madman. The trouble was he didn't know quite how to do that. The obvious solution would be to find Lucky Lucilla, but he didn't know where to look. He wasn't going back to St. Vincent Island no matter what. So if Lucilla was there, he would just have to remain there.

As the doctor walked down Reid Street, he decided he would try to enlist Chief Lane in his impending search. After all, Lucilla would probably be targeting Lane just as much as the doctor, and Lane was the only law enforcement officer the doctor entirely trusted. He had reason to believe that both Sheriff Roberts in Gulf County and Sheriff Duffield in Franklin County had been paid by Dr. Price to stay away from his moonshine business, as Jewel had suggested, and both seemed to the doctor more interested in winning their re-elections than protecting their constituents. Besides, since he didn't know where Lucilla was, he couldn't identify the appropriate jurisdiction anyway. St. Vincent Island was in Franklin County and therefore in Sheriff Duffield's dominion. Port St.

Joe was Chief Lane's purview. And the rest of Gulf County was Sheriff Robert's turf. But where was Lucky Lucilla?

The doctor was sweating profusely by the time he arrived at his office. Maybe it was time to talk to Sally Martin again. When they had captured Lucilla, the nut had claimed that he loved her so maybe he had contacted her. If anyone knew where the newly escaped lunatic was, it would be Sally. But the doctor had not talked to her for more than a year. And the last time he had asked for her help, she had refused him. He had no reason to believe that anything had changed. Still . . . maybe he should at least try.

The waiting room was full when he walked in. Nadyne was poring over her appointment book, and the doctor asked her to come back to his office so they could review the day.

"First off," she began, "you have Mrs. Cooper. Something's wrong with her eye. Did you notice when you came in? It's all swollen up. Then Curtis Palmer whose got all the symptoms of some kind of influenza. Marvin Larsen got bit by a dog. Mrs. Kilbourn believes she's pregnant. I'm not sure about Marge Horton, but I'd say she's got diphtheria, from what she told me. Liz Adams and her son Louis are here because Louis is all beat up. I think you and I know why. Then Mildred Jarvis has some sort of breathing problem. And then there're house calls in the afternoon. Max Sanders is fading fast, according to Elaine. Harold Morgan's syphilis is getting worse. Helen Myers fell yesterday and may have broken her hip. And another mill accident: Gerald Ray got run over by a truck backing up."

"A typical Monday," the doctor said. "Okay, Nadyne, send 'em in and I'll see what I can do."

Most of it was pretty routine. But nine year-old Louis Adams' injuries were not. His left eye was swollen and black with a nasty two-inch cut over his eyebrow. He had deep bruises over most of the rest of his upper body and possibly internal injuries.

"What happened?" the doctor asked him. But the boy only cried as the doctor cleaned his cut with gauze and Mercurochrome. After he had done all he could for him, the doctor motioned for his mother, a heavy-set woman with dull brown hair and sad blue eyes, to follow him to his office in the back.

"What happened?" he asked her.

"He fell down the stairs," she whimpered.

"Nonsense," the doctor snapped. "Who beat this boy?"

Liz Adams buried her head in her hands and sobbed.

"It was your husband, Norman, wasn't it?"

She did not answer and continued to cry.

"Look," the doctor said. "You convinced me not to do anything when this boy's big brother got beat up. And I agreed to keep quiet if you would stop your husband. But you obviously haven't so I have no choice but to report the bastard to Chief Lane."

"No, please, Doctor," she bellowed. "That'll only make it worse. He'll just beat me for tellin' on him."

"Then what do you suggest?"

"I don't know. Could you just patch Louis up and not say anything?"

"No," the doctor shot back. "No, we've already been through that. Have you ever thought about leaving the man, Mrs. Adams?"

"More times than I can count," she cried. "But I ain't got nowhere to go. I ain't got no family around here, and I ain't got no money. I've got eight kids to feed, and I ain't got no way to find a job. And Norman's usually okay, 'cept when he drinks too much. He at least puts food on the table, which is more than I could do."

"Okay," the doctor said, shaking his head. "Here's what I'm gonna do. I'm sick of seeing these children beat up and I'm not gonna stand for it anymore. I'm gonna talk to Chief Lane, and we're gonna try to figure out a way to stop this thing. I understand your concern about Norman taking it out on you so we'll try to figure out a way to avoid that. Now that I've sewed that cut up, that's about all I can do. The rest will heal with time, but you need to make sure he's given the time. Hide the bottle, withhold sex, buy a pistol, but do what you have to do. Because if I see this again, I'm gonna go out to your place and shoot the son of a bitch myself. You understand?"

"Yes, sir," she whimpered.

After the doctor had completed his house calls that afternoon, he drove to the police station behind City Hall and found Chief Lane just getting out of his patrol car. "Can I talk to you for a minute?" the doctor asked him.

"Sure," Lane answered. "Why don't we take a little walk down to the pier? I'll buy you a soda at the Texaco station on the way."

"Okay, sounds good. How's life treating you, Chief?"

"I can't complain. It's hotter than hell this time of year, but what are you gonna do? How about you, Doc?"

"Well, I've been better, to tell you the truth. Did Duffield tell you about Dr. Price and Gator Mica?

"Yeah, I'm supposed to keep an eye out for Gator. But you and I both know that he's out in the woods someplace, and we've got about as much chance of finding him as we do of finding Lucky Lucilla."

"Speaking of which, will you help me find that nut? I agree with you that our chances of finding Gator are slim, but the only way we can clear him is if we find the real murderer, who I believe is Lucky Lucilla. And, if I'm right, he's after you and me as well. So I figure you have almost as much to gain by finding him as I do."

"Hmm, maybe so," the chief replied. "But, like Gator, I don't have a clue to where we might find our old friend Lucky Lucilla."

"Well, I don't either," the doctor said. "But I was thinking maybe a good place to start would be the obvious."

"The obvious?"

"Yeah. Before we caught him, he was living out at the sheriff's old beach house on St. Vincent Sound. Maybe he's crazy enough to go back there."

"I doubt it," the chief said.

"Where else then?"

"I don't know. If I knew I would have arrested him by now."

"So?"

"What makes you think he's out there?"

"I don't know. I've just got a hunch and, frankly, no better ideas."

"Well, I guess I don't have a better idea either. Maybe it wouldn't hurt to drive out there and take a look. I have to go to a meeting in Wewahitchka tomorrow, but we could go on Wednesday, if you can make it."

"Okay. How about around three? I'll meet you at your office. With any luck, I'll be finished with my house calls by then, and that'll give us plenty of time before nightfall."

"Okay," the sheriff agreed. "Now let me tell you about another problem I have."

"Shoot," the chief said as he dropped a nickel into the Coca-Cola machine at the Texaco station.

As they walked down the pier from the Port Inn to St. Joseph Bay, the doctor told him about Liz and Norman Adams and their eight children, who were being beaten. By the time the doctor had finished giving the chief the details, they were at the end of the pier. The chief stared out into the gray waters of the Gulf of Mexico.

Finally, he said, "I've come across these things far too many times in my career. Especially during this damn Depression, when the stress of poverty tends to do strange things to otherwise good, hard-working men. There's no good answer, of course. The women should take the children and leave, but it's not always that simple."

"So what do we do?"

"Let's do this. Sometimes it works. I go out and pay a friendly visit to Mr. Adams. Just me and him, one on one. I tell him that when I was patrolling the school the other day, I noticed this boy who looked pretty beat up. So I asked him his name and where he lived and he told me. And then I asked him how he got all beat up, and he said he got in a fight with another kid at school. So then, I tell him, I went and talked to the principal and he said that the boy had not been in a fight as far as he knew. He said he didn't know what happened to the boy. This way no one gets the blame from Mr. Adams for snitching on him. But I let him know that I don't believe the boy and believe that he's the one responsible. Then I tell him that I've instructed the teachers and principal at the school to report any of his kids with even the slightest bruise. And if that happens, I tell him, I'm gonna come out and arrest him and throw him in jail, and I'm gonna make clear to the other inmates what he has done, and, furthermore, I'm gonna make it real easy for those other prisoners to get to him. And, finally, I tell him that I'm gonna be watching every morning as his kids get off the bus to make sure they all get off with big smiles on their faces, not a soul with a bruise or a limp or a single tear."

"The sounds pretty good, Chief."

"We'll see what happens. If it doesn't work, I'll lock the son of a bitch up and throw away the damn key."

Chapter 13

On Wednesday morning Jewel showed up at the doctor's house for breakfast. She looked beguiling as usual, with her hair pulled back and her white summer dress freshly starched. Vivian served them both a large slice of cantaloupe, cheese grits, a thick sausage patty, a glass of orange juice, and a cup of black coffee.

"Utensils," the doctor reminded Vivian. "And then quit fussing around and sit down at the table with us."

"Oh, I'm sorry," she said. "I got so excited seeing Jewel here that I plum forgot."

"So how was your trip to Raiford? How's your daddy?"

"The trip was okay . . . long. Daddy's sick. He's coughing a lot and he's lost a lot of weight. Peaked too. Just don't look right."

"Okay, bring him by the office today, and I'll take a look at him. What about Gabriel? Did you talk about that?"

"Yeah. He's still mad as farr. Says he doesn't want to have anything to do with Gabriel."

"What about Marcus?"

"He just shook his head, but Mama says she'll take care of that, 'cause she ain't gonna stop havin' Marcus around 'cause of Daddy. He better get used to the boy, she says, or he'll not be sittin' on the front porch but be out back in the doghouse instead."

"So where's Gabriel staying now that your daddy's back in the house?"

"Oh, he's out with his buddy Robert, who's got a farm on Old Parkwood Tramroad. But he ain't too happy about it."

"Good grits, Vivian," the doctor said. "What do you think, Jewel?"

"Not bad," she answered. "Could use a bit more cheese and a dash or two more pepper, but not bad."

"What else is new, Jewel? Since you been gone, I been real behind on the town gossip. What's goin' on?"

"Well, since I been runnin' back and forth between here and Raiford, I ain't heard much, but today I'll put out the word that we're lookin' for Lucky and Gator. Something'll turn up."

"I hope so," the doctor said. "Chief Lane and I are gonna check out Lucky's old house on St. Vincent Sound this afternoon to see what we can see. And I'm thinking maybe I'll pay Sally Martin a visit to see if she'll tell us anything. I have my doubts, but maybe it's worth a try."

"Are you sure you want to do that, Doc? You seen her at all since last year?"

"No. I've heard through the grapevine that she's doing real well at the mill. Already been promoted and doing something important there, not sure what."

"Let me check it out before you go see her," Jewel said. "I'll find out what's really happenin' there so you know the whole story before you face off with her."

"Okay, Jewel," the doctor said as he stood up and started clearing the table. "I have to get to work. See you when you bring your daddy by."

"All right, but you and Chief Lane be particular out there tryin' to find that nut."

Jewel was right as usual. Her daddy, Django Jackson, did not look well. Jewel had dropped him off at the doctor's office at around 11:00 and then had abruptly left to do some shopping, saying she would be back in about an hour.

"It's a pleasure to meet you, sir," the doctor said to Jewel's daddy as the man sat uncertainly on the doctor's examination table. "Before moving to New York, your daughter worked for me for three years, and she did a fine job. More than that, she's a good person. You should be proud of her."

"I am," the man said in a deep, gruff, no-nonsense voice.

"Before I examine you, tell me a bit about yourself, please," the doctor said.

"Ain't much to tell. I was born and raised over in Franklin County. My mama and daddy was slaves and when they was freed they went to work in a gum patch—that's what we called a turpentine camp back then. It was north of Eastpoint, near High Bluff. I was born in that camp and I probably would have died in that camp if my daddy hadn't told me when I was eighteen to go into Apalachicola and join the Army. That was the only way he could see me gittin' outta that camp, since we owed so much to the commissary. So in eighteen ninety-eight, I joined the Tenth Cavalry Regiment, what they called the Buffalo Soldiers, 'cause we was all colored, and fought with Teddy Roosevelt at San Juan Hill during the Spanish American War. And then when I got out of the Army, I went to Port St. Joe, where I heard the Apalachicola Northern Railroad was hiring veterans. I got a job as a laborer for 'em, and then I met Jewel's mama and then we had Jewel. It was a rough delivery, but she sure 'nough is the apple of my eye, that gal. Then that son of a bitch bluesman had to come to town and go and git her pregnant, and I ends up in prison for beatin' up some white men 'bout eight years ago, and then I got sick so they let me out early so I wouldn't infect any of the other prisoners. That's makin' a long story 'bout as short as I can make it."

"How long have you been sick?"

"For about the last year or so."

"Tell me about your symptoms. How you been feeling?"

"Well, at first I was runnin' a fever, then I got the chills, night sweats, and then I started coughing all the time, spittin' up some blood."

"What did they do for your sickness in the prison?"

"Well, they gave me a TB skin test that come out positive and then they gave me an X-ray that showed I had the disease. So they took me off the work gang and put me in the dispensary and had me rest and lay out on the porch most days. Then the dispensary got too crowded so some of us who had been in the longest got to go home."

"Okay, let's take a look at you. Take your shirt off so I can check your blood pressure and listen to your breathing."

Django Jackson was thin and a bit darker than Jewel, but with his shirt off, he looked gray and emaciated. Still, he was a handsome man, with Jewel's deep-brown eyes and straight nose and kinky black hair. His breathing was labored and his lungs obviously damaged. The doctor had no reason to disbelieve the prison's X-ray, but he decided to use his own portable X-ray machine that he was still paying for to take another picture.

"How long ago did they X-ray you?" the doctor asked him.

"Can't remember exactly, couple of months ago, I think, was the last one."

"I'm gonna take another one today so stand up and move over there in front of that machine there."

It took a few minutes for Nadyne to develop the photo, but it showed about the same number of lesions in the lungs as the prison's print.

"Okay, Mr. Jackson, you can put your shirt back on now," the doctor began. "I'm not sure how much Jewel has told you, but here's the deal. You're real sick. Your tuberculosis has advanced to the point that I would attempt to remove part of your lung if you were a younger man. But at your age it would be too dangerous. So the best thing to do is to make you as comfortable as possible for the time you have left."

"How long?" the patient asked.

"I don't know. If you rest, get lots of fresh air, eat well to bolster your immune system, you could beat this thing. But I'm not gonna lie to you. It's more likely that you'll die in the next few years."

The man did not blink so the doctor continued, "Here's what I want you to do. I want you to let your wife take care of you. Sit out on the porch whenever the weather is nice. Don't go out among a lot of people. Stay away from people as much as you can so you won't infect them. Keep your distance from Marcus, Gabriel, and Jewel."

"Won't be no problem with Gabriel."

"Well, that's your business. They'll all be goin' back to New York City soon, so it doesn't make too much difference anyway."

"Yeah, I know."

"Like I said," the doctor spoke softly to his dying patient, "it's none of my business. You have to do what you have to do. But if I were in your position, knowing that I was probably going to die sooner rather than later, and my only daughter and her son and the man she loves were leaving in a few days and I might never see them again, I would try to find it in my heart to make it right with them, swallow some pride, and do some powerful forgiving."

"Muriel, Jewel's mama, says the same thing so I been doin' some thinkin'."

"And?"

"Well, it's against my better judgment, but if that no-good blues singer makes an honest woman of her and finally marries her, I'll give her away and bless the whole damn lot of 'em, for the little boy's sake, if for no other reason."

"I think that would make your daughter very happy."

"Humph," Django Jackson replied, as he tucked in his shirt and resolutely marched out of the doctor's office.

Chapter 14

That afternoon was one of the hottest on record for poor little Port St. Joe. There was not a cloud in the sky, and the sun was blazing down and burning everything in its path. The breeze across the bay that ordinarily offered some relief was inexplicably absent. The heat and inescapable humidity put the doctor into an instant sweat as he drove over to meet Chief Lane.

"I appreciate your doing this," the doctor said as they rode out on Constitution Drive in the chief's black-and-white patrol car. "I know it's not your jurisdiction out there so this is definitely above and beyond the call of duty."

"Well, to tell you the truth, I'm not sure whether that old beach house is in Gulf or Franklin County. So I don't know whose jurisdiction it is, but, you're right, it's not in mine."

"How do you even know where it is?"

"Well," the chief answered, "I'm not sure I do. When I interviewed Lucilla in the hospital after we shot him, he told me the place had been abandoned by Sheriff Batson's father when the duPonts bought him out in thirty-three. Apparently the sheriff had told him about it and allowed him to stay there without the duPonts' knowledge. Lucilla said it was on St. Vincent Sound just east of the end of Jones Homestead Road. So we're gonna go out Sand Bar Road till we get to Jones Homestead, which I'm hoping is marked, and then go to the end of it at St. Vincent Sound, and we'll see what we can see."

The chief turned right off of Highway 98 and proceeded through a tunnel of thick palmetto and live oak, the glistening bay occasionally peeking through on their right. Then the road curved left at the Cape San Blas turnoff, and they were heading almost due east toward Apalachicola, past the Indian Pass Raw Bar and Indian Lagoon, out several miles until they saw the battered wooden sign that read Jones Homestead Road. The chief turned the patrol car onto the narrow gravel path that led to the sea.

"By the way," the chief said as he swerved to miss a deep pothole, "I had a little chat with Norman Adams this morning."

"Yeah, how'd that go?"

"I'm not sure. He was mad. Denied having anything to do with his son's bruises, but he knew that I knew. That's the important thing. I hope he doesn't take his anger out on any of his kids or his wife. If he does and I find out, I'll lock him up. I'm not sure what the judge will do about it, but I'm not gonna put up with it. So let me know if any of them come to see you again, okay?"

"Sure. I hope I don't have to."

"Me too."

Finally they came to the end of the gravel road, and there before them was St. Vincent Sound; far across it, St. Vincent Island; and just beyond, the top of the Cape St. George Lighthouse, cresting the slash pine forest, stark black and white against the azure sky. They found a sandy trail leading east on the mainland side of the dunes to a dilapidated, two-story cottage about fifty yards away.

"I don't know about this," Chief Lane said. "I think that sand looks pretty loose down that trail. We better park here and walk the rest of the way."

"I guess that's the place," the doctor said, opening the car's door.

"I think so," the chief said, removing his pistol from his holster.

They trudged down the trail, which was no more than parallel tire tracks with a ridge of sand sprouting sea rockets and primrose in between. Their shirts were soaked with sweat when they reached the white, weather-worn house boarded up with wide, pine planks nailed securely across each window. The steps up to the broad porch were sagging with rot, but the men made it to the porch without falling through. The covered porch extended out around the house on three sides. They walked around it, looking for an open window or an easy way in, but everything was boarded up. From the porch, they could see an old, listing shed in the backyard among a grove of saw palmetto and cabbage palm. Sea gulls squalled on the beach as the waves lapped the shore no more than thirty feet from them. *Someday soon,* the doctor thought, *a storm will take this entire house out to sea forever.*

They checked the back door, but it was boarded up just like the windows. The front door had only one pine plank across it. A foot wide and a couple of inches thick, the plank rested in a steel sleeve on each side of the door, with a thick bolt that appeared to run through the sleeve as well as the plank into the frame of the door. On the plank, in faded red paint, were the words "KEEP OUT."

"It looks like someone doesn't want us in here," the chief said. "Now what?"

"Well, if we had a wrench, we could unscrew those bolts and then just lift that plank out."

"I don't have a wrench in the car, but I guess we could check in that old shed over there."

"Okay, let's take a look."

Of course, the only door to the shed was locked. The chief jiggled the latch and, since it seemed pretty loose, backed up a step and gave the lock a powerful kick. The door sprung open and the chief pointed his pistol inside. But there wasn't much to point it at: an old wooden wheel barrow, a rusty shovel, several five-gallon tin cans, an oyster rake, and a lot of dust. On the workbench that extended along the longest side of the shed was a steel tool chest, and inside was a rusty adjustable wrench.

"We're in luck," the chief said.

It didn't take the chief long to unscrew and remove the two long bolts. Then together they lifted the plank out of its steel sleeves. The chief tried the lock on the heavy front door. It wouldn't budge. "Well, what do you think? This one's too sturdy for me to kick in, and the place looks pretty empty to me. Shall I shoot the lock open, or shall I buy you a beer at the Indian Pass Raw Bar?"

"We've come this far," the doctor said.

The chief shrugged, aimed his pistol at the door's lock, and fired. The doctor had never seen this done in real life, only in moving pictures, but, surprisingly, it worked. The door sprang loose, and the chief pulled it open. They stepped inside. A nasty barnyard smell hit them immediately, but with all the windows boarded up they couldn't see what was causing it. The chief took a flashlight from his belt and shone it around the room. It was empty except for an old brown couch covered with dust and piles of tiny gray pellets. The chief shone the flashlight up to the ceiling, and they saw where the smell was coming from. The entire ceiling was covered with small, furry creatures with beady, black eyes and slightly extended wings, hanging upside down, staring down menacingly at the two intruders.

"Holy shit," was all the doctor could say.

"More like bat shit," the chief replied. "Let's get this over with. This place gives me the creeps. And it smells like . . ."

"Bat shit," the doctor concluded.

"No shit."

With his flashlight in one hand and his pistol in the other, the chief walked from room to room, followed by the doctor, through the thick layer of guano on the uneven floors. Every room downstairs was empty, except for the bats and the one room with the old couch, so they started up the stairs to the second floor. It was the same scene in the two rooms there, nothing much more than dust, guano, and bats, thousands of them clinging precariously to the ceilings and smelly walls. There was a ladder at the end of the hallway leading to a three-foot-square hole in the ceiling.

"Shall we check out the attic?" the chief asked.

"Why don't you just climb up and put your head through the hole to make sure?" the doctor suggested.

Then they heard a chilling thud below. They hurried back down the stairs, the doctor following a step behind the chief. At the bottom of the stairs they found total darkness. The chief shone his flashlight on the front door. It was closed. Then they heard rapid footsteps on the porch outside. Then a new smell spread, all too familiar. It was gasoline . . . all around them. They both rushed to the door, pushed together to open it, but it was closed and locked, tight as a vice. Next came the frightening whoosh sound, like a sudden storm approaching, and the pungent odor of fire and smoke. The bats smelled it and began spiraling wildly from the ceiling, spraying guano everywhere. The two men swiped at them frantically, but the bats were panic stricken. The doctor tried to follow their path as the chief swung his flashlight erratically around the room.

"Up the stairs!" the doctor shouted, as the smoke grew denser and hotter. The chief shone his light at the square hole at the end of the hallway and saw the bats fighting desperately to fly through it.

"Let's go!," the chief said.

"You go first," the doctor said. He wasn't in any hurry to fight his way through the bats that were now streaming in waves through the opening.

The sheriff put his pistol back in its holster and climbed the ladder while the doctor shone his flashlight on him. The bats were crazed now by the smoke and the smell of the fire that was burning below. They looked like they were attacking the chief as he climbed the steps and finally disappeared into the attic.

The doctor started climbing, switching the flashlight back and forth between one hand and the other, trying at the same time to fight off the bats that were banging recklessly into him. Finally he was able to stick his head up through the hole as Chief Lane extended a hand and pulled him up into the attic. There he saw more bats and sunlight, beaming miraculously through the round, attic vent hole, its louvers long since rotted away, giving the bats, and maybe the two men, access to the outside world. The hole was about waist high and a yard across, and the bats were now streaming swiftly through it to escape the ensuing conflagration below. The chief rushed to the opening and stuck his head out into the bright light of the afternoon sun, bats battering him mercilessly.

"About ten feet down to the top of the porch roof and then another ten to the ground," he told the doctor. "Let's get out of here. It looks like the porch is burning but not the roof yet."

"You first," the doctor said. "You've got a wife and kid and I don't have anybody."

With the doctor's help, the chief swung a leg up into the opening, then the other, and disappeared below. With some effort the doctor followed him, the bats and thickening smoke upping his adrenalin level enough for him to push on when he really didn't want to. Finally, he wiggled through the opening and dropped to the roof below. He felt something crack. He didn't bother to get up since he didn't think he could; instead, he just rolled to the roof's edge and fell off it over the side, landing with a thunk in the sand next to the house's stone foundation. The chief pulled him up and dragged him, limping, away from the blazing building.

And there, in the shallow dunes and gathering dusk, Chief Lane and

Dr. Berber stood together and watched the frenzied bats dart into the smoky sky as Lucky Lucilla's hideout blazed away to embers.

Chapter 15

But there was no sign of Lucky Lucilla, just a smoldering, stone foundation and a few empty five-gallon tin cans strewn across the sand as the sun neared the watery horizon of the Gulf of Mexico.

"You still up to buying me a beer at the Indian Pass Raw Bar?" the doctor asked, peering into the ashes.

"I reckon," Chief Lane said.

The doctor's ankle hurt, but he didn't think it was broken. He could walk on it, but it wasn't easy. The chief's squad car appeared to be undisturbed, but the doctor insisted that they check under the hood before starting it. They couldn't see anything unusual there, so they got in, and the chief turned over the engine. They drove back the way they had come and stopped at dusk at the Indian Pass Raw Bar.

The roadhouse was busy as usual. Bob Wills and His Texas Playboys were singing "Ida Red" on the jukebox. The doctor and the chief had not considered how they looked before they entered, but the stares they received made them take a closer look at each other. It was not a pretty sight. The chief no longer looked snazzy in his pressed uniform and Panama hat. His wrinkled uniform and crushed straw hat were covered with a nasty combination of bat guano and black soot. The doctor could only imagine how he looked. It couldn't be any better.

"What on God's green earth happened to you?" Sadie McIntire asked from her perch behind the cash register.

"Fire," the doctor answered. "Out at the beach house at the end of Jones Homestead Road, where Sheriff Batson's father used to live."

"What the hell were you doin' out there?" she asked, blowing cigarette smoke out through her nostrils.

"Looking for Lucky Lucilla," the chief said. "Seen him?"

"Heavens, no," Sadie answered. "If I had, you'd be the first to know. You fellows okay?"

"We'll live," the doctor said.

"Well, get in the washroom and clean yourselves up. I'll git your supper ready while you're in there. What'll you have?"

"I'll just have a dozen raw oysters and a Pabst to start with," the chief said.

"I'll have the same," the doctor told her, "except give me a Spearman . . . or two. Thanks, Mrs. McIntire."

"Go," she said. "You're both a sight."

She was right. One look in the washroom mirror was enough to shock the doctor into the reality that they had very nearly been burned to death. Unlike the chief, who had had a hat to protect his face, the doctor's mug had taken the smoke and guano straight on. His thinning hair was a disgusting mess, his wrinkled face was black with soot and freckled with bruises, and his filthy clothes were foul and grungy. So the two took turns at the tiny sink until they were somewhat presentable. Sadie McIntire pointed to a table near the door when they finally emerged. On the table were twin trays of oysters and four brown bottles of cold beer. The men ate and drank.

"What next?" the doctor asked.

"I'm not sure," Chief Lane answered. "The state police, Sheriff Duffield, Sheriff Roberts, and all my men will be on the lookout, but frankly, Doc, I don't know where to look next. Which is probably just as well, since he'd probably set another trap for us anyway. Got any ideas?"

"No. Jewel is checking around, but Lucilla doesn't seem to have many contacts in the colored community . . . in any community, for that matter. So I don't know."

"Well, it's not very comfortable just waiting around for the lunatic to strike again."

"Tell me about it."

When the doctor limped into his office the next morning, he found Sheriff Duffield in the waiting room, peering through his green sunglasses at an old copy of *Look* magazine. Nadyne was poring over her appointment book while half a dozen patients in various states of disrepair sat waiting impatiently. She cocked her head toward the doctor's office.

"Be right with you," the doctor said to the assembled mass and followed Nadyne back to his office.

"The sheriff's been here waiting for the last half hour," she said.

"What about the rest?"

"Nothing that can't wait," she said.

"Okay, send the sheriff in, and I'll try to get rid of him as fast as I can."

Sheriff Duffield seemed peeved because he had been made to wait, so he dispensed with the usual pleasantries, sat down, and got right to the point.

"I've got two things for you this morning," he began, his right cheek bulging with a big wad of tobacco. "First, what the hell happened yesterday out at the end of Jones Homestead Road? Lane called me about it last night."

The doctor told him the entire story while the sheriff leaned back in his chair and shook his head. When the doctor had finished, the sheriff sighed and said, "I'd say someone is out to get you."

"No shit," the doctor replied.

"Lucky Lucilla?' the sheriff asked.

"That's my best guess, but I'm not positive."

"Any idea where he might be?"

"No," the doctor said, "I'm all out of ideas."

"Well, you can bet he's not, so be careful."

"You said you had two things."

"Oh, yeah," the sheriff said. "Guess who owns St. Vincent Island."

"I don't know," the doctor lied.

"Your friend Gator Mica."

"Really?"

"That's what the will says."

"I'll be . . ."

"The trouble is we don't know where he is. Do you?"

"Not a clue."

"Well," the sheriff said, looking around the room for a place to spit, "that puts everything up in the air. Price's children are in town for the funeral and they're crazy mad, both about the doctor's death and about their disinheritance. And they think Gator Mica is to blame for both, and they can't understand why we can't find him. Judge Denton doesn't know what to do. He's never seen a case like this before. Bob Huggins said he rewrote the will at Price's instruction, and Price seemed as sober and stable as a judge. The Price kids tried to hire him because they heard he was the best around, but Huggins told them it would be a conflict of interest, so they're looking for another lawyer. Looks like the whole damn thing is gonna end up in some courtroom somewhere and there's not a damn thing we can do about it."

"Well, I'll be."

"Look," the sheriff said, spitting a long line of tobacco juice into the doctor's waste basket, "after talking to Chief Lane and Bob Huggins, I'm willing to entertain the possibility that your friend Gator didn't kill Price, that maybe this nut Lucilla did, though I can't for the life of me think what his motive might be. And I couldn't care less about Price's Yankee kids. So if Gator would just turn himself in, with Huggins' help, we'll see what we can figure out. But the longer he's out there, the messier this thing gets and the less chance Gator has of being cleared and getting St. Vincent Island."

"What do you want me to do?"

"Convince Gator, if you can find him, to turn himself in. Otherwise, sooner or later we'll bring him in, dead or alive. And St. Vincent Island ain't gonna do him no good if he's dead or in jail."

"I'll do what I can," the doctor said.

"That's all I'm asking," the sheriff said and stalked out.

Chapter 16

The next morning, before the doctor could tend to his appointments, Millicent Foster brought her husband, Loren, in because he was having chest pains and shortness of breath. When the pain spread to Loren's stomach and back, the doctor determined he was having a heart attack. He gave him two aspirin and called the ambulance to take him to the emergency room in Panama City.

Mildred Weston was next. She had all the symptoms of acute sinusitis so the doctor wrote her a prescription for colloidal silver. Then Nadyne knocked on his office door. "Emergency at the Kenney Mill," was all Nadyne said as she poked her head through the doorway.

The doctor ripped Mrs. Weston's prescription off the pad and handed it to her, grabbed his black bag, and hurried toward the door. "Any more details?" he asked Nadyne.

"Nope, that's all I know. You want me to go?" she asked him, with a knowing look.

"No," he answered. "I'll do it."

The Kenney Mill was where Sally Martin had found a job as a receptionist after her husband had been murdered the previous year. It was just south of the canal across from the St. Joe Paper Company. It was a new sawmill, built about a year earlier, to help satisfy the new paper mill's insatiable appetite for pulp wood. Long logging trucks, trains, and ships from all over the Southeast hauled slash pine logs from wherever they could be found—further and further away as the nearby forests were decimated—to this and the other mills, where they were debarked and cut into the six-foot lengths required by the shredding machines in the state's five large paper mills. A daily demand of more than two thousand tons of pulp by these mills required more than two thousand units of pulping wood each day, the doctor had read in the *Star*. And about a million acres of land were required full time to meet this need. So it was just a matter of time until all the wood was gone.

But until then, it appeared that the Kenney Mill was consuming its fair share and operating at full capacity. Three slender smoke stacks belched black smoke; mountains of logs surrounded a long, unpainted, wooden shed, a large two-story barn, and a little pine clapboard cottage. The doctor's head bounced all the way up to the headliner when his old Ford crossed the rough siding of a single-track spur from the main Apalachicola Northern railroad line that ran to the center of the wood lot. A young man in denim overalls met the doctor when he pulled up to the cottage, which, according to the plank sign hanging from the front porch's eaves, served as the mill's office.

"Follow me," the man said and led the doctor to the long, low shed where the logs were being appropriately sized by a huge, shiny circular saw that was, at the moment, at rest in the center of a yard-high, wooden platform. In the far corner, he found a man lying on the dirt floor surrounded by three other mill workers, one none other than Sally Martin herself, red hair hanging in ringlets to her shoulders, holding the reclining man's head on her lap. A colored man was holding a small, tin first aid kit. The third, a tall white man, was holding what appeared to be a bleeding human hand, detached, the doctor assumed, from the man on the floor. The doctor looked to Sally for some explanation, but she avoided his stare and instead peered down at the injured man.

The doctor knelt next to the man and caught Sally's familiar scent: gardenia, arrowroot starch, and Ivory soap. The man whose head she was holding had his right arm wrapped in gauze, which was now thoroughly soaked in blood. The man was shaking, cold, and pale.

"Get blankets!" the doctor ordered. Then he grabbed his black bag, found a sterile syringe, filled it with morphine, and injected it into the remainder of the man's arm.

"Call the fire department and have them send an ambulance," the doctor barked to no one in particular. "We need to get him to the hospital in Panama City right now."

"We've already called," Sally Martin said. "It's on its way back from Panama City now. Somebody had a heart attack this morning. It should be here any minute now, according to the fire department."

That would by Loren Foster, the doctor thought. He had called the ambulance himself and had already forgotten all about it. He hoped Loren pulled through.

The handless man on the floor opened his eyes. They were bleary and distant. "You're gonna be okay," the doctor told him. The man closed his eyes, and the doctor took his pulse and checked his blood pressure. He was in shock, but it looked like the gauze wrapping and the natural clotting had stopped the worst of the bleeding. When, after a few minutes, the morphine had taken effect, the doctor unwrapped the gauze and examined the cut. The saw had done its job remarkably well. It was a clean, even cut through skin, muscle, veins, and bone—*a perfect specimen for an anatomy class,* the doctor thought. Too bad you couldn't just somehow reattach the man's hand. As he was cleaning the oozing cut with gauze and Mercurochrome, the colored man returned with a couple of blankets. The doctor asked the man nearest him, "Give me a hand, will you?"

The man holding the detached hand held it out to the doctor. "No, not that hand, you idiot," the doctor snapped. "Put down the damn hand and help me wrap this man up."

The man with the detached hand withdrew it, stared at it helplessly, embarrassed, seemingly confused as to exactly where he should place it. The colored man helped the doctor wrap the injured man in the blankets. In the process, the doctor's right hand brushed across Sally's soft blue dress. Then their eyes met for a brief moment. Damn, she was pretty.

The doctor continued dressing the wound, and just as he was taping the final bandages firmly in place, the ambulance pulled into the wood lot. They loaded the man in, and the doctor gave the young medic instructions on how to keep the arm elevated and the patient settled. Panama City was only thirty miles away, but to a man who had just lost his right hand it could be a very long way.

They all stood in the yard between the shed and the cottage and watched the ambulance back out and head toward Panama City: Sally Martin, her dress wrinkled and spotted with blood; the Negro; the two white men, one holding the first aid kit, the other, a bloody hand; and the doctor.

"So what happened?" he asked.

The colored man said, "I was the onliest one to see it. Jerry was out in the yard. Mike was in the barn. And Mrs. Martin was in the office."

"And?"

The Negro looked at Sally. She said, "Go ahead, Sam, tell him."

"Well, Ollie was on the saw. He stopped it to mess with the stopper that's all the time slippin'. When he was pushin' on it, a rat run across his foot and it look like he slipped, and his foot hit the foot pedal that starts the saw when his hand was next to it. It just sucked him right in. It was over before ya knew it."

"Who's in charge of this mill?" the doctor asked.

They all looked at Sally. "I am," she said. "Today. Max Kenney owns it, but when he's away, I'm in charge."

"Okay," the doctor said. "Sam, is there a safety guard on that saw?"

"No, sir," he said.

"And how about the foot pedal that starts the saw. Is there a guard on that?"

"No, sir, there ain't."

"How about an emergency shut-off switch?"

"Ain't got one," Sam said.

"Mrs. Martin," the doctor said. "May I have a word with you inside?"

"Of course," she answered. The doctor followed her up the steps and into the cottage, her round rump, with a slight trace of panty line and of sandy dirt from the shed floor, swaying enticingly only inches before his eyes. He wanted to brush the dirt away for her, but he did not.

She led him into the clapboard cottage, which consisted of a reception area with a high counter, two small offices, a bathroom, and what looked to be some sort of storage room in the back. Sally led the doctor into one of the offices, closed the door behind them, and motioned for him to sit in an uncomfortable oak chair in front of the desk. Sally took the chair behind the desk, facing the doctor. "Care for coffee, Van?" she asked.

"No, thanks," he answered. "I've already had my fill for today."

"Okay. How have you been?"

"I'm all right," he answered, "I guess. How about you? And the kids?"

"Everyone is fine. Out of school for the summer and probably at home getting into trouble."

"They're good kids," the doctor said.

"Yes, they wear me down sometimes, but they are good. Sometimes I think that the best thing that ever happened to us was losing Earl. Now we have the insurance money, and I'm enjoying my job here, and the kids seem to be thriving."

"Yes, congratulations, by the way, for being in charge of the mill, and after only a year here."

"Well," she said, brushing a stray curl from her forehead, "it's a small mill. Max likes the operations end of it, and I've been surprised to find out that I like the business end of it. So it works out all right."

"Then maybe it's Max I should talk to about the safety issues here."

"That would be better. He's not in today though. Decided to take the day off and go fishing."

"He do that often?"

"Yeah, when he feels like it. He's been at this for a long time. Frankly, he's pretty bored with it all."

"So you really do run this place then?"

"Well, I guess so. I do my best."

"Tell me then," the doctor said, "why is it your mill doesn't have any safety guards or emergency cut-off switches."

"To be honest with you, I don't know. I don't even know if such devices are available on the equipment we have. It was all installed like this when I got here."

"Sally, listen, I've seen more sawmill accidents than I care to remember. They're almost always nasty like this one this morning. And most of them could have been avoided if the mill's owner had gone to the expense of installing the necessary safety equipment and training his men how to use it, not to mention just getting a cat in there to kill the rats."

"I'm so sorry," Sally said, hanging her head. "I didn't know. I would have done anything to stop what happened to Ollie. I really would have."

"I believe you," the doctor said. "Unfortunately, the laws are very lax on requiring these safety measures. It appears that Max took the cheapest way out, and now it has cost Ollie his right hand."

"I'll talk to Max."

"That's a good idea. I'm gonna report what happened here this morning to Chief Lane, and I'm sure he'll want to meet with Max, maybe talk some sense into him. I don't think the law allows him to close this place down, but if Ollie and his family decide to file suit, it could get messy, and expensive, for y'all."

"I understand."

"There is one more thing," the doctor said, leaning forward to peer into Sally's glistening green eyes.

"What's that?" she asked.

"The matter of Lucky Lucilla, who, it seems, is trying very hard to kill me."

Sally lowered her head, averting her eyes from the doctor's.

"Where is he?" the doctor demanded.

"I don't know," she whimpered. "I don't . . ."

"Look," the doctor said, "I'm an old man and if Lucilla wants me dead then I'm ready to die. But trying to kill my friend Gator and then framing him . . . that's going too far. Gator didn't do anything to anybody."

"I told you I don't know where he is," Sally said as she raised her head to look at the doctor.

"I don't believe you."

Sally just shook her head and began to cry. And as much as the doctor wanted to comfort her as he used to, he did not.

"Look, Sally, I'm fed up with all this. And, as much as I love you and your children—yes, I still love you—I'm not gonna let Gator suffer for what your friend Lucky did. I don't give a damn anymore. Either you tell me where Lucky Lucilla is or I'm gonna tell Chief Lane everything I know about you and this homicidal nut, from the very beginning until now."

"Don't do that," she said, wiping the tears from her eyes, which were now blazing with anger. "You'll be sorry. I promise you."

Chapter 17

The doctor drove straight to Chief Lane's office at Port St. Joe's City Hall and sat in his car in front of the building. He had to think about Sally's threat. *What would she do if the doctor told Chief Lane everything?* he wondered. He was not sure he wanted to find out. It appeared that Lucky Lucilla was out to kill him either way, and he had to do something to save Gator. But what? He wasn't sure, so instead of telling the whole story to the chief as he had threatened, the doctor decided to go home, have an early dose of morphine, and think on it some more. And so he did.

Despite the morphine, he had a hard time falling asleep. He realized, as he lay staring at the ceiling, that he may have acted rashly by talking to Sally Martin. So he decided, lying there in the dark, not to divulge to Chief Lane just yet what he knew about Sally Martin and Lucky Lucilla. Instead, he would do the only two things he knew might help. He would somehow find Gator Mica and convince him to turn himself in before Sheriff Duffield found him and either arrested him or killed him. And he would intensify his search for Lucky Lucilla, who he was by now convinced had murdered Dr. Price and had tried to kill him, Gator, and Chief Lane. Maybe somehow he could save them all.

He heard her voice below in the kitchen and thought he was dreaming or having a historical—or hysterical—hallucination. But it was morning and, yes, it was definitely Jewel's voice and it was real. He downed his morning dose of morphine, showered, and dressed quickly.

She was sitting with Vivian at the kitchen table, drinking coffee, when the doctor entered the kitchen.

"Good morning, Doc," she greeted him.

"Good morning, Jewel. Good morning, Vivian. To what do we owe the pleasure?"

"I've got some news," Jewel said.

"I work here," Vivian added.

"I know, Vivian. So what have you been working on for breakfast?"

"Cantaloupe from Curtis Palmer, grits, and ham," she answered as she got up and went to the stove.

"And what's your news, Jewel?"

"Well, first off," she said, "I gotta thank you for talkin' to Daddy. He's like a whole new man. Says that if me and Gabriel tie the knot, he'll forgive us everything and give us his blessing. So we're gittin' hitched."

"When?" Vivian exclaimed as she placed a full plate in front of the doctor.

"This Sunday afternoon. Day after tomorrow."

"So soon?"

"Well, we're headin' back to New York in a few days, so we decided to do it here before we take off so our families can come, maybe even some of Gabriel's people from over in Eatonville. But we're gonna keep it small, 'cause we don't want Daddy to infect all of colored North Port St. Joe with TB. We'll just have us a little party for our northern friends when we get back to New York. So I'm here to invite y'all. It's at four o'clock at the New Bethel A.M.E. Church, and then we'll have a potluck supper afterwards in the church basement."

"I'll be there," Vivian said.

"You better be, 'cause you're gonna be a bridesmaid."

"Oh, my!"

"Congratulations," the doctor said, none too cheerfully. "What else, Jewel?"

"Well, let's see. Nobody has seen this Lucky guy. He's like a nasty mole, just diggin' around, doin' all kinds of damage but no one ever sees him. And Gator, nobody seen hide nor hair of that Indian neither. And Sally Martin. Well, that gal is doin' okay from what I hear from Sam Myers' wife, Maggie, who lives down the street from Mama. She pretty much runs that mill where she went to work just last year, accordin' to Maggie, and Sam says he's pretty sure that Sally and the owner of the mill—Max, I think his name is—have a little somethin' goin' on the side, if you git my drift. Besides that, this Max guy's been teachin' her how to shoot a pistol. Anyway, she's been buyin' up every stand of timber she can git her hands on to cut up and sell to the paper company. Maggie says Sam says that she won't be satisfied until she owns every stick of pine in the dadgum Panhandle."

"Hmm," said the doctor, chewing a piece of ham. "Coffee, Vivian?"

"Oh, I'm so sorry. Jewel and I done drunk it all before you even got here."

"Well then, just sashay over next door to Mrs. Shriver's house and ask her if you can borrow enough for a fresh pot. She won't mind a bit."

"Okay," Vivian said.

When she was gone, the doctor said to Jewel, "I didn't want her to hear what I'm about to tell you. If she knows too much, her life could be in danger too."

Then, between bites, the doctor told Jewel about everything that had happened to him in the last few days. "So," he concluded, "I'm afraid I may have incurred the wrath of Sally Martin, so I'm gonna do everything I can to find Gator and Lucky Lucilla. They're our only hope. And if I don't find them soon, I'm afraid Lucky just might find us first. And if he does, I think we're in big trouble, because now Sally will stop at nothing to keep us quiet."

"Damn, Doc," Jewel said. "I thought you was gonna leave Sally Martin alone."

"Oh, I was, but I let my emotions get the best of me when I thought of what they'd done to Gator and how he was probably gonna get screwed out of the place he loves the best. And what they might do to you, Jewel, when they realize you're back in town and that I've probably told you the entire story."

"I told you, Doc, not to worry about me. I can take care of myself. But how are we gonna find Gator and Lucky? I don't see that we're gittin' any closer."

"You're right, Jewel. We're not. And I told myself I wasn't gonna do it, but I'm going to Tate's Hell as soon as I get done seeing you and Gabriel get married."

"And what about Lucky Lucilla?"

"I decided in the middle of the night to go to Tampa, where he's from. I don't think he's returned there. I think he's still around here, looking for his next chance to kill someone, but who knows? He hasn't turned up here in the last few days. The least I can do is talk to any remaining family or people in his neighborhood so I can try to understand what makes him tick. For some reason, I find it fascinating why someone would turn out the way he has. He seems to have no compunction at all about wreaking havoc whenever and wherever he wants. There's got to be some kind of reason for that."

"I'll give you a reason, Doc," Jewel said. "He's crazier than a Bessie bug. That's the reason."

Chapter 18

The doctor thought about going to Tate's Hell the next day, Saturday, but he knew he wouldn't have time to mount any sort of decent search and then get back and cleaned up before the wedding on Sunday afternoon. He only wished he knew somebody else like Gator who could go with him to Tate's Hell. He could locate it on a map, but that was about all he knew about the place. So he would try to relax on Saturday, go to Jewel's wedding on Sunday, and then have Nadyne cover for him and take off to Tate's Hell the first thing Monday morning.

Sometimes the doctor thought he must have, as well as early onset dementia, some sort of aberrant masochistic streak, because on Sunday morning, instead of suffering with the Joads as they pulled into Bakersfield, he turned on the Philco radio in the parlor and listened to the news. As German troops amassed on the Polish border, the British and the French, in a last-ditch effort to deter Hitler, promised again publicly that they would defend Poland, Romania, and Greece if the Nazis invaded any of them.

Another reporter told a story about a Czech figure skater named Vera Hruba, who was performing at the New Yorker Hotel in New York City. At one of her performances, the German Consul was present and ordered her to stop dancing to the Czechoslovakian national polka. At which point, according to the reporter, the very beautiful Miss Hruba "sneered a very beautiful sneer" and shot back, "Mr. German Consul, not for one small moment can you tell me what to do," and then proceeded to finish the dance. Apparently, however, this was not the first time the fiery skater had insulted a high-ranking Nazi official. At the 1936 Winter Olympics in Bavaria, she had met Adolf Hitler himself. And when he had asked her if she would like "to skate for the swastika," she had looked him in the eye and told him that she would rather "skate *on* the swastika." The Fuhrer had been furious, the reporter said. *Furious enough,* the doctor thought, *to invade and take over the skater's native country two years later.*

All this talk of war made the doctor more depressed than he was about Jewel's impending marriage. He had all but talked Django Jackson into instigating the proposal. He might as well have dropped to his knees and proposed for Gabriel himself. What the hell was he thinking?

Now he had to get all dressed up, smile, and pretend he was happy for the young couple when, in fact, he wished they had never met. Oh, well, he hoped at least the nuptials would make Jewel happy. The doctor knew she loved Gabriel, but she had never been sure about marrying a traveling bluesman. That and her daddy's total rejection of Gabriel had caused her not to press the matter. But now, with Django's change of heart, the doctor understood that this was probably the best way to keep peace in the family and placate her dying father.

The doctor wasn't sure how Gabriel felt about the bonds of matrimony. He had come and gone as he pleased for a long time now and seemed perfectly satisfied with the less-formal arrangement. Now, perhaps from relief that the old man was no longer trying to blow his brains out more than anything else, he was apparently going along with Django's magnanimous offering of peace.

At any rate, despite these trepidations and the peculiar circumstances of their union, it looked like they were going ahead with the hastily arranged ceremony. So the doctor showered, dressed in his best blue serge suit, which was only a little snug, and, at the appointed hour, drove over to the little, pine African Methodist Episcopal Church in North Port St. Joe.

If this was a small ceremony, as Jewel had contended, then the doctor couldn't imagine what a large one would look like. By the time the doctor arrived a few minutes before four, nearly every pew in the narrow sanctuary was filled with women in big hats and men in dark suits, nearly all attempting to create some sort of communal breeze by briskly waving Royal Undertaking Company fans in front of their flushed faces. An elderly colored man in a black suit and red tie met him at the door and led him to the front pew on the left side of the long, carpeted aisle, where Jewel's mama was seated with some other colored people whom the doctor didn't recognize. Jewel's mother, whose first name the doctor could not recall, if he, in fact, had ever known it—Jewel always just referred to her as "my mama"—motioned for him to sit next to her. The doctor complied, dodging the wide, white rim of Jewel's mama's hat, which he was sure was the largest he had ever seen, not only in width, but also in height, with a garden of multi-colored silk flowers sprouting upwards toward the church's hand-hewn rafters. The woman's suit matched the doctor's in color, if not in style. She was already dabbing the tears from her eyes with a lacy white handkerchief when the doctor eased in next to her. She squeezed the doctor's palm with her free hand and smiled. "Thanks for coming," she whispered above the organ strains that were softly wafting through the packed chapel.

Presently, a middle-aged man rose from a high-backed, red cloth-covered chair on the low platform before them and stepped in front of the choir who was seated in pews behind the organ. On cue, about a dozen women and six men dressed in long, bright blue robes rose as one. And, as the organ increased in volume, the director raised his arms and the choir began to sing "I'd Rather Have Jesus." *What an odd choice,* the doctor thought. "It's her favorite," Jewel's mother explained, as if hearing what the doctor thought had been a silent query. Had he mistakenly said it out loud?

Then, after the hymn, three ushers came forward and passed a peck basket down each pew as the organist, her eyes closed and head raised, played a pretty song the doctor did not recognize. He fished a dollar bill out of his billfold and tossed it in the plate and remembered that he had not bought a wedding present for the newlyweds. Oh, well, cash was always appreciated, he was sure.

Then another tall man in a black robe, who the doctor assumed was the preacher, rose from his chair and walked over to the wide, wooden pulpit. "Ladies and gentlemen, boys and girls, uh-huh" he expounded in a deep Southern drawl, "let us pray."

Everyone stood up as the preacher continued. "Our most gracious heavenly Fatha," he pleaded, "uh-huh, be with this congregation gathered here this fine, summer Sunday afternoon to celebrate the union of these two Christian young people who are about to be joined together in the sacred vows of holy matrimony."

As the preacher paused to draw a breath, a spattering of amens, as well as a stream of tears from Jewel's mama's eyes, urged him on. "Surely, Lord, we are humbled by the immense profundity of their undertaking, and we know, Lord, uh-huh, that they'll not be entering into this momentous bond without the deepest solemnity and humility. And we know, Lord, uh-huh, that even in the best of times, the stress and strain of economic hardship and rampant racism can test even the strongest of bonds. So we pray, dear God, uh-huh, that you bind these two young people with the densest, most durable cement in your celestial storehouse." Now the Amens were coming fast and furious as Jewel's mama's handkerchief became drenched and useless. The doctor noticed and gave her his unused handkerchief from his suit coat pocket.

"And we thank you, Lord Jesus, uh-huh," the preacher continued, "for bringing this family together again, from the bride's daddy, who has recently returned to our flock after a long and lugubrious absence, to the young couple recently returned from New Yo'k City, to young Marcus, who will now be blessed by the warmth and understanding of a close Christian family, uh-huh. May they all flourish as this new union is formed and may it be forever bountiful as you, dear God, bless them with your everlasting love and absolution. In the name of the Father, the Son, and the Holy Ghost, we pray that you hear our prayers, oh, Lord, uh-huh. *Amen!*"

"Amen!" the congregation shouted as Jewel's mother's bawling reached an unshackled bellow.

Thankfully, the preacher then nodded to the organist, who immediately broke into a loud and lusty version of "Here Comes the Bride." The crowd's collective head turned to see Jewel and Django, arm in arm, stroll slowly down the aisle to face the beaming pastor. By the time they arrived there, two bridesmaids in pink crinoline dresses, one being his own Vivian, and Gabriel and Marcus and another man, all in dark suits, had appeared from nowhere to stand beside the preacher.

"Who gives Jewel to be married to Gabriel?" the pastor asked.

"Her mother and I do," Django answered and coughed. Then he sat down on the other side of Jewel's mother and whispered something in her ear. Whatever it was—a threat or a word of reassurance—it quieted her, at least for the time being, with the tears falling silently as Jewel and Gabriel were married.

And, of course, Jewel, like all brides, did look beautiful in her long white dress, which was so much more stunning against her brown skin than it would have been on a pale white woman. The rest of the ceremony was a blur, as they say, and, before he knew it, she and Gabriel kissed, turned, smiled broadly to the congregation, and filed back up the aisle and out the door, as the organist boomed out Handel's "Allegro Maestoso." Just like that, and it was all over. And Jewel was gone.

Chapter 19

But not for long. There was the blasted reception in the church's basement to contend with. The doctor was seated at a round table next to the wedding party's table. At his table were the preacher, the choir director and his wife, and, on either side of him, two women about the doctor's age whom he had treated at some point in the past for ailments he had long since forgotten, but he was sure they hadn't.

At least the basement was cooler than the sanctuary upstairs, and it smelled like a heavenly feast. When everyone was seated, the preacher rose and gave another long and flowery prayer. Then the wedding party stood and walked down the long row of food tables that lined the entire length of one side of the room, where they piled generous mounds of fancy fare on their plates and smiled self-consciously to the crowd and each other.

The two old ladies on either side of him gushed about how beautiful Jewel was and how charming the ceremony had been and how very nice everyone looked. The doctor just nodded and smiled.

After the wedding party had served themselves, a large woman in a spotless white apron told the people at the doctor's table that they were next. The doctor followed the others to the long line of tables covered with white tablecloths and bowls and side-by-side platters packed with more food than the doctor had ever seen at one time and in one place in his one life. First came the salads: chicken, several varieties of potato, black-eyed pea, egg, coleslaw, tomato and cucumber. Next were the vegetables: green beans, assorted casseroles, okra and tomatoes, greens, corn, scalloped potatoes, and candied yams. Then the meat: a whole roasted turkey, a giant ham, piles of fried chicken, meat loaves, stuffed peppers, boiled shrimp, and grilled grouper. And the bread: yeast rolls, dinner rolls, cornbread, and biscuits. Finally, the desserts, which were left largely untouched in this first pass-through since the guests' plates were overflowing by the time they arrived at the cakes, pies, zucchini and banana breads, cookies of every sort, and thick slices of cold watermelon. By the time the doctor got back to his table, all of the glasses were filled with sweet tea. The two old ladies at his table knew who and how almost every dish had been prepared and shared each cook's secrets with the doctor. He just sat there between them, stuffing himself and trying to look interested.

He was about to make some excuse so he could go home when Gabriel and his best man, whom he introduced as Robert, scooped him up and led him up a back stairs to the church's backyard. There were a few other men already there, standing around under a large live oak, loosening their ties and belts, smoking and drinking, some from Kerr Mason canning jars, others from flasks, and still others from bottles in brown paper bags. Gabriel reached into his inside coat pocket and pulled out three fat cigars, passing one to Robert and one to the doctor. The best man lit each man's cigar, then retrieved a flask from his inside jacket pocket and passed it around. The whiskey was sweet and smooth, and the doctor was glad he was there instead of between the two old ladies, who were suffocating him with the unpleasant smell of their perspiration and perfume, not to mention their banal chatter. Here he could breathe a little, enjoy the cigar smoke, and let the alcohol take effect.

"Damn, I'm glad that's over," Gabriel said.

"Me too," Robert agreed.

"Congratulations, Gabriel," the doctor said.

"Thanks, Doc. And thanks for comin' too. I know y'all bein' here means a lot to Jewel."

"I wouldn't have missed it for the world," the doctor lied.

He listened to the men talk: of weddings past, baseball, work or the lack thereof, and the possibility of another war in Europe. In wasn't too long before Marcus appeared to deliver a message.

"Mama wants to go home," he said. "Says you should invite whoever you want over to Big Mama's house for a little after-party, but she's gittin' tired and wants to get outta her fancy dress and have a drink."

"Okay," Gabriel said. "I already know who's boss in this family, so I ain't about to argue. Doc, I know all this must be a pain for y'all, but I'd sure be honored if you'd put up with us for just a little bit longer and come on over to Jewel's mama's place for a few more drinks."

"Under one condition," the doctor said.

"What's that?"

"You sing a few songs for us."

"Well, it'd be my pleasure." Gabriel smiled and handed the doctor the flask.

The doctor drove home first to get rid of his coat and tie, retrieve a bottle of moonshine that he had saved in the kitchen cupboard, take a fifty-dollar bill from a cigar box in his bottom dresser drawer, and take a small nip from his brown bottle of morphine. Of late, he was always more than a little afraid when he entered his empty house, half expecting Lucky Lucilla to be hiding behind a door someplace with a raised ax, ready to relieve him of his head with one fatal, final blow. But today he had drunk enough from Robert's flask that he really didn't care that much. Besides, Jewel was married, Gator was gone, and he just didn't give a damn anymore.

He drove back to North Port St. Joe, past Damon Peters' grocery store and his brother Nathan's Cozy Bar and Pool Room and the Cozy Taxi Company, which hauled Negroes back and forth between North Port St. Joe and Port St. Joe to work in the town's white neighborhoods. By the time he located Jewel's mama's house further down on Avenue C, the party was in full swing. Gabriel was sitting on an old oak chair on the front porch, strumming his guitar and singing in his baritone blues voice, something about lost love and an evil woman. Jewel, in a simple white dress, was dancing with Marcus. Vivian was dancing with Robert. And Jewel's mother and father were sharing the porch swing and looking proudly on. Another twenty or so people danced or leaned on the porch railing or just milled around the dusty yard.

The doctor sat on the top step of the porch and leaned against the railing. He always enjoyed Gabriel's singing, and these blues songs he sang always had a firm, steady beat that he found reassuring. From his vantage point on the top step he could watch Jewel dance, her skirt swirling up occasionally to show the top of her stockings and the bottom of her black satin garter belt. He liked her ass the best, of course, but her legs weren't bad either. Such thoughts—about a married woman, and at his age—but he couldn't help himself. When Gabriel took a break, he eased up beside her.

"Congratulations," he said.

"Oh, Doc, thank you so much. Thanks for comin'. Thanks for everything."

And she hugged him. And he held her for a moment, perhaps a moment too long, because he knew this might be the last chance he would ever have to do that. As he released her, she kissed him gently on the cheek, and the doctor thought for a moment that now he was going to cry.

Jewel circulated. The doctor found Gabriel and gave him the fifty-dollar bill. Then he noticed that Jewel's father was sitting alone on the porch swing. He walked over to him and asked if he could join him.

"Yes, please do," the old man said. "I believe my wife has had enough of this revelry. She's gone in to take a nap."

"Congratulations," the doctor said.

"Thank you. And thanks for your advice. I'm not sure if I'll ever forgive the man for doin' what he did to my daughter, but I guess there's not much I can do about it if she loves him."

"No, that pretty much trumps everything, doesn't it?"

"Yep, 'fraid so."

"How have you been feeling?" the doctor asked.

"Better, actually. The fresh air and Mama's good food seem to agree with me."

"Good. You do look better. Just keep at it, and get plenty of rest. That's the key."

"I'll do my best."

"Well," the doctor said, "I guess I better be getting home. I have a big day tomorrow."

"Oh, yeah?"

"Yeah, I'm trying to track down my buddy who's in trouble with the law."

"Jewel mentioned that. Gator the Injun. Where is he?"

"Well, that's the trouble. I don't know exactly where he is. He told me when he took off that he was going to someplace called Tate's Hell, but I've never been there and I don't exactly know where I'm gonna look when I do get there."

"Tate's Hell, huh?"

"That's what he said."

"You ain't gonna find him there," Jewel's father stated matter-of-factly.

"No?"

"Uh-uh, not unless you know where you're goin'."

"Well," the doctor said, "I sure as hell don't. But what makes you think so?"

"I worked more than a decade in Tate's Hell on Cash Creek, not far from High Bluff. In a turpentine camp. I know the place like the back of my hand."

"And?"

"And there ain't no way y'all gonna find your friend by yo'self. It's just too wild out there."

"Well," the doctor said. "I don't know what else to do. If I don't find him soon and get him to a good lawyer, I'm afraid the sheriff over there is gonna find him and kill him."

"Hmm," Jewel's daddy said. "When did you say you're gonna go over there?

"Tomorrow is my plan."

"Well, the last time I checked I didn't have nothin' on my calendar for tomorrow. Want some company?"

"You feel well enough?"

"To tell you the truth, Doc, I'm goin' plum stir crazy just sittin' around here. If I don't git out of here pretty soon, I'm gonna die of sheer boredom."

Chapter 20

The doctor stopped by his office the next morning and made sure Nadyne was prepared to deal the new day's calamities. Fortunately, there were no emergencies, so he drove over to the Jacksons' house in North Port St. Joe, where he found Django sitting in his front porch swing in denim trousers and a blue work shirt buttoned tight around his neck. He jumped out of the swing and was off the porch before the doctor stopped his car.

"Top of the mornin' to you," he said.

"Good morning, Mr. Jackson. How are you today?"

"Ain't complainin'. Call me Django."

"Okay," the doctor said as the man eased in beside him. "Y'all party late last night?"

"Oh, yeah, the young-uns danced the night away. But me and Mama went to bed right after y'all left. You told me to git plenty of rest."

"That I did," the doctor said.

They headed out Constitution Drive east toward Apalachicola on Highway 98. It was already hot, but as the old Ford picked up speed, the wind through the open windows kept the pair fairly comfortable. When they were well out of town, Django coughed and looked at the doctor. "So," he said, "let's see if we can narrow down where your friend

Gator might be. As I said, Tate's Hell ain't nothin' but a big ol' piece of wilderness out in the middle of nowhere. Did he give you any clues about where in Tate's Hell he might be headin'?"

"No, not really. He just said Tate's Hell."

"How was he traveling?"

"What do you mean?"

"Well, was he drivin' a car or what?"

"No," the doctor said, "he was going by boat. He left St. Vincent Island in a little boat, what he called a glade skiff, and it had just this tiny one-and-a-half-horsepower engine."

"Really? Okay, that's a start. Let's take him at his word then and assume he really was goin' to Tate's Hell and that he would of entered by water, and let's also assume that he would want to get out of the open ocean, where he could be easily spotted, as soon as he could. The first place he could get to Tate's Hell by water would be at East Bay this side of Eastpoint. Once inside of East Bay, he could either go west into West Bayou toward Creels or he could go east up East Bayou to Cash Creek toward High Bluff, which would be more in the direction of Tate's Hell and further from civilization. So let's just keep assumin' here and assume, since he said as much, that he'd go toward Tate's Hell."

"But how do we get there without a boat?" the doctor asked.

"Well, there's some roads that cross Cash Creek, so I guess we oughta drive down 'em and see if we can see anything. It's a startin' point anyway."

"Okay," the doctor said. "Just tell me where to go."

The drive from Port St. Joe to Apalachicola and then across the John Gorrie Bridge into Eastpoint is referred to as the Florida West Coast Scenic Highway for good reason. Once out of Port St. Joe, the road is lined with a thick slash pine and saw palmetto forest, except for occasional swampy, stump-filled fields that the greedy timber and paper mills had abandoned. Then after Highway 98 joins Sand Bar Road near St. Vincent

Sound, the route parallels the coast almost all the way into Apalachicola. The pines and scrub-covered dunes block the view of the ocean for most of the way, but occasionally the view of the dark waters of Apalachicola Bay peek through. As they neared Apalachicola, the doctor asked Django about his days in the turpentine camp.

"Well, it's been a long time," he said, coughing again into his handkerchief. "I was born there in eighteen eighty. After the Civil War, a fellow by the name of Windrow, Bobby Windrow, bought up most of the land around there that my parents' owners, the Jacksons, were trying to farm with about a hundred slaves. This Windrow man decided—I guess because of all the pine forests on the place—to get into making turpentine. Back then the pitch, tar, and rosin was used in makin' ships, what they called naval stores. But now it's put into soap, paint, ink, roofing, and all kinds of stuff.

"Anyway, this Bobby Windrow hired a bunch of Jackson's former slaves. A lot of them just scattered to the wind when they was freed. But my parents stayed on to work for him. Too bad for them, 'cause them camps was awful, at least Windrow's was. Ya see, the white folks, which is mostly the foremen, the boss men, the commissary men—we just called 'em all "the man" or "Captin" to they's faces—they all lived in some nice houses on one side of the camp, and the colored folks, which is the ones that did all the hard work, we lived on the other side in two- or three-bedroom cabins or board houses. Ain't none of 'em had 'lectricity, heat, plumbin', runnin' water, or nothin'.'"

"So why did y'all stay under those conditions?" the doctor asked.

"Well, I was gittin' to that. Here's how all that mess worked. The man, ya see, he paid all the Negroes on a piecemeal basis. So the chipper—he's the one that makes them slanty cuts on the trees so the gum can come out and drain into a box. He was paid a penny a tree. A puller, well, he chips the trees above where the chipper can't reach with this long-handled ax called a puller. He got two cents a tree. A tree is chipped and pulled for three years and then it gits chopped down and sold to the mills or burnt up to fuel the still. The dipper is the man who takes the box off the tree, scrapes out the gum with a dippin' iron, and then puts the box back on the tree. The dippers were paid eighty-five cents a barrel for gum and ten barrels a week is good dippin'.

"Now all these mens got paid once a week, and with their pay they'd go to the commissary, that's owned by the man, and buy food fo' themselves and they families. The commissary charged whatever it liked. The camp's out in the middle of nowhere. Ain't no other stores around. Ain't nobody got a car to go nowhere else anyways.

"Now all that might be okay, but here's the problem. There ain't no dippin' or chippin' or pullin' when it's rainin' or stormin', and there ain't none of that neither from November to March. That's when they scrape the trees and rake around them to keep them from catchin' fire. Only need a few mens for that. But during all this time, a family's gotta eat. So there's no pay comin' in, but you be buyin' stuff from the commissary anyway. So everybody's in debt to the commissary. They can't go nowhere until they pay their debt, and they ain't paid enough to pay their debt."

"Sounds a lot like slavery to me," the doctor said.

"Worse," Django continued. "At least in slavery, you didn't owe nobody nothing. But in the camp, if you tried to leave owin' a debt to the man, which everybody did, then they'd hunt you down, beat you up, and bring you back to work off the debt. And if the law caught you, they'd put you in jail and keep you there until the foreman or the woodsrider come and git you and bring you back."

"So how long were you in these camps?"

"From the time I was born until I was eighteen. I started out as a water boy. Then I done some chippin' and boxin', and dippin'. I even worked the dip squads that went through the woods with a team and a wagon topped with barrels. We'd fill the barrels with gum, thick as syrup, and haul it off to the still to be refined. My daddy said if I was a white boy I'd of been a foremen, but there ain't no colored foremen. That ain't allowed."

"So you left?"

"Yeah, I hated to leave my family there to pay off their debt, but I didn't have no money until I got back from the Army and got a job with the railroad. Even then, it took a few years before I'd saved enough to get Mama, Daddy, and my little sister and brother outta there for good."

"Anything good come from all of it?"

"Not much," Django answered. "We got the weekends and winters off, so there was huntin' and fishin' in the woods. That's how I learnt my way around Tate's Hell. Saturday night all the men went to the jukes and gambled and got drunk and fought. And on Sunday mornin' some jackleg preacher would come in and we'd have church outside or in somebody's house."

The road turned into Avenue E in Apalachicola. The town wasn't much—a sleepy fishing village at the mouth of the Apalachicola River.

"You hungry?" the doctor asked.

"I could stand a bite. Might as well git somethin' here, 'cause once we git into Tate's Hell there won't be nothin' unless you want to hunt it down."

"Well, I don't get over here that often, so I'm not sure what's here."

"You mean you don't know where there's someplace that'll serve a colored man, don't you?"

"Well, yeah."

"Next Negro you see on the street, pull over."

When they were at what appeared to be the center of town, Highway 98 took a sharp right onto Market Street. They saw a prim colored woman with a shopping bag and large purse waiting to cross the street. The doctor pulled over as Django had instructed.

"Excuse me, ma'am, but could you tell me what's the best place to eat in town?" Django asked her.

The woman looked from the doctor to Django and back again, obviously confused.

"For colored folks," Django told her.

"My house," she said.

"Your house?"

"That's what I said."

"Hop in," Django said, stepping out of the car to open the door for the woman. She wasn't hopping anywhere, for it was easy to see she was a lady and a pretty good-looking one at that: middle-aged, slim, refined, and as confident as a queen. He helped her and her bags into the backseat and, when she was settled, said, "Where to, ma'am?"

"Turn around and go back the other way on Market Street," she instructed. "Keep going . . . past those fish houses . . . now take a left on Avenue M . . . a little further. Yes, here, to the left . . . on to Sixth. There on the right . . . the last house."

The doctor pulled to the curb and turned off the engine. Django helped the woman out of the car and the doctor grabbed her bags. She led them up the dirt path that led to a gray shotgun shack sitting in a grove of live oak and saw palmetto. They followed her down a narrow hall that went from the front of the house all the way to the back, where she took a left into a sparkling kitchen with a round table and four chairs planted squarely in the center.

"Sit," she ordered. "Lemonade or tea?"

"Tea, please," they both said at once.

"My name is Louisa Lee Randolph," she said. "Welcome to my kitchen."

"Pleased to meet you, Miss Randolph. I'm Django Jackson, and this here is Dr. Van Berber. Thanks for having us in your home."

"The pleasure is all mine, I'm sure," she said, pouring tea into their glasses. "Now tell me what brings you to Apalachicola. I don't believe I've ever seen either one of you in town before."

The doctor and Django looked at each other. Finally the doctor shrugged and said, "We're looking for a friend of mine, an Indian fellow, who has disappeared. We have reason to believe that he's somewhere in Tate's Hell, so we've come to look for him."

"Oh, my," she replied, peering over the top of her wire-rimmed spectacles, "how mysterious. My late husband was part Indian. Do you have any idea what you're getting into by going to Tate's Hell?"

"Well, it's been a number of years since I worked a gum patch on High Bluff," Django said, "but back then it was a wild and wonderful place where bear, otter, deer, wild turkey, quail, and fox roamed, even a few wildcats and panthers. All kinds of woods, scrub oak and slash pine, streams and swamps with cypress and willow and thickets so tight you needed a saw to git through 'em."

"What about the serpents?" the woman asked as she tied a starched, white apron around her tiny waist and began to prepare lunch.

"Oh, yeah, how could I forget? Snakes of all kind, water moccasins as big around as yo' arm, rattlers too, and alligators just as mean as the snakes."

"And y'all goin' into that today?"

"Yes, ma'am. That's what we're fixin' to do."

"May God be with y'all then," she said, shaking her head.

"What about you, Mrs. Randolph?" the doctor asked. "Are you an Apalachicola native?"

"Yes, I am, born and reared here on the Hill. That's what we call the colored part of town here in Apalach. Mama and Daddy were slaves way before I was born. Their granddaddy was one of the few that survived the big explosion up river at the Negro Fort back in eighteen sixteen. That was when the army shot a red-hot cannonball into the fort's main gunpowder magazine. They say folks in Pensacola heard the blast. Of the three hundred and twenty freed slaves and Choctaw Indians in the fort, only fifty survived, my great granddaddy, just a boy at the time, included. At any rate, after the rest of his family was blown up, he was returned to slavery, not far from here.

"Now, my daddy fished for a livin' after he was freed for the same man who owned him, H.C. Deavers, while Mama raised six kids. Mama was a cook for the same white family that owned Daddy. Mama taught me how to cook. Now I do most of the fancy bakin' for this little town. Somebody, colored or white, need a birthday or wedding cake, or some pies for Thanksgivin', or some cookies for a tea, they all come see Miss Louisa."

"And your parents?" the doctor asked.

"Oh, my, they've long since passed. As has my husband, Gerald; he left this earth five years ago. Died in a storm while he was out tonging for oysters in the bay. I'm all by myself now. All my brothers and sisters have moved away."

It was quiet for a while as the slender, genteel woman worked at her kitchen counter and the men sipped their tea. A mockingbird whistled merrily away outside the open window. Presently, Miss Louisa sat a large, round tin tray of chucked oysters in the middle of the table between Django and the doctor. Also on the tray was a bottle of Ed's Red Hot Sauce, a little white bowl of mashed horseradish, and several lemon quarters scattered among the oysters. She refilled their glasses and hurried back to the counter. "Enjoy," she said.

"Ain't you gonna join us?" Django asked her.

"Not right now. I'm working on the next course. Y'all go ahead, please."

"I believe these are the plumpest, sweetest oysters I've ever tasted," the doctor said between slurps.

"Yes, indeed," Django grinned.

"Tonged this morning, fresh out of the bay. I get 'em from Jimmy Deavers, son of the man who owned by mama and daddy. He gives me a burlap bag full of 'em anytime I ask."

When the men had finished all the raw oysters, the woman sat a big bowl of chowder in front of each of them. They tasted it.

"Oh, my," Django cooed, "what . . . what in the world is this?"

"Well, I gotta do somethin' with all them oysters so I made y'all some oyster soup. Like it?"

"'Like it,'" the doctor said, "is much too mild an appreciation. This is the best soup I've ever tasted."

"Hmm," was all Django could get out as he shook his head in agreement, "amazin'."

"Your recipe?" the doctor asked.

"I'm embarrassed to tell you," she said.

"Oh, come on."

"Just oysters, cream, chicken broth and, ah, paprika."

"That's it?"

"That's it," she said. "Maybe a little love too."

"I should say so," the doctor said.

While they finished their soup, Miss Louisa continued to work away at her counter. When she heard no more quaffing from the men, she turned and removed their bowls. Then she returned to the counter and continued her preparations. Soon the kitchen was filled with the most delicious aroma. She was frying something that smelled really good, and then the oven opened and closed and she sat down at the table with the men. "Ten minutes," she said.

"I don't think I can wait," Django said. "After what you've already fed us and that smell . . . my mouth is waterin' like a overflowin' fountain."

"I have a little garden out back," she told them. "I grow tomatoes, beans, corn, some herbs, onions, shallots, okra, potatoes, and I have a Meyer lemon tree too that produces sweet, juicy fruit almost year round."

"And then you have all this fresh fish from the sea that's only a couple of blocks away."

"Yes," she said, "that's the secret to any good cooking, using fresh food. I used to do some canning, but now I mostly just eat what I can get from the garden and the fish from Jimmy Deavers."

Miss Louisa asked about Port St. Joe, since she had not been there in several years, so the doctor told her about the new mill and how rapidly the town was growing. Django admitted that he had been away for a while and had just recently returned to a town he could hardly recognize. Somehow, before she had served the next course, she had wheedled the marriage status out of the two men, as well as Gator's and why he was hiding out in Tate's Hell.

The doctor and Django were surprised by the next dish, which appeared, steaming there in the middle of each of their plates, to be nothing more than a small, puffed brown paper bag, tied closed with a piece of twine. "Pompano en papillote," she announced.

"What?" Django asked.

"Slice the bag open with your knife and take a look," she said.

"Oh, my, I've never smelled anything so good," the doctor said, when he had cut open his bag of pompano, covered in slivers of fried onions, sliced shallots, lemons, and some sort of herbs.

"Bon appetite," she chirped as she placed a saucer of sliced tomatoes next to each of their plates.

"This is so good I think I'll eat the bag too," Django said.

"Superb!" the doctor said. "Where in the world did you come up with this?"

"Believe it or not," she answered, "there used to be an honorary French consul in Apalachicola. The last one was here, upstairs in the

Grady Building downtown, from eighteen eighty-nine until nineteen oh-five, when I was just a young bride. A man named Antoine Jean Murat. He loved to cook. When he heard that I was the best cook in town, he found me and we traded recipes and cooking tips. He was a lovely man and a very good cook. He told me he got the basis for this recipe from a chef in New Orleans, a man named Jules Alciatore, who worked at a restaurant called Antoine's. I learned a lot from him, including this pompano, which is plentiful here in our bay. Tasty, don't you think?"

"Outrageously so," the doctor said.

"I'll never look at a brown paper bag the same way again," Django laughed.

But Miss Loiusa had saved the best for last. She served each of them a generous slice of a yellow custard pie. It was both sweet and tart in exactly the right combination.

"Sorry, I didn't bake this morning," their hostess said, "but I saved this in the icebox from yesterday."

"It's wonderful," the doctor said.

"Hmm . . . yes," Django nodded. "What is it?"

"Lemon chess pie," she said.

"I never had chess pie like this!"

"Well, I do use a few secret ingredients."

"Like?"

"They wouldn't be secrets now, if I told you, would they?"

"Well," the doctor said, "I can taste that you've put some of your Meyer lemon juice in there."

"You're right about that, and some buttermilk too."

"The sweet taste is different than I ever tasted in a chess pie," Django noted.

"Okay," she smiled, "I'll tell y'all what the secret to most of my baking is, if you promise not to tell."

"We won't."

"What?"

"Honey," she whispered. "Tupelo honey, instead of sugar. It's the sweetest, most delicate of all honeys, and it's harvested in April and May just a few miles from here in the swamps in the Apalachicola River Valley. I buy it from a man named L.L. Lanier, who keeps bees not far from Tate's Hell. Stuff is so pure it never crystallizes."

"Well, I'll be," the doctor said. "It's surely wonderful!"

"Miss Louisa," Django said, "I thought up till now that my wife was the best cook in the world, a far sight better than my mama, that's for sure, but just between you and me—you got 'em both beat."

"Well, thank you, Mr. Jackson. I don't believe I've ever had a kinder compliment."

The doctor pulled out his pocket watch as he finished scraping the last of the crispy piecrust from his plate. "As much as I'd like to spend the rest of the day with you, Miss Louisa," he said as he pushed back from the table, "we should be going now."

"I understand," she replied. "You've been most pleasant company, and you're welcome here on your way back or anytime you're in the area. And if you find your friend Gator, tell him he's welcome too."

"Thank you," the doctor said, "for your hospitality, your food, for everything. Can we pay you something? If you had sent us to a restaurant, we wouldn't have had enough money to pay for the kind of meal you just served us."

"Oh, heavens no," she said. "You live in the South now, Doctor, so you must know about our Southern hospitality. You're welcome here anytime. And if I ever get back to Port St. Joe before I die, I'm sure that y'all will reciprocate."

They exchanged telephone numbers and hugged good-bye. Django and the doctor, sated, loosened their belts, got back in the car, and forged ahead to whatever awaited them at the ominous, looming gates of Tate's Hell.

Chapter 21

It was about twenty miles between Port St. Joe and Apalachicola, but by the time the doctor had checked on Nadyne, picked up Django, and been served an early dinner by the best cook in north Florida, it was past noon when they began crossing the Apalachicola River and then Apalachicola Bay on the four-year-old John Gorrie Memorial Bridge. It was a long—six and half miles—two-lane span across the mouth of the river, over Little Towhead Island, and then out over the choppy, brown waters of the broad bay. There was even one section near the middle that rotated to allow ships with high masts to pass through. Fortunately, the rotating section was not open when they reached it so it was an easy ride into Eastpoint on the other side of the bay.

"Who's John Gorrie?" Django asked.

"I think I read somewhere," the doctor answered, "that he was a doctor in Apalachicola way back when who invented an ice maker and some way of cooling a room. He thought it would help cure malaria and yellow fever. It didn't, of course. He couldn't find any backers to manufacture his invention so he died bankrupt, but apparently the people here still remember him."

"Well, if he could cool down a room in a Panhandle summer, then he deserves to be remembered, and this here bridge is a fittin' honor.

Why, it used to be the only way across this bay was by ferry," Django said, "when I lived around here. Took more than an hour. Run by a man named Wing, if I recollect correctly. Now here we are in Eastpoint in no time."

Eastpoint was another sleepy fishing village much like Apalachicola. They were through it in no time as the highway snaked up the coast toward Carrabelle. The Gulf of Mexico stretched out to their right as Django coughed and squinted into the bright sunlight, trying to spot the road north into Tate's Hell.

"There," he said finally. "Take a left here. The sign says they're calling it State Road 65 now, but I don't recall if that's what it was called when I was here. But that's it, all right."

Now they were on a narrow gravel road that was bordered by denser and denser pine forest closing in on both sides. As the trees all but blotted out the sun, the doctor strained to stay on the road and out of the muddy ditch beside it. Then the road sloped off to the left, and Django told him to slow down. There didn't appear to be anything out here—just the doctor and Django sliding around on the narrow gravel path deeper into the woods.

Soon they came to a one-lane wooden bridge. "Stop here," Django told the doctor.

So the doctor found a little clearing, just to the left, on the other side of rickety bridge and pulled over into it. "Let's have a look," Django said.

They got out of the car and, from the bridge, looked up and down the dark stream. There was a swampy backwater and a small island to the west and a meandering salt marsh–enshrouded waterway to the east. "Cash Creek," Django announced. "The gum patch that I worked at is right up there."

"I don't see anything except trees, water, and marsh grass," the doctor said.

"Me neither. Could Gator's little boat navigate a stream like that?"

"Oh, yeah," the doctor said. "No problem. We've fished many a stream like this."

"Okay, let's drive on a little further. Let's see if there's anything left of that ol' camp."

They got back in the car and continued northwest up the gravel road, still not a car, a human, even an animal in sight.

"Keep it slow," Django ordered. "We're lookin' for a little dirt road off to the right somewhere around here."

The doctor drove on.

"How about there?"

"Nope," Django said. "If memory serves me, that's Jeffie Tucker Road. Go on to the next one."

In about another quarter of a mile, they came to another sandy, dirt path heading off to the right.

"That's it," Django said. "Take a right. This here's North Road, I think. We're gonna go about half a mile down and then take a right onto Rake Creek Road."

There wasn't much left of what Django had identified as Rake Creek Road—just two parallel tire trails with a low, overgrown ridge between them. On either side was a dense thicket of wax myrtle, cabbage palm, saw palmetto, scrub oak, and Florida privet. The so-called road was bumpy, muddy, and filled with potholes so it was slow going. After about half a mile, it just "petered out," as Jewel would have said, and there they were, somewhere in the midst of Tate's Hell.

"Looks like the end of the road, literally," the doctor observed. "Now what?"

"A couple a hundred yards or so into them woods ahead is Cash Creek and what's left, if anything, of that gum patch. Be a good place for a camp."

"Let's have a look," the doctor said as he opened the car door and the mosquitoes swarmed upon him like a flying flock of tiny, buzzing, bloodthirsty vampires.

Django found a narrow deer trail through the brambles and high grass, and the doctor followed him into the woods. As the trail became fainter and fainter, the doctor asked, "You know, I've been meaning to ask you. I think I'm beginning to guess the answer already, but why do they call this place Tate's Hell?"

"Oh, you ain't never heard the story?" Django asked as he held a buttonwood branch away from the doctor's face.

"No. I probably don't want to know, but go ahead."

"Well, somewhere back when, around eighteen seventy-five, they say, a fellow by the name of Cebe Tate had a cattle ranch over 'round Sumatra. A panther was killin' his cows so he took off with his three hunting dogs to kill the panther. That turned out to be no easy job. When they got deeper and deeper into the woods, they got turned around. Then a panther attacked them and killed the dogs, and Tate lost his rifle. He kept on wandering around, lost, tryin' to find some way out. When he tried to get some rest at the base of an ol' cypress tree, he got bit by a snake. So, lost and snake bit and hounded by swarms of hungry mosquitoes, just like these here, he wandered around in the swamps for a week or so. When he finally did straggle out somewhere near Carabelle, some twenty-five miles southeast of Sumatra, he came upon two hunters. They were surprised by what a mess he was and asked him what happened. All he could say was, 'My name is Tate, and I've just been in Hell.' And then he just upped and fell to the ground and died right there at their feet, as dead as a graveyard corpse."

"My God," the doctor exclaimed. "Is that a true story?"

"I don't know, but maybe I should've told you it before we started out on this hunt," Django said as he bent over into a coughing, laughing fit.

The path was gone now. It appeared to the doctor that they were just wandering around in the mud and ever-thickening woods, not unlike old Cebe Tate. As the ground grew softer, the buzz of the mosquitoes grew louder and more annoying. Both men had buttoned up their shirts tight around their necks, leaving their sweating heads as open targets for the pests to feast upon. The men, miserable by now, flung their arms in self-defense. Why hadn't the doctor thought to bring beekeeper helmets or at least some DMP oil?

They slogged ahead through cypress stumps, blueberry bushes, and railroad vine. The doctor's shoes were heavy with mud and probably ruined for good. His shirtsleeves were streaked with spots of blood from the attacking buttonwood branches. The lower half of his pant legs were torn and covered with burrs. He was bent over, huffing for breath, flailing at the mosquitoes, his eyes bleary with sweat and maybe even some tears.

"How much further?" he panted.

"I ain't sure. I thought we would have been to the creek by now. It's been a long time since I been out here. I think maybe I disremembered exactly where it was."

"So what do we do?"

"I don't know. Let's keep goin', I guess."

So they slogged on. The ground grew muddier and the brambles sharper. The doctor wasn't sure how much further he could go. His heart was pounding and his face was a bloody mess from all the mosquitoes and errant branches. He hadn't been out here for more than an hour and he was already feeling like he had been damned forever to the perdition tagged so gruesomely by the wayward hunter Cebe Tate. He was about ready to give up and suggest to Django that they return to the car, if they could find it, when Django suddenly stopped before him and pointed ahead. There, about thirty yards away, between them and what looked maybe like the creek's bank, sat a mother black bear and her cub feasting on a thick stand of blueberries.

"Oh, no," the doctor whispered.

"Stay still," Django ordered.

But the doctor was shaking, uncontrollably. They watched each other for a long time—the two bears and the two men—long enough for the doctor to clearly contemplate his death by an angry mother bear and his stupidity for not bringing along his shotgun. *Maybe,* he thought, *if we just wait quietly, the bears will grow bored and go away.*

But then he heard the noise in Django's throat, that nasty, rasping sound so familiar to tuberculosis patients who are about to commence a coughing fit. And he could tell by the weird guttural noises that Django was making that he was doing his best to contain it, but it was no use. The coughing began as a strained groan, then a stutter of a gasp, and then the explosion that Django could not control.

The startled bears turned, and the mother bear rose from her sitting position into her running position. For a moment, the doctor thought that Django's coughing might scare the bears so much it would cause them to run away. But he was wrong, because the big bear was now picking up speed through the blueberry thicket and heading directly for them. If the doctor had been a religious man, this would have been the point at which he would have offered up a prayer. But instead he froze in fear and watched in terror as the bear rapidly bore down on them.

Then a loud crack echoed through the woods, and the bear turned and simply fell over on its side to the ground, not more than ten yards from the doctor and his companion. At the blast, the cub scurried away into the woods. The doctor looked around, trying to figure out what miracle had just occurred. And then from behind a thick, tall slash pine tree, Gator Mica, thin and weathered, rifle in hand, appeared as if from nowhere, a wide smile on his red face.

"Well, I'll be damned," the doctor said. "I'll be goddamned."

"You fellows sure know how to make an entrance," Gator said. "Follow me before you get yourself into any more trouble."

"Boy, am I glad to see you," the doctor said. "This is Django Jackson, Jewel's daddy."

"Pleased to meet you, sir. I'm Gator Mica."

"The pleasure is mine, especially after that good bit of shootin' just now."

The two shook hands and Gator set out toward the creek bank with the doctor and Django wearily in tow. As they approached the creek, the doctor saw Gator's glade skiff hidden under a pile of pine boughs. Then they came to a tallgrass clearing; at least the undergrowth was not as high and thick as the surrounding area. At the edges of the clearing were several piles of rotted lumber covered by vines. Gator had set up camp in the only brick structure in the area, a twelve-by-twelve, windowless shed with an opening but no door and no roof. Gator had apparently spread some scavenged lumber across the top of the walls for some cover but hadn't gotten around to fashioning a door yet. There were, however, the remains of a fire in front of the hut and a cypress log for sitting next to the fire, facing the clearing.

"Have a seat," Gator said, pointing to the log. "Sorry, I ain't got nothin' much to offer you, unless you like bear meat."

The doctor and Django sat on the log as Gator pulled over a stump that looked like he'd been using as a chopping block. He sat down and asked, "How the hell did y'all find me? I thought I was pretty well hidden out here. Not that I ain't glad to see you. I've been powerful lonely out here with no one to talk to or drink with."

"You won't believe this," the doctor said, "but Django led me pretty much directly to you."

"I worked a turpentine camp right here where you're campin' when I was a kid," Django explained. "In fact, that little brick building there was where the still was, if I ain't mistakin'. Looks like that's about all that's left. But I figured it might make a pretty good hideout for someone travelin' by boat from St. Vincent Island. Actually, it was just a lucky guess."

"Well, I know now," Gator said, "where Jewel gets her investigatin' skills from. I'm mighty impressed. But, tell me, why have y'all come all the way out here?"

"Listen, Gator," the doctor began. "If we could find you, sooner or later someone else is gonna find you and then tell the sheriff where you're at. And the sheriff, when he finds out, he's gonna come and get you and either put you in jail or shoot you. Probably shoot you, since I doubt you'll go without a fight."

"So what do you want me to do?" Gator asked.

"There's more, Gator. Listen. Guess who Dr. Price willed the island to."

"Who?"

"You, you numbskull. You. You own St. Vincent Island."

"I do? But the sheriff thinks I killed Price."

"Well, he's not so sure now. He knows that Lucky Lucilla is on the loose and trying to kill me and God knows who else. Maybe even Dr. Price, though we haven't figured out why yet. Bob Huggins thinks he can mount a good defense for you, but only if you turn yourself in. If you stay on the run and the sheriff finds you and arrests you, then your chances of getting off are slim, according to Huggins. But one thing's for sure: You're not gonna get the island if you're hiding out here."

"What a fuckin' mess," Gator said.

"Yeah, and this is no way to live, Gator, you know that. Foraging like an animal out here in the woods. You've lost a lot of weight and you don't look healthy. You need to come home and work with Huggins and me to straighten the whole thing out. I've already talked to Sally Martin, but she's not saying anything. She warned me not to say a word about what we know."

"So what do we do?"

"I don't know."

"Sally knows from Sheriff Batson that I killed a man in Florida City. She's gonna tell Lane about that if she's cornered, not to mention your own little secret, partner."

"I know," the doctor admitted. "I didn't think about that when I confronted her. I was just so pissed that you were taking the rap for Price's murder instead of Lucilla that I decided to go see her. I'm sorry."

"Oh, that's okay, but it sounds like the only chance I have now is if we find Lucky Lucilla and get him to admit he killed Dr. Price, if he in fact did."

"That's right. And then we get Huggins on the case about you assaulting Sheriff Duffield and that man in Florida City. He got you off before; maybe he can do it again."

"I don't know," Gator said, shaking his head. "I gotta think on all this. I ain't so sure we can find Lucky Lucilla, and I ain't so sure, if we did, he would admit to killing Dr. Price, and I ain't so sure Bob Huggins can get me off for killing a man and slugging a sheriff. Seems to me there's a lot goin' against me."

"Well," the doctor said, "look at it this way. You can either continue sufferin' out here in the woods by yourself, hoping the sheriff doesn't find you, or you can come back with us, turn yourself in, and face the music. At least then you have a chance of getting off and inheriting the island of your dreams."

"Hmm," Gator said. "Mr. Jackson, excuse me for broachin' the subject, but you've got some experience with goin' to prison. Say it don't turn out as pretty as my partner here would like to think and I end up in prison. Would that be any better than being out here in the woods free?"

"That's a mighty good question. And the answer is probably different for every man you ask it to. And if you was out here with somebody else, say a purty woman, then that's one thing. But to be out here all by your lonesome and always lookin' over your shoulder, that's another. I believe I'd rather be in prison. Leastwise, I'd have someone to talk to. But then again maybe there's another way."

"Yeah?" Gator asked.

"You could come back with us. Hide out someplace closer. And then in a few days ride back to New York City with Jewel and Gabriel and Marcus. Then disappear in the crowd there. I ain't never been there, but I hear tell that a man could hide there forever without nobody takin' a notice of it. Now, I ain't talked to Jewel or Gabriel about that, but it's an idea."

"New York City . . . I don't know," Gator said. "I git to feelin' too closed in when I'm in Port St. Joe. I think I'll take my chances out here for the time being."

"Okay, Gator," the doctor said. "Let me talk to Judge Denton and Bob Huggins and see what kind of deal we might be able to work out if you were to turn yourself in at this point. Then I'm gonna go to Tampa to see what, if anything, I can find out about Lucky Lucilla. We haven't heard from him for a few days now, so maybe he went home. Who knows? Then let's talk again, see where we stand."

"Okay," Gator muttered.

"Meanwhile, Django and I'll drive back to Eastpoint right now and bring you back some gasoline for your hothead, some decent food, some liquor, and whatever else you need. Then I'll come back in a few days and let you know where we're at. If you want to get in touch with us before we come back, try to get to a phone and call me or Jewel collect. I'll write down the numbers for you. Also, there's a nice little lady named Louisa Randolph who lives in the last house, a gray one, at the north end of Sixth Street in Apalachicola. It's only a couple of blocks from the fishing docks at Scipio Creek. She's got a phone and the best kitchen in the Panhandle. We told her a little bit about you, and she said you'd be welcome there anytime."

"Oh," Django said, "and one more thing. Thanks for saving our lives today."

"No problem," Gator said with a tired smile. "Just bring me back a couple of Partagas cigars and a bottle of Old Crow and we'll call it even."

Chapter 22

The doctor and Django drove back into Eastpoint and found a store to buy the cigars, whiskey, and other provisions for Gator. By the time they had delivered them and tried again, unsuccessfully, to talk Gator into returning to Port St. Joe with them, it was dusk. They were tired and hushed as the doctor squinted through the dusty windshield of his old Ford into the setting sun.

When he finally dropped Django off at his house, the sky was gray and the bay was black. With the doctor's newfound disregard for death, he ignored the enveloping gloom of his old house. He just traipsed through the empty kitchen, ignoring what Vivian had left him on the counter for supper, pulled himself up the dim stairs, undressed, measured out the morphine, drank it, and went to sleep.

He awoke to the welcome sounds of women's voices downstairs in the kitchen. Vivian and Jewel were laughing about something he could not quite make out. He lay there and listened. All he could do was catch a word here and there, but the pleasant, rhythmic, feminine chatter was reassuring enough.

After the doctor had consumed his morning dose of morphine, showered, and dressed, he joined the two women at the kitchen table.

"Good mornin', sleepyhead," Jewel greeted as Vivian got up and moved to the stove.

"Good morning, Jewel, Vivian. What's for breakfast?"

Vivian answered by placing a plate of crisp bacon, two fried eggs, and a bowl of blackberries in front of him. She filled his cup with black coffee and sat a glass of orange juice next to his plate.

"Utensils?" the doctor said.

"Oh, sorry. Jewel and I just got to talking, and I plum forgot all about them."

"What were y'all talking about?"

"You, of course," Jewel replied with a smile as Vivian hurried to the silverware drawer. "'Bout how you and Daddy near got yo'self kilt in Tate's Hell lookin' for Gator Mica."

"So your daddy told you about our little adventure, huh?"

"Yeah, I guess y'all thought I didn't have enough worriment—what with Gator and Lucky Lucilla and all—so now I gotta worry 'bout you and Daddy wandering off in the woods someplace."

"Well," the doctor said, "so far we're still alive, thanks to Gator."

"Yeah, but no thanks to yo'selves," Jewel said, "and now Daddy says you're gonna go down to Tampa to see if you can find Lucky Lucilla there. Why, I ain't sure. If he's down there, which I doubt, why don't you just leave him be, down there by hisself?"

"Because if we don't find him, he's gonna kill me, Gator—if he can find him—and probably you. And because, without him confessing, Gator's gonna remain the main suspect in Dr. Price's murder."

"Well, if he's gonna kill me, he better hurry 'cause Gabriel, Marcus, and me are headin' back to New York City the first thing Saturday mornin'."

"So soon?" the doctor asked.

"Yeah, Gabriel's got to get back to work next week so we gotta go, as much as I hate not helpin' y'all out down here."

"I wish you could stay."

"Me too," Vivian said.

"Me too," Jewel said. "Me too. But I'm a married woman now, and my place is with my husband, and his job is in New York City."

"I know," the doctor said, resigned, "but I'll do my best to be back from Tampa on Friday to say good-bye. If the trains are runnin' on time, it won't be a problem. Maybe y'all—you, Vivian, Gabriel, Marcus, and your mama and daddy—could come over here Friday night for a little going-away party."

"You're gonna be tired from you trip, Doc. Why don't y'all come to our place? Mama and me'll make supper and we'll have a good ol' time."

"Okay," the doctor said. "But I'm still not happy about seeing you go. I was really hoping that once you got back down here, y'all would decide to stay," he added, momentarily ignoring Vivian's paranoia.

Outside it was cooler than usual, with a line of high clouds somewhat tempering the sun's mounting heat. The doctor walked to work and found the waiting room full. He motioned for Nadyne to follow him to his office.

"How'd everything go yesterday?" he asked her.

"Fine," she answered. "Nothing unusual, except . . ."

"Yes?"

"Chief Lane dropped by to see you."

"What'd you tell him?"

"The truth, of course," she said, "that you were taking the day off."

"Thanks."

"But he seemed skeptical."

"Okay, I'll call him. What else?"

"Want to hear what's going on today?"

"Of course. What do we have?"

"Mrs. Dawson has another migraine. Bill Butler cut his calf some way or another. Mavis Williams is here with her daughter; she won't say why. Percy Wilkens can't breathe very well. Lauren Morrison wants you to check a bruise that won't go away. Max James thinks his arm's broken; he fell off his roof. Haddie Michaels' son Junior has a pink eye. Then house calls in the afternoon."

"Okay, thanks, Nadyne. And before we get going today, can you cover for me again tomorrow and the next day? I gotta go to Tallahassee for a conference," he lied.

"Sure," she answered, but the doctor could tell she suspected something other than a conference since the doctor had never been absent more than one day in a single week. The simple fact was he didn't want to scare Nadyne about Lucky Lucilla. If the doctor told Nadyne he was going to Tampa to find him, then she would want to know why and he would have to go into the entire story. Besides, the whole trip seemed more and more like a wild goose chase. No use sharing his foolhardiness with Nadyne if he could avoid it.

Mavis Williams was a small, stooped woman in a flowery housedress and practical, well-worn black flats. She started crying as soon as the doctor closed the door of the examining room behind her. Her taciturn daughter stared angrily at her.

"Okay," the doctor said. "What's wrong here?"

"I want y'all to see if Millie's in a family way," she whimpered. The girl continued to stare at her mother with hate in her eyes.

"How old are you, Millie?" the doctor asked.

"She's sixteen," her mother answered.

"That's a damn lie," the girl blurted out. "I'll be thirteen in September."

The doctor looked at the woman and then back at her daughter, who appeared to be about ready to attack her mother. By the looks of her, the daughter was probably the truthful one.

"What makes you think she's pregnant, Mrs. Williams?"

"I seen her," she sobbed.

"Seen her what?"

"I seen her . . . you know, havin' sex."

"At her age?" the doctor asked. "With whom?"

The mother, now sobbing uncontrollably, and her daughter, fists clenched and furious, sat staring at one another, neither offering an answer. The doctor let them sit like that for a while.

"Look," he finally said. "It's against the law to have sexual relations with a child as young as Millie. And when I know the law is being broken, I have to report it to the police. So you might as well tell me now."

"No!" Millie screamed. "No, Mama, don't tell him!"

Now they were both in tears. What the hell was going on here? Nadyne had apparently heard the scream and was knocking at the door.

"Everything okay in there?" she asked.

"Come in," the doctor told her, thinking maybe he could use a little help with this one.

"Hey, Mrs. Williams, Millie," Nadyne said. "Is there anything I can do?"

The mother and daughter sat and sobbed.

"I'll get the urine sample bottle," Nadyne said calmly. "Follow me, Millie."

The girl did as she was told. The doctor just sat there, helpless, looking at her crying mother, waiting for some logical explanation. But one never came, at least not from the mother. Soon Nadyne and Millie were back, and Nadyne told them that they should come back Friday afternoon to get the results of the pregnancy test. Then they left, and the doctor asked Nadyne to close the door behind them and sit down.

"I'm afraid to ask," he said.

"As well you should be," Nadyne replied, removing her spectacles and wiping her eyes. "A few years back, before you came here, her older sister, Barbie Jo, about Millie's age then, came in with her mother. Same issue. Luckily, she wasn't pregnant, but she was just as angry as Millie. The next day, she went after her daddy with a butcher knife, but he got it away from her before she could do much damage, and then he beat her up. I fixed her up the best I could, but no one's seen her since. Apparently she just took off."

"Now this," the doctor said.

"Yeah, I told the mother back then that she better do what she had to do to put a stop to this or the same thing would happen to Millie, but I guess she didn't listen."

"And the police?"

"Yeah, I reported it to that fool before Chief Lane. Mathis was his name. Never been a more worthless human being in all of north Florida. He didn't do anything. Said he had no proof, and, with the girl gone, there wasn't anything he could do."

"What an awful shame."

"I know. I wish now that I had gone out there and shot the son of a bitch myself."

"You did what you could, Nadyne."

"I guess. Sometimes, Doc, I just don't know about people. You'd think in such a pretty, quiet, little town like ours that stuff like this couldn't happen, but . . ."

"But it does, doesn't it?" The doctor shook his head. "Let's just hope that Millie's test turns out as good as her sister's. When I see Lane this afternoon, I'll tell him what's going on. And if he doesn't stop it, I will."

The doctor had dinner at the Triangle Restaurant—meatloaf, mashed potatoes, gravy, green beans, and coconut cream pie—and started his afternoon house calls. Madge Dooley had bronchial pneumonia and needed to be moved to the hospital in Panama City. Morris Fulgate had twisted his neck when someone had rear-ended his car in front of the

Port Inn. Jim Matteson had malaria. Naomi Liston had left her three year-old daughter alone at home while she had gone shopping. The child had somehow turned on the stove and burned a festering red hole in her tiny, right hand.

Chapter 23

When he had finished his house calls, the doctor drove over to Chief Lane's office in City Hall. The chief looked tired, but the doctor told him about Millie Williams and his suspicions regarding her father.

"I don't know," the chief said, shaking his head. "That family is one of the poorest in town. The father was injured several years ago in a railroad accident and can't work. The mother is not quite right in the head. The older daughter, as you said, disappeared a few years back, before I got here. I'm not sure how they get by."

"Is there anything we can do?"

"We're in a difficult spot. If the mother or the daughter would press charges against the man, then I could arrest him. But if they don't, I don't have any evidence to prove he did anything wrong. If I try to scare him into admitting it and he doesn't, then he'd probably take it out on both his wife and his daughter."

"If Mrs. Williams tells you what her husband is doing to her daughter, then you can arrest him?"

"Yes, or if the daughter tells me."

"Okay," the doctor said. "When they come back in on Friday to get the results of the pregnancy test, I'll do my best to convince one of them to tell you exactly what happened. And, if on the off chance it was someone besides the father, at least we know and can deal with it."

"Let's just hope she's not pregnant," the chief said.

"We'll see," the doctor said. "One more thing . . ."

"Yeah?"

"I just wanted to let you know that I'm going to Tampa tomorrow to see if I can find Lucky Lucilla or at least something more about him that might give us a clue to where he is."

"Hmm . . .what makes you think he's there?"

"Well, no one around here has been attacked in the past few days, as far as I know, so I'm thinking maybe he's decided to give up and go home."

"Tampa's a mighty big place."

"Well, when I read the police report, I wrote down the address of the house where he murdered his family, someplace in Ybor City. An aunt lives nearby. I thought I would try to find her."

"Maybe I could get you a little help," the chief said, reaching for the telephone on his desk. "You do remember, don't you, that I used to work for the Tampa Police Department before I came here?

"Well, to tell you the truth, I had forgotten all about that. But now that you mention it, I do recall that someone told me about that. Your wife, I think."

"My father works down there as a union organizer, and I still have a few friends left in the department. I'm gonna call one of them right now and see if he can give you a little head start on your search."

It didn't take long for Edna, the town's day telephone operator, and the chief to locate his friend, a Sergeant Bert Wiley, and for the chief to tell him about Lucky Lucilla and the doctor's planned visit. "So see what you can find out, Bert, if it's not too much trouble," the chief concluded. "Dr. Berber will be there. . . when, Doc?"

"My train's supposed to arrive late tomorrow night."

"Can he meet you at the station first thing Thursday morning, Bert? Okay, thanks a million. Say hi to Susie. Okay, bye."

"Thanks, Chief, I really appreciate that."

"Bert's a good guy. He'll do what he can to help you, but he's got other things to do, so don't expect miracles."

"I'm not. In fact, I've been thinking that the whole trip is more than a little foolish. It's just that I feel so helpless not being able to help Gator. I know he didn't kill Price, and I suspect Lucky Lucilla did, but I don't know why. So I'm doing the only thing I can think to do at this point."

"Well, if Lucilla's still around here, at least you won't be his target for a few days."

"There is that," the doctor said.

When the doctor returned to his office, he phoned Louisa Randolph in Apalachicola.

"Why, what a pleasant surprise," she purred. "It's so nice to hear from you, Doctor."

"It's a pleasure talking to you again too. How have you been?"

"Well, very well, and you?"

"Oh, fine, thank you. I'm calling to ask if the man we were looking for yesterday may have paid you a visit yet?"

"Why, no," she answered. "Should I be expecting him?"

"Well, I'm not sure. We did find him, and we told him to look you up if he got to Apalachicola. So he may show up."

"All right. I'm sure it will be a pleasure to meet him."

"Mrs. Randolph, if he does visit you, would you ask him to call me or Jewel? Your operator can call our operator here in Port St. Joe—her name's Edna Edwards—and she'll find one of us. I have to be out of town for a few days, but Edna will connect him to Jewel while I'm gone."

"Of course," she said. "He should call you or Jewel."

"That's right."

"I'll tell him."

"Thank you so much."

"Oh, and thank *you* for calling. Just remember you have an open invitation to drop by anytime you like."

"Thank you, Mrs. Randolph. Thanks so much."

"Louisa, Doctor. Call me Louisa."

"Okay . . . Louisa. Thanks again. Good-bye."

"Good-bye, Doctor."

Was she making a play for him or was she just displaying her customary Southern hospitality? Sometimes the doctor couldn't tell the difference. At any rate, if Gator did get as far as Louisa Randolph's house, there was a good chance that his will was weakening and he might coax his friend to come out of hiding to help him track down the elusive Lucilla. At least, that was his hope.

Chapter 24

The Apalachicola Northern Railroad ran only two passenger trains from Port St. Joe to Chattahoochee each day. The first left at 8:00 A.M. and the second at 1:00 P.M. The doctor had told Vivian to take off the two days while he was away. He planned to indulge in the guilty pleasure of having breakfast in the train's dining car instead of having Vivian make it. But she had insisted on fixing him a sack lunch, which she had left in the icebox.

So he took the lunch and his suitcase, an old brown, cracked leather bag that was one of a set he had bought, one for Annie and one for him, each with a scrolled, gold-embossed monogram, his now chipped and fading, hers maybe still visible on her half of the set, which had disappeared with her a dozen long years before. He left his black bag and his shotgun in his bedroom at home. Then he drove to the depot on First Street in downtown Port St. Joe. It was an imposing, two-story clapboard building that the railroad shared with the St. Joseph Telephone and Telegraph Company, both of which were owned, like most of the rest of the town, by the duPonts and the St. Joe Paper Company. He parked his car across the street and went inside to buy his ticket. Fourteen dollars and twenty-eight cents was a lot of money for a round-trip ticket to Tampa, but he didn't want to drive that far by himself. It was more than three hundred miles one way, and he wasn't sure his 1934 Model B Ford sedan, with its balding tires and second-hand battery, could make it there and back. Besides, he had always enjoyed train travel, having time to read, ruminate, and relax without having to worry constantly about someone running into him.

A colored porter helped him up the stairs into the Pullman car and directed him to his seat. He placed his suitcase and lunch on the overhead rack and headed back to the middle of the train to find a place in the dining car. There were a dozen tables, each with a white linen tablecloth, a vase of fresh flowers, and four wooden chairs. The waiter asked him how many were in his party and, when the doctor said "one," led him to a table next to the kitchen where a stern, middle-aged woman in a dark blue suit was already seated. He took a seat across from her and nodded.

"This must be the singles table," she said with a Yankee accent, "where that Negro sticks all the people who are traveling alone."

"Apparently so, back here by the kitchen."

"Maybe we'll get fed first then."

"I hope so. I'm starving. My name's Van Berber."

"Geraldine Whitaker."

"Pleased to meet you."

"The pleasure is mine."

"I'm not much of a traveler," the doctor said. "How does this work exactly?"

"Well, what you do is decide what you want from the menu and then you write it down on this little pad, tear it off, and give it to the waiter."

"Sounds easy enough."

The doctor looked over the menu and wrote on the pad:

Ham

Grits

Toast

Melon

Coffee

While he was writing, his tablemate asked, "Where are you going, if you don't mind me being nosy?"

"To Tampa," he answered. "To visit a friend. And you?"

"Buffalo," she said. "I'm returning home."

"And what brought you all the way down here to Port St. Joe?"

"A funeral. My father's funeral."

"Oh, I'm so sorry," the doctor said, as he handed his order to the waiter. "He lived in Port St. Joe?"

"Well, not exactly. He lived on St. Vincent Island."

Oh, my God, the doctor thought. He had no idea what to say to her next. He just stared out the window, watching the outskirts of Port St. Joe disappear into the morning mist.

"What's wrong?" she asked. "You look like you've seen a ghost. Did you know him?"

"I did but not well."

"Tell me more," she said.

"He was a patient of mine. He was recovering from Eastern equine encephalitis when he died."

"Oh, you're a doctor. Tom, my father's servant, told us Dad had been ill."

"Us?"

"Yes," she said as the waiter delivered their food and poured them coffee from a silver pitcher. "Me and my two sisters. They came down together by car with their families, but I'm alone since my husband died last year. I couldn't stand to be in a car that long with their children, so I came alone by train, which I much prefer to automobile travel anyway. This is much more civilized, don't you think?"

"Yes, I agree. I don't travel that much, but this seems very agreeable."

"Can you tell me anything else about my father? I'm afraid we'd grown apart over the years."

"He was a fine man, a good employer, and he loved that island more than it probably deserved to be loved."

"I know," she nodded. "I can't understand what he saw in it, isolated down here in the middle of nowhere. He was always after us to come down and visit him. But frankly it was just too wild and mosquito infested for us. He and Mom raised us in the city, so that little hellhole was just not for us, I'm afraid."

"I can understand that," the doctor said.

"All three of us tried to convince him to sell the place to a lumber or paper company so he could move to Miami or someplace nice, as long as he insisted on living in the South. God knows why. But he wouldn't hear of it so he died there surrounded by all those bugs and trees."

After they had paid him, the waiter refilled their cups and cleared their table. Muddy, treeless fields that had been decimated by the lumber and paper mills whizzed by their window. *This is what St. Vincent Island would look like if this woman had her way,* the doctor thought.

"Tell me, if you don't mind," he said, measuring his words carefully. "Because I was his doctor, I know the circumstances of your father's death. Do you have any idea who might have wanted him dead?"

"Well," she huffed, "according to the sheriff, a wild Indian that they can't seem to find wanted to inherit St. Vincent Island. For some reason God only knows, my father had willed the place to him."

"I see," the doctor replied. "So what happens if they can't find him?"

"That's unclear," she snapped. "You're from the North, right? You don't speak like the rest of these Southerners."

"Yes, I grew up near Boston."

"Well, you understand then that they're more than a little backwards down here. This judge from over in some little Podunk town whose name I can't pronounce . . ."

"Wewahitchka."

"Yeah, that's it. Well, he says that if they don't find this Indian in ninety days, then the will will go to probate court, which apparently is him, and he'll decide what to do."

"What if they do find him?"

"Then he goes to trial, and if he's convicted, the will goes to probate court too."

"And if he's not convicted?"

"Well, that would seem highly unlikely," she sneered. "But I suppose the island would become the savage's. God knows how that could happen, but I guess anything's possible down here where this boondocks judge can do pretty much what he damn well pleases."

The doctor stared at the woman for a moment and wondered how her open-minded, preservationist father had produced such a pretentious reactionary offspring. He didn't know exactly how to respond, but finally he rose from his chair and said, "I hope, madam, that it pleases him not to grant you one single millimeter of that mosquito-infested little hellhole. Good day."

The doctor didn't know why he got so defensive when Northerners berated Southerners, not to mention his friend Gator, but he did. He guessed that he had lived in the South so long—fifteen years now—that he felt more like one of them than he did a Yankee. But at least now he understood why Dr. Price had changed his will to give St. Vincent Island to Gator Mica.

The doctor's seat was next to the window, and he had to disturb a sleeping man in the aisle seat to get there. But before he could settle in, the man was asleep again, which was fine by the doctor. He had already had enough conversation this morning and just wanted to look out the window and finish *The Grapes of Wrath.* The empty, desolate fields passed by, mile after discouraging mile. It was just about a hundred miles from

Port St. Joe to Chattahoochee so they would be there soon.

The doctor wondered how Nadyne was doing back in his office. He hoped nothing serious would happen while he was gone, but Nadyne was a fine nurse and would take care of whatever arose. He drifted off as the train chugged ahead across the Panhandle.

The doctor needed to change trains at the Chattahoochee depot so when the train squealed to a stop there, he grabbed his bag and sack lunch and found a porter to ask where he could find the Atlantic Coast Line train south to Tampa. It wasn't there yet, he was told, but he could wait for it in the station. As he was entering the station's waiting room, he saw Dr. Price's daughter lugging a heavy suitcase to a train heading north, and for some reason that made him think of Annie. He had watched her board a train in Tallahassee twelve years earlier, never to return. She had last been seen by a conductor somewhere around Charleston, but, despite the doctor's fervent search, she had never been found. He wondered about her now as Dr. Price's daughter was helped up the train's steps by a colored porter. Was she still alive out there somewhere? What, he wondered for the thousandth time, had become of her?

He waited in the station for about thirty minutes until he heard the announcement for the train to Thomasville, Georgia. He boarded and rode north to Climax and then east to Thomasville, about sixty-five miles altogether. In Thomasville, he had to change trains one more time to go south back into Florida again. This final train was newer and better appointed than the previous two, with broad, red velvet seats and shiny aluminum ceilings and walls. He sat next to an old woman who knitted intently and didn't even bother to look up as he eased past her to his window seat. So he read and watched the scenery sail by. There were a few more pine stands now between the gutted fields, some cotton fields in full bloom, vegetable farms, and eventually large orchards of orange, lemon, and grapefruit trees.

As the train pulled into the Monticello station, he noticed the clock there read 1:00 P.M. He got down the lunch Vivian had packed for him and started walking through the train until he found a conductor who could direct him to the club car, where he found an empty table. He ordered a Spearman beer from the waiter and opened his lunch. He found a ham-and-cheese sandwich on thick slices of Vivian's homemade wheat bread, two hard-boiled eggs, an apple, and a note that read simply:

Dear Dr. Berber,

I hope you are having a pleasant trip. I know you are going on a serious matter, but please take time to relax. I'll see you when you get back.

Sincerely yours,
Vivian

P.S. It is better to travel alone than with a bad companion.

He finished his lunch and ordered another beer, and the train slowed again as it rolled into Perry. Now he understood why the 275 miles between Thomasville and Tampa was scheduled to take so long: This train was apparently going to stop at every dinky station in north central Florida.

He returned to his seat and thought a bit about what he would do when he returned to Port St. Joe. He would have to find Gator and then try again to talk him in to turning himself in. That would be no easy task. And if he didn't locate Lucky Lucilla in Tampa, which he seriously doubted he would, or uncover some clue to his whereabouts, then he would just have to wait to be killed by the nut. He only hoped it wouldn't be in too painful a way.

He drifted off as the train left Cross City and was then jolted awake as it lurched to a jerky stop in Wilcox, then, as the afternoon passed and it grew dark, Dunnellon, Trilby, Vitis, and Thonotosassa, all little Florida towns that he had never heard of and that smelled of moss and citrus and the unseen sea.

Finally, at a little before 8:00 P.M., the train pulled into the Tampa Union Station. He retrieved his suitcase and walked through the depot's cavernous waiting room and out onto the street. It was busy even at this hour of the evening, with cars and people hurrying somewhere under the yellow streetlamps into the dark night. He found a taxi queue and took a taxi the few blocks north to the Floridan Hotel, the tallest building in the state, with 19 floors and 316 rooms, according to the friendly bellboy who led him through the opulent lobby, with its carved-wood ceiling, marble floor, and crystal chandeliers, to a bank of elevators and up to his room.

He lay back on the bed and stared at the stamped-tin ceiling. It had been a long day, and he was tired and hungry. He still felt foolish and a little guilty about taking this trip, since he had no good reason to believe Lucilla was here. But here he was anyway, with nothing to do now but make the best of it.

So he went back downstairs to the crowded Crystal Dining Room, ordered a Spearman, and looked over the extensive menu. He thought the fix-priced menu, which offered a variety of selections for each of three courses, was the best deal at one dollar. So he pored over his choices for the first course: tomato juice, honeydew melon, cumato juice, clam chowder, cold soups, cherrystones, cantaloupe, pine melon juice, consommé, and fruit supreme.

The doctor decided to go with the cherrystones. The menu for the next course included these specials:

Individual Black Sea Bass Sauté, Waffle Potatoes, New Corn
Fried Filet of Sole, Julienne Potatoes, Coleslaw
Scrambled Eggs Country Style, New Corn off the Cob
Chicken Tivoli en Bordure, Asparagus Tips
Loin Lamb Chop Combination, Fried Tomato
Minced Sweetbreads, Olives and Chipolata Sausage

Since it was August in the South, there was also a variety
of cold specials:

Bon Ton Salad
Floridan Fruit Plate
Italian Ham, Vegetable Salad
Tomato filled with Tunafish Salad
Crystal Salad Bowl (Baked salmon, hard-boiled egg, mixed salad,
Thousand Island dressing)

The doctor, after much vacillation, selected the black sea bass, waffle
potatoes, and coleslaw. Next, he didn't know how he could possibly
decide among the dessert choices:

Floridan Deep-Dish Fresh Blueberry Pie
Fresh Cherry Pie
Macaroon Custard Pie
Fresh Peach Cake, Whipped Cream
Lemon Fluff Cream Pudding
Floridan Devil's Food Date Cake
Stewed Fresh Apples
Fresh Peach Ice Cream
Fresh Strawberry Ice Cream

Sherbets
Floridan Chocolate Ice Cream
Famous Raspberry Ice
Cheese with Toasted Crackers or Ry-Krisp

But he did. Who could pass up fresh blueberry pie? The doctor was treating himself. It had been a rough couple of years and he expected to die soon, so why not enjoy his few remaining days? After the pie, which was delicious, he was stuffed but decided to visit the hotel's famous Sapphire Room before turning in.

The joint was jumping, to borrow a phrase from one of his favorite Fats Waller songs of a couple of years earlier. The Bill Lacey Orchestra was blasting out its version of "Little Brown Jug." The dance floor was crowded with soldiers, women in tight, bright dresses, and men in baggy suits. It smelled like cheap perfume, cigarette smoke, and overpriced liquor. The doctor found an empty stool at the bar, ordered a Cuba Libre, and watched. He sure wasn't in Port St. Joe anymore. A staggering soldier bumped the doctor as he passed by.

"See that beauty over there?" he mumbled to the doctor. "I'm gonna have her for the next dance and maybe, if I git lucky, for the night."

"Good luck."

"Thanks. You know what they call this place back on the post?"

"Isn't it called the Sapphire Room?" the doctor asked.

"Well, we call it the Surefire Room!" The soldier laughed and stumbled toward his target.

The doctor enjoyed the band, the pretty people, the liquor, and the pleasant sense of freedom that comes from being incognito in a crowd of strangers in a big city. By the time he returned to his room and drank his nightly dose of morphine, he was ready to fall into bed and go to sleep.

And so he did.

Chapter 25

The next morning, the doctor took a long hot shower, dressed, and had a leisurely breakfast. Then he packed, checked his suitcase with the bellman, and asked the doorman where the police station was.

"It's only a few blocks away," he told the doctor. "Just go south on North Florida for six blocks, take a right on Jackson, and in one block you're there."

It was a beautiful morning, not yet hot. At 9:00 the sidewalks were already crowded with pedestrians and the streets with honking cars and lurching delivery trucks. The police station was exactly where the doorman had said it was, and the patrolman at the front desk directed the doctor to an office on the second floor.

Bert Wiley was a tall, lanky, middle-aged man with unruly black hair and a half-smoked cigar in his mouth. He stood when the doctor entered his cramped, windowless office and offered his right hand. "Welcome to Tampa," he said, shaking the doctor's hand. "Please sit down. How was your trip?"

"It was long," the doctor said, "but I arrived in time to pass a pleasant evening at the Floridan.

"Good. You picked a fine hotel. Would you like coffee?"

"No, thank you. I've already had my limit."

"How's my old friend John Herman Lane?"

"He's well," the doctor said. "We're lucky to have him in our little town."

"That you are. Our loss is your gain, as they say. He's one of the finest officers I've ever worked with. In a department rife with corruption—don't quote me on that—he was somehow able to stay above it all. When he quit because they ordered him to arrest that lector in Ybor City, I lost a good friend."

"Well, he's done a fine job in Port St. Joe. I don't know what we would've done without him."

"It looks like this Lucky Lucilla is trying to find out."

"Yeah," the doctor said. "It seems he's determined to rid our town of both the chief *and* me."

"We've been on the lookout for him here, but I'm afraid there've been no sightings so far," Wiley said as he relit his cigar and puffed mightily to get it going again. "I was able to find his aunt, though, his mother's sister, the one who led the police to the bodies Lucilla butchered back in thirty-three. She's moved since then. One of our Italian cops asked around and was finally able to find her in a little cottage in Ybor City she shares with two other old, Italian women. Afraid that's all we got so far."

"Well, that's something," the doctor said. "I wasn't sure I'd find anything here. I have to admit this is a bit of a wild-goose chase."

"Sometimes, Doctor, wild-goose chases end up in cooked gooses. In this business, you do what you can and hope for the best. So should we go pay this Italian auntie a visit and see what we can find out?"

"Sounds good to me."

"Let's go then," the policeman said as he stood up and grabbed his hat and gun belt.

If the doctor thought downtown Tampa was a busy place, it was a rural crossroads compared to Ybor City. Here, people of all hues and stripes hustled down the sidewalks and through the stalled traffic; men huddled on street corners, their heads shrouded in swirling clouds of thick, gray cigar smoke. The streets were lined with cigar factories, social clubs, grocery stores, all permeated by the aroma of tobacco, rice and beans, and sweet espresso from the Columbia Restaurant and other cantinas along the way. People shouted from upstairs windows. Latin music coursed from crowded cafes, where dark-skinned men sipped coffee and argued. The smell of freshly baked Cuban bread wafted from La Segunda Central Bakery. The bustling neighborhood was piquant and loud and noisy and full of life. And the doctor loved it.

Even though they were attempting to traverse the busy streets in a black-and-white Tampa police car, the brick roads were too narrow for them to move any faster than the cars and streetcars ahead of them. But Wiley slowly maneuvered around the delivery trucks and pushcarts loaded with cigars, heaps of boxes, and fruits and vegetables of all kinds.

"All these people," the doctor said. "Where do they come from?"

"From everywhere," Wiley answered. "Originally from Spain to work in the cigar factories, then Cuba, Italy, all over Europe and Latin America. The largest immigrant groups have formed their own mutual aid societies and hospitals to take care of themselves in a country that hasn't always been that friendly to them. There's the Centro Espanol over there, the oldest one, with those old men playing dominos all day out front. The largest is El Centro Asturiano around the corner. There's also a couple for Cubans, one for light-skinned ones and another for those with darker skins. There's even a Deutscher-Americana Club for German and Eastern European folks. And, of course, L'Unione Italiana. A few blocks from there and Our Lady of Perpetual Help is where we're going. You can see the steeple over yonder."

Wiley wove in and out of the traffic and took a right down a pretty street lined with palm trees and colorful cottages set well back from the bougainvillea-lined sidewalk. He stopped the car in front of a small, pink clapboard cottage with a wide, covered front porch. The doctor followed him to the front door. He knocked and they waited.

Finally, after a few minutes, a tiny, gray-haired woman in a long black dress opened the door and peered questionably at them through the screen door.

"Are you Mrs. Aquilla?" Wiley asked her.

"Yes, I'm her."

"I believe Officer Mangione spoke to you yesterday . . . about your sister's family."

"Si."

"I wonder if we might ask you a few questions. Don't worry. You're not in trouble. But I'm afraid the son who committed the crimes, Anthony, has escaped from the state hospital in Chattahoochee."

"Again?"

"Yes, I'm afraid so. This is Dr. Berber. He lives in a little town in the Panhandle called Port St. Joe, where Anthony lived for a while. He is trying to help the boy."

"Okay," she whispered as she opened the screen door. "Come in."

She led them to a cramped parlor to the right of the front door and motioned for them to sit down on the old brown sofa whose armrests were covered with large white doilies. She sat stiffly in front of them in a padded chair. The place smelled like furniture polish, olive oil, and old age.

"Thank you very much for talking to us," the doctor said. "You have not seen Anthony recently, have you?

"No, I no see him since they take him away molti years ago."

"I see," the doctor said. "Do you have any idea where he could be?"

"No," she said, shaking her head wearily.

"As a doctor, I'm trying to understand why Anthony acted so

violently. Do you know what might have prompted him to act that way?"

"My sister, Maria," she began slowly, "she marry bad. Her husband's famiglia is matto, you know, crazy. So Anthony, he gets his crazy from them, the Lucillas.

"And was there anything in particular that would set him off?" the doctor asked. "Besides his family, what made him so . . . so angry?"

She stared hard at the doctor, her eyes beginning to mist over.

Then finally she blurted, "The saw."

"The saw?"

"Si, the saw. Anthony's padre run a sawmill. And when his kids are bad, he tells them he gonna cut them with the big, loud, round saw."

"Did he ever do that?"

"No," she said, "but if they was really bad, he would put them up on the platform where the wood go and he tie them down and he start the saw and he push them to the saw. He stop, but the kids, especially Anthony, would scream, afraid he gonna cut something off. It was not a good thing for a bambino."

"You say Anthony was especially scared of the saw?"

"Si," she said and began to cry softly and did not continue for several minutes. The doctor heard only her sobs and the grandfather clock in the corner ticking relentlessly. Finally, she spoke with her head down, through the tears, "Anthony, he wet the bed, until he was old. His padre yell at him and yell at him, but he kept doing it. Then he tell him he gonna put him on the saw and cut . . . and cut his pene off. He put him up there, with Maria and me screaming for him to stop, but he pushed us away, and took Anthony's pants off and tied him up and pushed him to the saw."

"And?"

"He stopped just in time, but Anthony . . . he couldn't stop sobbing. After that, the boy always seemed to have a tear in his eye."

She wept softly. The doctor rose and walked over and put his arm around her shoulders. "I'm so sorry," he said.

"Me too," she cried.

The sun blinded the doctor as he left the dim parlor and followed Wiley back to the car. Unlike most of the streets of Ybor City, this one was quiet. Only a mockingbird broke the silence with its unsullied singing. The doctor and the policeman did not speak for a long time.

"No wonder," Wiley finally said.

"Now we know."

"And wished we didn't."

They drove back through the middle of Ybor City, which was just as noisy and vibrant as it was earlier, despite the pain that the doctor now realized resided there. As they neared downtown, Wiley asked, "What next?"

"I think I've heard enough."

"Want to grab a bite to eat?"

"No, thanks. I seem to have lost my appetite for once. I think I'll just head home."

"When's your train?"

"I have an open ticket," the doctor answered. "I'll figure it out when I get to the station. If you can stop by the Floridan so I can get my bag and then drop me at Union Station, I'd be much obliged."

"No problem, Doctor," Wiley said, fishing a cigar from his shirt pocket. "I'm just sorry we didn't find out more."

"We found out plenty," the doctor said. "Maybe too much."

Chapter 26

With all the traffic, it was a little past noon when Bert Wiley dropped the doctor off at Union Station. As it turned out, there were a number of Atlantic Coast Line trains that would take him back to Chattahoochee, but there were only two Apalachicola Northern passenger trains a day running from Chattahoochee to Port St. Joe, one at 11:00 A.M. and the other at 3:00 P.M. So it was too late for him to get to Chattahoochee to catch either one of those. He was, however, just in time for an express train to Thomasville and then another to Chattahoochee that would get him there by 7:00 that evening.

The doctor rushed down the platform and appeared to be the last one to board the Gulf Coast Special bound for New York City. This train was fast. Once they gained speed, the doctor felt like they were almost flying, ripping past all those little stations they had stopped at on the way down. The doctor had a comfortable window seat all to himself and maybe enough time to finish *The Grapes of Wrath*.

But something was bothering him besides his visit with Lucky Lucilla's aunt. He stared out the window, but the train was now moving so fast that he didn't have time to focus on the passing landscape. Then it hit him: Chattahoochee, home of the Florida State Hospital, from which Lucilla had escaped for the second time only a few days earlier. And his train to Port St. Joe tomorrow didn't leave until 11:00. Why hadn't he thought of this before? He could pay a visit to the hospital in the morning before his train left and see what he could find out about Lucky Lucilla from his doctors there.

He finished *The Grapes of Wrath* a few minutes before the train pulled into the station in Chattahoochee. He was so repulsed by what Lucky Lucilla's aunt had told him and how the Joads and the other victims of the Depression were treated that he had forgotten all about eating. But now he was hungry again and needed a place to spend the night.

Trouble was, Chattahoochee was such a small town there wasn't one single hotel there. The station master told him that his only choice was the Azalea Boarding House, a couple of blocks from the depot. Following his directions, the doctor walked over to Azalea Street and found who he assumed were the house's residents sitting on the front porch in rocking chairs, looking out at the street as if awaiting his arrival.

A tall, stout woman in a long, gingham dress and white apron, somewhat resembling a poor man's Queen Victoria, opened the front door for him and invited him in. The house smelled like soap and supper.

"Welcome to the Azalea Boarding House," she said. "How long will you be staying?"

"Just one night," the doctor answered.

"Okay. Are you hungry?"

"I'm starved."

"Good, you're just in time for supper. We hold it every night until the train comes, just in case a traveler like you shows up, so come on in. I'll show you to your room and where the bathroom is. Then you can wash up and join us in the dining room. Just follow your nose. I'll be serving it up while you're washing up."

His room for the night had a narrow, single bed, a dresser with a bowl and pitcher on it, and a small desk in front of a window that looked out onto the house's dark backyard. The shared bathroom was at the end of the hall. Everything was modest but neat and clean. The doctor washed up and went down to the dining room.

The Queen Victoria landlady was placing bowls of steaming food on the table as he entered. She motioned for him to sit in one of the empty chairs. Then she sat at the head of the table and looked at the man to her right.

"Reverend Boyd," she said, "would you say grace, please?"

"Why, of course," the reverend said and launched into a flowery thanks for everything from the food to the day, his housemates, and his dead wife.

Then the landlady started passing the bowls around. There was crispy fried chicken, mashed potatoes and rich brown gravy, green beans with tomatoes, sliced cucumbers and onions in vinegar, and big hunks of steaming cornbread. One of the men at the table poured himself a glass of sweet tea and passed the pitcher on. As all of this passing was going on, the landlady made introductions.

"This here to my right," she began, "is Reverend Floyd Boyd. He was pastor of the United Methodist Church here for near forty years. When his wife passed and his children moved to Atlanta and he retired, he moved in here with us, some four years ago now. And next to him is Leonard Shifler. Leonard works for the Apalachicola Northern railroad as a laborer in the yards. When his mama died back in thirty-six, he came to live with us. And then there's you, sir."

"Yes, well," the doctor said. "I'm Van Berber. I'm a doctor who lives in Port St. Joe. I'm returning there from Tampa, where I was visiting a friend. I plan to catch the eleven o'clock train in the morning."

"Then across from you is Mike Nelson, the one with the messy hair. Mike works as an orderly at the Florida State Hospital. He moved in here two years ago, when he and his wife divorced. And next to Mike is Carl

Ostrum. He's worked at the Gulf station downtown for twenty years and lived here for the last ten, since his parents passed in a car accident. Then to Carl's right is Alexander Gaeta, who was injured in the Great War. He helps me out around here, cleaning, gardening, and fixing things that need fixing. And then there's me. I'm Millicent Carson. My husband's dead and all my children have moved away. I've run this place by myself, except for Alexander's help, for the last twenty-three years now."

"I'm pleased to meet y'all," the doctor said, wiping fried chicken grease from his chin. They all nodded and continued eating. There was some other idle conversation as they all ate, most of which the doctor couldn't follow since he couldn't hear that well and the talk seemed to revolve around private matters pertaining to the interlacing lives of Mrs. Carson's longtime guests: who was to bathe when, whose alarm clock was the loudest, who played his radio too late and too loudly, who held a grudge against whom for some long-forgotten slight.

"If you'd just read your Bible for once," the pastor was saying to the Gulf service station attendant, "you'd know your hollering is all wrong. 'And be ye kind to one another, tenderhearted, forgiving one another, even as God for Christ's sake hath forgiven you,' the Bible says. So if Mike forgets to clean out the sink after he's shaved, would it kill you not to scream at him at six o'clock in the morning, for Christ's sake?"

"Don't you be quotin' scripture at me, you jackleg preacher, or I'll come over there and beat you over the head with your damn holy book!"

"Why, you ignorant grease monkey. . . ."

"All right, that's enough," the landlady interrupted. "All of you skedaddle now and let me clear the table. I'll bring you watermelon out on the porch."

They all did as instructed, and on the porch the doctor pulled a rocking chair next to Mike Nelson, the orderly at the Florida State Hospital with the disorderly brown hair. They were sitting far enough away from the others that no one could hear their conversation. "So how long have you been at the hospital?" the doctor asked.

"Almost seven years now," he answered. "Care for a smoke?"

"No, thanks. How do you like it?"

"It's okay. I'm just an orderly, so it's mostly just cleaning up and doing the stuff the nurses and doctors don't wanna do."

"Like?"

"Oh, helping patients who can't take care of themselves, restraining patients who are violent, just trying to keep everything clean and orderly . . . Get it? Orderly?"

"I get it," the doctor laughed. "Ever come across a patient named Lucky Lucilla?"

"Well . . ."

"It's okay. Whatever you say, I'll hold it in confidence."

"Hmm . . . ," the orderly said as he blew cigarette smoke from his nostrils and the tree frogs began their evening chorus. The doctor decided not to push it and waited to hear whatever the man wanted to tell him. The landlady brought them both a slice of watermelon and then went back inside.

"There's nothing better than ice-cold, ripe watermelon," the doctor said.

"It's true."

After they had finished their watermelon, the orderly took their rinds back into the house. The doctor was about to get up and go to his room when the man returned. He again sat in his rocking chair next to the doctor, lit another cigarette, and in a low voice began to speak.

"There are certain things that happen out there. . . ."

"At the hospital?"

"Yeah . . . that I would not like to be quoted on."

"I understand," the doctor said. "Whatever you tell me is between you and me. I'm just trying to keep this Lucilla man from hurting anyone else in Port St. Joe. That's the only reason I'm asking about him."

"Well, good luck with that, 'cause Lucilla is one deranged son of a bitch. He never hurt me, but he hurt plenty of others. Some seriously. Even killed a man the first time he escaped. Stabbed a nurse this last time."

"So what did the doctors do about it?"

"Well, that's what I need you to keep quiet about. Leastwise don't involve me, 'cause, as much as I hate it sometimes, I need the job."

"We never spoke."

"Well . . . the doctors . . . they did about everything, short of killing him, to try to keep him calm."

"Like what?"

"You sure you wanna hear this?"

"No, but go ahead."

"Well," the orderly whispered. "At first they just had us strip him, put him in a straitjacket, and throw him in the hole."

"The hole?"

"Yeah, a little room with nothin' in it. Just concrete walls and nothin' else. They'd tell us to keep him in there for days, weeks at a time. Just take him out and feed him and take him to the bathroom three times a day."

"And?"

"Well, that didn't work too good. He'd bang his head against the wall until it was a bloody mess, and then when we brought him something to eat, he'd throw it on the floor and go crazy. So then they tried medicating him."

"With what?" the doctor asked.

"At first, insulin, enough to produce major convulsions. And then Metrazol, which produced even stronger convulsions. For some patients, these drugs worked, frankly, I think, because they would do almost anything, including being nice, to avoid convulsions, which, to be honest, scare the shit out of me, and I'm not even having them."

"They still do this then?"

"Yes, especially with the violent patients."

"And Lucilla was one of these?"

"Oh, yeah, except on him these so-called shock treatments didn't work. Made him worse, in fact."

"So?"

"They came up with something else, something experimental, something even worse."

"What?"

"They're calling it electroconvulsive shock therapy."

"What the hell is that?" the doctor asked.

"They strap the patient down and then they hook his head up to a bunch of electrodes and then they shoot him full of electricity. They shock the shit out of him basically. It's an awful thing to watch."

"And this is supposed to help the patient?"

"Yeah, that's what they claim. And, to tell you the truth, sometimes it does. The patient is less violent, easier to control. But for Lucilla it had the opposite effect. He couldn't take it. It took a bunch of us to restrain him. Once we started to strap him down on that platform, he went crazy. It was the day after he had his last treatment that he checked into the dispensary, stabbed the nurse, and escaped."

"I see," the doctor said.

The doctor went back to his little room, took his dose of morphine, and tried to sleep. But it was slow in coming. When he closed his eyes, all his mind seemed to present to him was a chilling image of a boy tied to a platform, helpless, crazed with fear, awaiting his fate.

So it was no surprise, when he finally did go to sleep, that he dreamed of a bloody monster chasing him in the cool night air through the back alleys of Port St. Joe, to the sea, to his death, with nothing but stark fear in his heart. He woke drenched in sweat and wanting badly to be back home, even if it meant that he would probably have to confront the monster face to face in real life.

He had breakfast in the dining room with the other boarders, except for Mike Nelson, who was now nowhere to be seen. Then he walked in the summer sunlight to the Florida State Hospital, which was a large compound of old white houses and new large buildings scattered about a quiet green campus.

A gardener directed him to the main administration building in one of the stately old houses. He told the woman at the reception desk that he was a doctor in Port St. Joe and that he wanted to talk to Anthony Lucilla's doctor.

The woman, slim and pretty in her starched white nurse's uniform, asked him to wait while she found the doctor. There were deep brown leather chairs in the waiting area, but the doctor was too agitated to sit. So he paced back and forth in front of the tall windows that looked out on the bucolic grounds.

Soon the woman returned and led him down a long hall to an office at the very back of the house. She introduced him to Dr. H. Mason Smith, who rose slowly from his chair to shake the doctor's hand.

"How may I help you?" the nervous, middle-aged man asked as he lit his pipe. "Please sit."

"I have reason to believe that a recent patient of yours, a man named Anthony 'Lucky' Lucilla, may have returned to Port St. Joe, where I practice medicine," Dr. Berber said as he eased into the brown leather chair. "And I was hoping that you might be able give me some insight into his personality that might help me locate him."

"Well, I wish I could help you, Doctor, but I don't know where he could be."

"Could you tell me what his diagnosis was?"

"Well . . ."

"I assure you that whatever you tell me will remain strictly confidential."

"Ordinarily no, but since this is such an extraordinary case, I'll give you all the information I can, not only as a matter of professional courtesy but also as a matter of public safety. This man Lucilla was diagnosed with dementia praecox with serious homicidal tendencies."

"And your treatment?

"Hmm . . . well, we tried several things to calm him. First opiates and barbiturates of various types and dosages. Then insulin and Metrazol."

"To induce convulsions?"

"Why, yes."

"To what end?"

"To calm the patient and hopefully restore him to a more normal existence. We're not sure how it works, but it does seem to."

"With Lucilla?"

"Yes, at first the shock treatments were effective, but as we continued to use them, the patient regressed."

"What about electroshock treatments?" Dr. Berber asked.

"How do you know about those?"

"I try to keep up."

"Well, then, you know they're experimental at this time."

"My question is," Dr. Berber asked, "have you been experimenting?"

"I'm afraid that I'm not at liberty to tell you that."

"I think that answers my question," Dr. Berber said as he hoisted himself out of the chair. "Thanks for your help, and thanks for allowing Lucilla to escape again."

Chapter 27

The doctor walked back to the boarding house, thinking about Lucky Lucilla's troubled life. He was going to retrieve his bag, walk to the station, and return to Port St. Joe to meet his fate at the madman's hands. Not a very inviting prospect. If he had any sense at all, he would stay right there in Chattahoochee at the Azalea Boarding House and live out his remaining days with Queen Victoria and her sorry subjects. But he didn't.

Instead he boarded the train to Port St. Joe and watched the world, such as it was, pass by. He dozed and brooded. By the time the train pulled into the Port St. Joe station, he was tired and despondent. And it didn't help when there was no one to meet him at the station. No one to welcome him home. No one who cared. So, without checking for explosives, he started his car and drove over to the Black Cat Café for dinner. Friday was fish day at the café so he ordered the fried catfish, hushpuppies, and coleslaw and then wolfed it all down so he could get back to his office and Nadyne.

She met him at the door.

"Thank God, you're back," she said.

"Why? What's going on?"

"You name it. Everything went fine yesterday, but today all hell's broken loose."

"What?"

"Well, I don't know where to start. About an hour ago Jewel's daddy and her new husband came by looking for you because Jewel and Marcus have gone missing."

"What?"

The doctor suddenly felt sick. The greasy catfish and hushpuppies seemed to settle into the bottom of his stomach with a ferocious vengeance. He wanted to run to the toilet and vomit, but Nadyne was explaining.

"They said Jewel and Marcus went out to do some shopping first thing this morning but haven't come back. They thought maybe they had come to see you."

"What time was this?"

"Like I said, about an hour ago . . . that would make it about one o'clock."

"So they've been gone for about three or four hours?"

"I guess," Nadyne answered.

"Well," the doctor said, with a slight tinge of relief, "that's not that bad. They could have just taken a drive, or Jewel could have got to talking with someone and lost track of time."

"I hope so, but you better drop by and see if they've found them yet when you're finished delivering Katie Mulligan's baby. She just called and said her water broke and the contractions are coming fast and furious. Since this is her third, I told her to come here right away instead of trying to make it to the hospital in Panama City."

"Okay, why don't you get the emergency room set up? I'll clean up. What else?"

"Well, you're not gonna want to hear this, but . . ."

"What?"

"That Williams girl, Millie. . . . She's pregnant."

"Shit."

"Yeah, I broke the news to her and her mother this morning, after I operated on the rabbit."

"And?"

"It was not a pretty sight," Nadyne said. "Both of them were in hysterics. When they finally calmed down, I explained their options to them."

"And?"

"They'll be here first thing Tuesday morning for an abortion."

"Jesus. Okay. Anything else?"

"Isn't that enough?"

"Too much," the doctor said, shaking his head and walking back to get ready to deliver a baby.

It came relatively easily, not more than an hour after Katie Mulligan waddled into the office. Nadyne had been right in not sending her to Panama City. The mother was a perfect baby-making machine: strong, young, and relaxed, having gone through it two times before, with wide hips and an ample birth canal. With no trouble at all, she pushed out the little baby girl, who screamed heartily as Nadyne cleaned her up and the doctor cut the cord. In the midst of all of this calamity, seeing the beaming mother hold this child for the first time somehow made it all worthwhile.

The doctor went to the waiting room and told the father and his two sons that everyone was well and they could now go see their new baby girl. He saw a woman comforting a whimpering little girl—about seven or eight years old, the doctor guessed—who had a towel wrapped around her head.

"Follow me," the doctor said, leading them back to the examining room. "What happened here?"

"Patty was swimming off the Port Inn pier and dove in and hit her head on a rock," the woman reported.

"Okay, let's take a look."

The doctor unwrapped the towel and assessed the damage: a deep cut on the upper right temple. He cleaned it up, stitched it together, and bandaged it with clean gauze.

"Where'd you dive in?" he asked the girl.

"'Bout halfway down the pier."

"It's obviously too shallow there. You can only dive from the end of the pier. Who were you with?" the doctor asked Patty.

"Kathleen," she answered.

"Who's that?"

"It's her little friend," the mother answered. "She came and got me."

"Where were you?"

"Having lunch with Kathleen's mother at the Port Inn."

"She's too young to be swimming in the bay without an adult," the doctor told her.

"I know," the mother said, "but she's an excellent swimmer."

"I don't care. If she had passed out when she hit bottom, she would have drowned."

"I'm sorry," the mother sniveled.

Sometimes the doctor had to question what parents were thinking. *It's no wonder,* he thought, *that these little people grow up to populate a world full of such senseless adults.*

The doctor checked on Katie Mulligan and her new baby and then released them to go home with their family. Maybe at least one good thing would come from the day.

Then he drove over to North Port St. Joe to see if Jewel and Marcus had turned up yet. Jewel's mother came out on the front porch to meet him as he got out of the car.

"Found them yet?" the doctor asked as he climbed the porch steps.

"No," she answered. "I don't know where they could have got to.

They said they'd be back before noon. Now it's . . . what?"

The doctor checked his pocket watch. "Coming on to five," he answered.

"Oh, my, I ain't got a good feelin' about this," she said.

"Me neither. Where's Django and Gabriel?"

"They's out drivin' 'round, lookin' for 'em?"

"Where at?"

"Relatives, friends, anyplace they can think of."

"Okay," he said. "You stay here in case they come back. I'm going over to Chief Lane's office and tell him about this. Then I'm going home in case they show up there. When Django and Gabriel come back here, tell them to come to my house if they haven't found them yet, no matter how late it is, okay? And call me if they show up."

"Do y'all think they's all right?" Jewel's mama asked.

"I don't know. I just don't know."

Chief Lane was in his office when the doctor arrived a few minutes later. He was reading something on his desk and looked up when the doctor tapped on his office doorframe.

"Come in," the chief said. "How was your trip to Tampa?"

The doctor sat down in one of the two uncomfortable oak chairs in front of Chief Lane's desk and told the chief all about his trip, including his meetings with Lucky Lucilla's aunt, his doctor at the Florida State Hospital, and the orderly.

"Sounds like we've got more of a nutcase here than we thought," the chief said.

"Yeah, and that's not all of it."

"Whatta you mean?"

"Jewel—you remember, my former housekeeper—and her son, Marcus, are missing."

"So? I don't get the connection."

"I think Lucilla is out to get me," the doctor said, "and everyone around me, including you, Gator, and now Jewel and Marcus."

"So you think he's got Jewel and Marcus?"

"I don't know, Chief. But I'm afraid."

"Okay, you go home and get some rest. You look horrible, by the way."

"It's been a long day," the doctor said wearily.

"I'll radio all of our men, Sheriff Roberts', and Sheriff Duffield's to keep an eye out for these two. Just give me a full description, and we'll start looking."

It was when he started describing Jewel to the chief that he again realized how much he really cared for her and how bad he felt about getting her involved in all of this. If she hadn't been such a good friend, he wouldn't have shared the conspiracy details with her, and maybe, just maybe, she wouldn't have been a target of Lucky Lucilla. He was becoming confused by the entire mess, like he was when Annie had disappeared. His senseless bewilderment, wandering aimlessly from train station to train station, had done nothing to help him find Annie, and now he felt just as disoriented and helpless looking for Jewel.

By the time he finally arrived back at his house, he was not only befuddled but also dead tired. In the gathering twilight, he trudged up the back porch stairs, unlocked the back door, and entered the dark kitchen. He had long since given up worrying about being killed by Lucilla, but now, in the dim light, he felt a strange presence that permeated his soul. He didn't mind dying but not before finding Jewel and Marcus. What scared him was that Lucky Lucilla would kill them all. So first he needed to find Jewel and Marcus and make sure they were safe, and then the lunatic could murder him for all he cared.

Lugging his suitcase up the stairs, the doctor was prepared for anything. But there was nothing—too much nothing, in fact. His black bag still rested on top of his dresser where he had left it, but his shotgun was no longer leaning against the wall next to his bed. He checked in his closet; maybe he had put it back in there and forgotten. But it was no place to be seen. He checked under the bed. Nothing. Someone had taken his shotgun and apparently left everything else undisturbed.

He went into the bathroom and threw back the shower curtain. Nothing. He undressed and turned on the shower. Now was the moment, he thought, as he stepped into the shower and closed the curtain. *I'm going to die clean,* he thought, *or I'm going to wash this travel dust and steam engine soot away, drink a dose of morphine, and wait for Django and Gabriel.*

It was not a good idea to mix morphine and alcohol. But that's what he did anyway. Not a lot of either. Just a nip of the opiate and half a glass of moonshine as he waited for Django and Gabriel on his screened-in back porch, with the crickets and tree frogs wailing a cacophonous lullaby in his ears.

The morphine and alcohol induced weird, fantastical dreams. He wanted to reach out to them, Jewel and Marcus, as they floated around in his backyard like two dark wisps of clouds, in and out of the live oak branches, their shadows sailing across the moon. They didn't seem to notice him looking up at them or Sally Martin, sitting next to him, holding his hand firmly, and smiling up at them knowingly. Instead they wafted overhead and then down and through the mesh of the screens and drifted around his head. He tried to reach up to them, but then they were gone into the bleak, black night while Sally snickered wickedly and squeezed his hand.

He didn't hear Gabriel's car stopping or him coming up the stairs and onto the porch. But he did feel his nudge on his shoulder as he awoke and looked into the tall bluesman's brown eyes.

"Evenin', Doc," he said.

"Oh, hi, Gabriel. What time is it?"

"Little past ten. You okay? You look a little strange."

"I'm fine," the doctor told him. "Just old and tired. Did you find them?"

"No, not yet. We've done looked everywhere I can think of, and nobody's seen 'em."

"Where's Django?"

"I took him home. He was worn out, both from the long day and worryin' about 'em."

"How about you? You doing all right?"

"I ain't too good, Doc," Gabriel whispered, sinking into the white, wicker chair next to the doctor. "It ain't like Jewel to go off like this, especially with Marcus, not this long. So I'm thinkin' the worst. But I don't know what else to do. We've done looked everyplace I can think of."

"I told Chief Lane and he radioed the sheriffs, so they're out looking too. There's nothing else we can do tonight."

"I guess not."

"But tomorrow," the doctor said, "if they haven't showed up by then, could you and Django go to Tate's Hell and see if you can find Gator? Django knows where he was and maybe he's still there. Tell him about Jewel and Marcus. Tell him we need him here. Tell him Huggins thinks he can clear him on the Price murder. I'm not sure what he's gonna do if he does come with you, but I have an idea."

"What's that?"

"I've decided just now—I had this dream—that the only thing left for me to do is to talk to Sally Martin again and see if I can force her hand. I'm not positive that she knows where Lucky Lucilla is, but I think she does. And I don't know for sure that Lucilla has anything to do with Jewel and Marcus's disappearance, but I have a hunch. Jewel has told you about Sally and Lucky, right?"

"Yeah, I know all about them, and from what I know, I'd say you could be right about this. At any rate, it's 'bout all we got left, I guess."

"When you find Gator, come here first to see what I've found out from Sally. If I'm not here, go to her house. It's on Sixth Street, number four sixty-three, a white two story with a big magnolia tree in front. Since tomorrow's Saturday, I expect she'll be there. But if the mill's operating on Saturday, then I may have to go there to find her. So if I'm not at her house, go to the Kenney Mill, right across the canal from the new paper mill. Okay?"

"Okay, Doc," Gabriel said, pushing himself up from the chair. "I guess it's worth a shot."

"We'll soon find out."

Chapter 28

After Gabriel awakened him, the doctor had a hard time going back to sleep in his bed. He kept hearing noises, and he didn't have his shotgun anymore, and he kept worrying about Jewel and Marcus and wondering where they were and what they were doing. And he felt sick again.

He awoke with a start, the light shining brightly into his room, and looked at his alarm clock, which he had failed to set. It was already past ten. Damn, he had planned to get an earlier start since he didn't know where Sally Martin was or how he was going to find her. He hurriedly showered, dressed, and made himself a cup of coffee. He stomach still ached, and he wasn't sure he could keep anything solid down, so he didn't eat. Instead he phoned Jewel's house. Jewel's mama answered and told him that Jewel and Marcus had not turned up yet and that Django and Gabriel were on their way to Tate's Hell to get Gator.

He drove directly to Sally's house on Sixth Street, arriving there without a clue as to how he was going to convince her to help him. He could see her car parked in the driveway behind the house, so he guessed she was home. He knocked on the door and waited.

And there she was, as pretty and prim as he remembered, her crimson hair pulled back in a ponytail and her eyes wide with surprise. She wore a form-fitting, blue cotton dress that showed her slim figure off to good advantage. The doctor was speechless.

"Why, Van," she said, wiping her hands on a dish towel, "what brings you back again?"

"I need to talk to you," he answered. "Are your kids here?"

"Yes, they're inside, helping me clean."

"Maybe we could sit out here on the porch for a few minutes then."

"Okay. Would you like something to drink?"

"No, I'm fine."

So they sat in the wooden rocking chairs next to each other, as peaceful as the summer morning, with the birds singing and the doctor's stomach churning.

"I've come to see you," he started tentatively, "because my former housekeeper, Jewel—I'm sure you remember me talking about her—and her son have disappeared."

"Yes?"

"And I have reason to believe that Lucky Lucilla may be responsible for their disappearance."

"What reason?"

"There's simply no other explanation. He's been out to get me, Gabriel, Chief Lane, and now them."

"I warned you," she said.

"Well, it's time to put a stop to it all. I can understand why he wants to get back at the chief and me, but Gabriel, Jewel, and Marcus are all innocent. They haven't done a thing to him."

"What do you expect me to do?" she asked him.

"Tell me where Lucilla is."

"What makes you so sure I know?"

"Sally, listen to me," the doctor said as he stood up in front of her. "Enough of these games. I know you framed Gator, so I've decided to tell Chief Lane and Judge Denton about your involvement in all of this."

"Okay," she said tentatively, "do what you have to, but, you know, no matter what you tell them, they still don't have any hard evidence. And as far as I can see, they're not likely to find any, so I'll still be free and clear of it all."

"Maybe," the doctor whispered, glaring into her wet, green eyes, "but . . . if I keep talking to enough people, maybe the word will get around that you aren't who you pretend to be. Maybe some people will start to believe that there's a kernel of truth to what I say. Maybe people in a small town like this will begin to believe the stories. Maybe it'll become harder and harder for you to get ahead like you want to. Maybe I'll tell them about you making Lucky kill Dr. Price."

"You wouldn't."

"Why did he do it?"

"Why should I tell you?"

"Because it's all over, Sally."

She hesitated, thinking. Finally, she whispered, "Wood."

"Wood?"

"The mill wanted to buy the timber rights to St. Vincent Island. It's probably the last virgin stand in Florida and right here under our noses. Price wouldn't hear of it, but we had reason to believe his heirs would, so . . ."

"So you had Lucky murder him for wood?"

She did not answer, only stared down at her lap, expressionless.

"Well?" the doctor prompted.

"Listen," she finally said. "I tried to play the game like I was supposed to. I listened and minded my daddy, like my mama told me to do. And when both Mama and Daddy went and died during the Dust Bowl and left me all alone out in West Texas, a helpless orphan, I still did what I thought they wanted me to do. I got married and minded my husband, just like they would have me do. I even listened to that lying philanderer Sheriff Batson. Then I thought you and me had something worth keeping, but you had to keep digging, even when I warned you not to. And where did it get me, all this kowtowing to you stupid, self-centered, arrogant men?"

The doctor did not answer as Sally's skin grew redder and redder and the tears began to flow down her face.

"Nowhere, that's where," she cried. "Out on that godforsaken sand spit with four kids and not much else to show for it all. The sheriff was the last straw. I decided right then and there that I was gonna do it my way. To hell with Mama and Daddy! They left me all alone and at the mercy of a bunch of selfish oafs. To hell with all you so-called men! I finally got smart and made up my mind to do it my way and get what I wanted, and, in this case, I wanted wood."

"This information will clear Gator," he said.

"No, it won't, because if you breathe a word of it, you'll never see your housekeeper and her son again. I warned you before, and I'm warning you again."

"Okay, Sally, all you have to do is tell me where he is. If I go there and I'm able to kill him, you've eliminated a crazy man who can tell a whole hell of a lot about your involvement in a lot of mayhem. If, on the other hand, he kills me and Jewel and Marcus—if he hasn't already killed them—then you've finally gotten rid of me, which is what you and Lucky have been trying to do for a long time. Either way you can't lose."

"Hmm . . . you have a point," she whispered, drying her tears. "I might be inclined to go along with you if I was sure what would happen if you killed Lucky, though I seriously doubt you will. What would keep you from telling these stories about me anyway?"

"What would be the point? You're right. I have no hard evidence against you. Besides, I hold no animosity toward you or your children. In fact, despite all this, I still love you. I just want to get Jewel and Marcus back and stop Lucilla from hurting anyone else."

Sally stared at the doctor for a moment and then looked as though she had made a decision.

"I'll make a deal with you then," she said. "If you survive this and promise to keep your mouth shut about my involvement, I'll tell you a secret."

"A secret?"

"Yes, I have some information that you might find interesting."

"What?"

"If I tell you, will you promise to keep your mouth shut about me? If not for my sake, for my kids'?"

"Okay, I'll keep quiet. What is it that you know?"

"You promise?"

"Yes, damn it, I promise."

"I know where Annie is."

"What?"

"When Sheriff Batson was looking into your past, he not only found out about your morphine habit—when exactly were you going to tell me about that, by the way?—he also found your long-lost wife."

"How?"

"I'm not sure. He had friends with all kinds of records in all kinds of places."

"Where is she?"

"Not a word about me to anyone?"

"Not a word, I swear. Where?"

"Remember, you cross me on this, all your friends are dead," she said, staring at the doctor. "Understood?"

"Yes."

"One more thing: no police. I don't want to chance Lucky confessing to any lawman. I don't think he would, but you never know. But I do know that Lucky will kill them immediately if he sees any lawman."

"So they're still alive?"

"Only if you go alone."

"Where?"

"Kenney Mill."

"And Annie?"

"You promise, no police, no more talking about me?"

"Yes, yes, where is she?"

"The Florence Crittenden Home in Charleston."

The doctor was up and out of his chair before she finished speaking, but as he was descending the stairs he heard her call, "Van, wait . . . I love you too."

He just kept right on going.

Chapter 29

The doctor had to find a gun fast. He drove over to Bob Huggins' house at the end of St. Joseph Drive and found him pushing a lawn mower across his yard and sweating profusely. He explained his situation to the lawyer.

"Doc, I'll be damned if you don't get yourself into the weirdest predicaments I've ever heard of. How do you do that?"

"I don't know. I have a talent, I guess. Can you loan me your shotgun or not?"

"It's against my better judgment," Huggins said, wiping his face with his handkerchief. "And, as your attorney, I'm advising you against it."

"Bob, it's Jewel and her kid, for Christ's sake. Come on!"

"Okay, wait here. But I never saw you today."

"Not a glimpse."

With the gun and a box of shells, the doctor drove toward the Kenney Mill, wondering where Gabriel and Django and Gator were. He didn't have time to track them down. He just wanted to get to Jewel and Marcus before it was too late.

The Kenney Mill looked abandoned as he drove up through the mountains of logs and parked in front of the little pine cottage that served as the mill's office. There were two other buildings: the long, narrow sawmill shed where he had treated the man with the amputated hand and a two-story barn behind the mill. He loaded the shotgun, released the safety, and stepped up onto the porch of the office building. He tried to open the front door, but it was locked. He looked in the windows on each side of the door, but it was dark inside and the windows wouldn't budge. He walked around the cottage, peering in each dark window, until he got to the back and tried the back door. It too was locked.

The sawmill and the office were the two buildings that were used daily so it was unlikely that Lucky was hiding in either of these or else he would have been noticed by the mill workers. The doctor had never been in the windowless barn in back so he didn't know if there might be a hiding place in there, but it seemed the mostly likely spot. He walked all the way around the big barn and determined that there was only the one door. He slowly tried to open it, but it was locked too.

Before he started shooting locks off and alerting Lucky to his presence, he decided to check the sawmill. The windowless mill was a high, untreated clapboard building about fifty feet long with big swinging doors at both ends to allow logging trucks in and out. Both doors were closed and secured with heavy chains and padlocks. The doctor stood at the rear door, the one nearest to the barn, and listened. He didn't hear a sound coming from any of the buildings or from the scrub thickets surrounding them. He waited in the midday sun, thinking that Lucilla might show himself or that some clue might materialize. But nothing happened. He stood there alone, becoming more and more fearful by the moment.

He had to do something. He walked over to the barn's heavy door and aimed his shotgun at the lock. He backed off a few steps so the pellets wouldn't ricochet off the door and hit him, aimed again, and pulled the trigger. The door sprung open, and the doctor cautiously peered in. All he could see was a shaft of light streaming from the door down a narrow aisle, lined with floor-to-ceiling shelves. He stepped inside and thought he heard something at the back of the building. He tiptoed down the aisle toward the noise. As he got further into the barn, the sunlight shining through the door began to fade, but his sight was beginning to adjust to the gloom. He heard another noise, like scratching on the floor, so he moved more rapidly down the aisle toward it. A gray rat sprung from the darkness and crossed his path, stopping his heart. And then everything went black.

When he awoke, he had no idea how long he had been unconscious, but it was apparently long enough for someone to move him to the sawmill, and tie him to a chair, and gag him. He turned and saw Jewel and, next to her, Marcus, both tied and gagged. Jewel's eyes were filled with fear and tears, her white dress soiled and wrinkled. Marcus had his eyes closed and, despite his gag, was sobbing uncontrollably. The doctor tried to move his hands and feet, but they were tied too tightly to the chair. He might be able to push the chair over, but then what? All he could think to do was to continue wiggling his hands and wrists in hopes of somehow loosening the ropes. Jewel peered pleadingly at him while Marcus continued to cry.

They all jerked when they heard the lightning snap and then a rumble of thunder rolling across the bay. The rain began a minute later, pounding madly on the tin roof above them. And then the wind came in angry gusts against the sawmill's walls.

The doctor was not sure how long this deluge continued before Lucky Lucilla appeared before him. He was tall and lanky, with wild green eyes and a full head of black, unruly hair. He wore blue cotton work clothes and heavy, steel-toed boots and cradled the doctor's shotgun in his hairy arms. He spoke in a hoarse whisper that made the doctor tremble.

"Welcome to the slaughterhouse," he sneered as the gale hammered the walls and the rain continued to pummel the roof in wave after relentless wave. "What took you so long?"

The doctor tried to speak, but the gag was as tight as the ropes. All he could do was shake his head and make angry, growling, incomprehensible noises.

"When I couldn't find you at your house," Lucilla continued, "I figured I'd lure you out. I knew if I couldn't find you, you'd find me—and your friends here—sooner or later."

The doctor shook his head violently in the direction of Jewel and Marcus. Lucky Lucilla just looked at them and snorted.

"Oh, they ain't goin' nowhere," he grunted. "Once I tied the boy on the crosscut sled and started the saw, she told me all she knows about me and Sally . . . and it's way too much. Too bad the boy had to hear it too, 'cause now all three of you gotta go."

The doctor struggled with all his strength to break free as the howling wind and drenching rain shook the building and rattled its roof. A deafening clap of thunder cracked above them just as Lucilla raised his gun butt and slammed it into the doctor's jaw. The pain went through his head and down his spine. He felt the loose teeth with his tongue and tasted the blood as it mounted in his mouth and rolled down his chin. For a moment he thought he would lose consciousness, but he could still see Lucilla standing blearily before him through the tears.

"Okay, who goes first?" he growled, looking from the doctor to Jewel and then to Marcus. "I was thinkin' the boy, so's I can see the look on your faces. Which part of his puny, little body you think we should start with? His head? How 'bout a foot? Maybe an arm?"

Jewel was screaming mutely through her gag, tears streaming down her face. Marcus, defeated, just hung his head and whimpered. Lucilla, seemingly tired of talking, moved fast. First, he went to the wall and pulled a large red switch, and then another one under the saw platform, and still another next to the saw itself, and suddenly the big circular saw, at eye level before them, came to life with a high, whirling, howling scream, all but drowning out the storm that continued to swell around them. Lucilla rushed to Marcus and picked him up, chair and all, and carried him to the in-feed table next to the saw. He then untied him, slammed him onto the crosscut sled, and strapped him down with the heavy leather restraints so that his right arm was out in the path of the saw. Then, with a vulgar grin, he slowly pushed the sled toward the spinning saw's hungry teeth.

Lucilla's eyes were wide and frenzied as he shoved the sled forward. Marcus strained and looked away. Jewel continued her muffled scream. And the doctor closed his eyes and prayed, to what God he did not know.

Then everything stopped, except the wind and rain outside, and everything was black. The saw was silent, the lights went off, and the rain continued to batter the building in sheet after incessant sheet. In that moment, the doctor, for the first time in his life, found himself, he was sure, in the presence of God.

But it was Gabriel and Django, not God, whom he saw next, flinging open the wide door at the front of the mill and rushing forward, each with a flashlight in one hand and a shotgun in the other. Gabriel ran down the side of the table saw where the doctor had last seen Lucky. Django came toward the doctor and Jewel. When he reached them, he dropped his gun and fished a pocket knife from his pants pocket and started cutting the ropes around the doctor's wrists.

Then a shot rang out on the other side of the saw. A bolt of lightning struck nearby and a flash of light momentarily streamed through the open door. The doctor saw no Gabriel, but he did see Lucilla atop the table that held the saw, coming fast toward them. Django had apparently seen him too because he swung the beam of his flashlight on him as Lucilla launched himself off the table and onto Django, whose flashlight flew across the floor. Then Lucilla picked up the flashlight and the doctor followed its beam as Lucilla shone it first on Django, who was lying still on the floor, then to Jewel, who was still tied to the chair with terror in her wet eyes, and then to the doctor, who was still in his chair, the ropes only partially cut before Django was attacked.

Then Lucilla shone the flashlight on Marcus, who was still strapped securely to the crosscut sled, his eyes wide with fright. The flashlight's beam flickered to the other side of the table, but there was no Gabriel, who must have been shot when the gun went off.

Lucilla jumped up onto the table and shone the flashlight down on the floor on the other side of the table out of the doctor's line of sight. He jumped down onto the floor, leaned over, and came back up with a shotgun in his hand. He slowly climbed back onto the table, stepped over Marcus, and faced the doctor and Jewel and Django, still lying on the floor. He was panting and his shirt was soaked with sweat, his eyes still wild and unfocused. He slowly raised the shotgun and nestled its butt against his right shoulder, holding in his left hand the barrel and the flashlight, its sharp beam blinding the doctor.

The doctor kicked the floor as hard as he could with both feet, and the chair fell over. He kicked and rolled with all his might. He heard the shot but didn't feel any pain except in his shoulder where he had hit the floor. He was under the table now, he thought. It was too dark to know for sure. He could no longer see the beam of Lucilla's flashlight. He lay there on his side on the hard dirt floor, listening and twisting his hands and wrists against the rope, which, with Django's cuts, were beginning to give a little.

Suddenly he was blinded again as the lights in the mill blinked back on. Then the saw was humming and then twirling and then roaring at full speed. The doctor looked over and saw Jewel, still bound and crying in her chair. And then he heard footsteps coming across the dirt floor toward him. Oh, no. He struggled to get free.

"Easy, partner," Gator said, leaning into his face and loosening his gag. "Don't hurt yourself. I'll cut them ropes."

"Gator," the doctor gasped as Gator began slashing the ropes around the doctor's ankles. "Where have you been?"

"Better late than never," he said.

Then Lucky Lucilla landed on top of Gator with a crushing thud. Gator rose and flung him to the floor, but Lucilla was up again before Gator could attack. The two stood toe to toe and swung viciously at one another. From his vantage point on the floor, the doctor couldn't tell who was winning and who was losing. He only knew that there was blood and sweat flying everywhere and that he was finally beginning to slip out of his ropes. Then Gator fell to the dirt floor next to him, battered and bloody and unable to move.

The doctor looked over Gator's head and saw Lucilla pushing himself up from the floor. He stumbled around the table saw and was soon back with a shotgun in his hands. He stood directly over the doctor and aimed at his head.

"Well, Doc," he said with a malicious sneer. "This wasn't exactly how I planned it. I wanted to watch your face while I sawed up your friends. But now that we've been interrupted, maybe I'll just blow your head off and then shoot the rest, except maybe for the boy, of course, since I already got him tied to the in-feed table, and then maybe his mama too. But maybe you'd rather stay alive a little longer and watch. You ever seen what a saw like this one can do to human flesh? Quite a sight. On second thought, I think you might enjoy it."

Then he lowered the shotgun and started back toward Marcus. The doctor kicked out his right foot, which he had finally wriggled free, and landed a hard shot on Lucilla's left shin. Lucky looked down at the doctor in surprise and groaned in pain. The doctor kicked again . . . and again . . . and still again. Lucilla, backing away from the doctor and howling in anger and agony, dropped the gun, which landed on top of the table, where it slid toward the buzzing saw. He finally managed to stagger away from the doctor's kicking attack and crawled up onto the table to retrieve the shotgun.

As Lucilla limped toward the gun, the doctor freed himself from the rest of the ropes. He looked for a weapon and saw Django's pocket knife lying next to his body. He grabbed it and flung himself up onto the table with Lucilla, who had now reached the gun and was raising it to shoot. The doctor lunged at him with the knife and buried it in his side before Lucilla could get off a shot. The doctor felt the dampness of his victim's blood, withdrew the knife, and wildly plunged it again as Lucilla pounded the doctor's head and shoulders with the butt of the shotgun. Despite the pain, the doctor pulled the knife out and plunged it again in an adrenalin-charged rage. Lucilla continued to back up toward the buzzing saw as the doctor swung the pocket knife wildly toward him. When the doctor raised his arm to bury the knife in Lucilla's heart, Lucilla slammed the butt of the shotgun squarely into the doctor's forehead. He went down, and the knife slid casually across the table.

As Lucilla put the shotgun to his shoulder and aimed at the doctor's head, the doctor heard a distant pop and saw a red hole appear in the middle of Lucilla's sweating forehead. With a surprised look on his face, the madman lurched backwards and twisted around as his stomach crossed the whirling saw.

Chapter 30

Lucky Lucilla's flesh and blood flew everywhere. The doctor went to Marcus first, slipping on a gory piece of Lucilla's intestines. The boy had passed out, but he was breathing easily. He was covered with blood and pink pieces of the dissected man. The doctor left him strapped there for the time being, jumped off the table, and cut the power switches to the saw. Now the mill was quiet except for the constant pounding of rain on its tin roof.

He found Django's knife, went to Jewel, removed her gag, and began cutting ropes.

"How's Marcus?" she cried.

"He's okay," the doctor answered. "Out cold but unharmed. I hope he fainted before he saw what happened to Lucilla."

Once loose, she rushed to her son and began releasing him from the leather restraints. The doctor found Django coming to and hurried on to Gator, who was still lying on the floor next to Django with a dazed look on his face.

"You okay, Gator?" the doctor asked him.

"Uh . . . I ain't sure," Gator moaned. "I ain't never been hit that hard before."

"Rest here. I'll be right back. Let me check on Gabriel."

The doctor hurried around the table saw and found Gabriel lying on the floor on the other side. He was covered in blood and gore and looked gray. The doctor felt for a pulse and found none. He put his ear to Gabriel's bloody chest and felt nothing. Jewel ran around next to the doctor and knelt with him beside her blood-soaked husband.

"Is he alive?" she bawled.

"No," the doctor told her.

Jewel threw herself on her new husband and cried. The doctor watched her helplessly. After a while, he put his hand on her shoulder and said, "Come on with me now."

She reluctantly followed him to the saw, where Marcus still lay unconscious. He told her to clean him and make him as comfortable as possible until he woke up. He did not tell Jewel that he was most concerned about the boy at this point. He didn't know what he had seen or exactly what he had been through. But if Lucilla was telling the truth and the boy had been strapped to the crosscut sled before, then his level of trauma would surely leave lasting effects.

He couldn't find any serious bleeding on Django, who was still groggy, so he gave him some smelling salts as he eventually came around. Then he tried to pull Gator up off the dirt floor.

"What happened?" Gator wanted to know.

"You didn't shoot Lucky?"

"Shoot? I can't even stand up."

"Who then?"

"Beats me."

"Well, it looks like you finally lost a fight, Gator," the doctor said.

"I missed the whole thing," Django said.

"Just as well," the doctor sighed.

Then, as the storm finally let up, a Port St. Joe patrolman and Chief Lane arrived. Apparently someone had heard the shots and the roaring saw through the storm and called the police. The doctor described what had happened as the two listened with astonishment.

"You just got here?" the doctor asked the chief. "You didn't shoot Lucilla?"

"Nope. I would have been happy to, but it wasn't me."

"Who then?"

Chief Lane just shrugged and walked over to the sawmill to access the damage. Marcus came to just as the police arrived, and Jewel helped him off the crosscut sled and held him tightly and whispered in his ear as they sat on the floor in a corner by themselves. The doctor checked Gator and Django again. They, like Jewel and Marcus, were shaken but alive.

The doctor led them all to his car, leaving Gabriel and the two bloody halves of Lucky Lucilla in the mill. He put Jewel, Marcus, and Django in the backseat and Gator in the front next to him. Chief Lane followed them in his patrol car. The doctor took them to Jewel's parents' house in North Port St. Joe. Luckily, neither his car nor the chief's got stuck in the muddy streets. Jewel's mama was waiting for them on the front porch. The doctor helped Django to the door, and Jewel led Marcus in. The doctor told Jewel's mama what had happened to Gabriel and instructed her to put the rest of them to bed and to take care of them like only a mother could.

He and Gator said goodnight to Chief Lane and drove on to the doctor's dark house. They both showered and then sat on the back porch and listened to the rain. The doctor poured them both a glass of moonshine. Gator looked pretty beat up, and the doctor was more tired than he had ever been in his life.

"Seriously, Gator, you didn't shoot Lucilla?"

"I told you, I could barely move."

"Well, where have you been?"

Gator sighed and took a long swallow of the liquor. "After a few days out there in Tate's Hell," he said, "I began to realize why it had that name. And as much as I like the wilderness, after swattin' them skeeters and flies all the time and sleepin' with snakes and scorpions, I was thinkin' maybe they'd have to rename the place Gator's Hell. So I decided to accept your invitation to stop by Louisa Randolph's place. I sailed my ol' skiff right back into Apalachicola Bay and up Scipio Creek to within a few blocks of her house. I hid it in a marsh there, walked to her house, and presented myself, all filthy and bug bitten, like a goddamn prodigal son or something. And I been there ever since. Well, until this mornin' anyway."

"Well, I'll be, Gator. And to think I've been worrying myself almost to death about you out there in that swamp. Louisa Randolph promised me that she'd call me or Jewel if you showed up, but I never heard a word."

"I convinced her otherwise. It was so cozy there and the food was so good, I was in no hurry to be found again."

"So how did Gabriel and Django find you?"

"They looked first in that camp I had in Tate's Hell, where y'all found me before. But when I wasn't there, they went to Louisa's house. That's what took us so long. They had to backtrack into Apalachicola to find me. Then we went to Sally Martin's house, but your car wasn't there so we went to the mill, like y'all told 'em to."

"But where were you when Gabriel and Django burst in?"

"Oh, I was outside in the rain. When we heard the saw whirlin', I told Django and Gabriel to get ready to rush in when I found the mill's main power supply and cut it off."

"I thought the storm must have taken down the lines," the doctor said.

"Nope, it was only me. I figured if I cut the power, the saw would stop and we could surprise him."

"You saved Marcus's life and probably all of ours. Thank you."

"Oh, no problem, partner. I just wish Gabriel had made it and I was a better fighter so you didn't have to tangle with Lucilla."

"Well, we're done with him now."

"Yeah, thank God," Gator said. "I guess now I gotta face the music about Dr. Price's murder. I was expectin' the chief to arrest me when he saw me."

"I think he recognized that you had probably had enough excitement for one night. Besides, Bob Huggins thinks he can get you off. And Judge Denton doesn't seem dead set on hanging you quite yet. Sheriff Duffield is still pissed at you for slugging him and taking his gun so we still have that to deal with. We'll talk to Huggins tomorrow and try to figure it all out."

"Maybe I should just go back to Louisa's place."

"You like that cookin', don't you?"

"I ain't never tasted anything so good."

"Stay here in my spare room. Stay away from the sheriff," the doctor said as the wind picked up again and the thunder echoed across the bay. "We'll work it out. I promise."

"Okay," Gator said. "I'm too tired to fight it anymore. They can do what they want to. I just wanna go to bed."

"Me too."

And so they did.

Chapter 31

But not for long. The phone started ringing about the time the doctor's head hit the pillow. Marie, the night operator, told him to get over to Mervin Penner's house on Yaupon Street, where a tree had fallen through the roof of Grandma Penner's bedroom and pinned the old lady in her bed. By the time the doctor arrived, her son Mervin and a neighbor had sawed the limb away from her, and she was lying on her back under a heavy quilt, moaning in pain. Her wrinkled thigh was fat and flabby to begin with, and now it was swollen and red—either broken or badly bruised. The doctor couldn't tell which so he called the fire station to send the ambulance to take her to the hospital in Panama City.

Then when he was driving home, he saw Raymond Lewis, the old night watchman at the marina, waving to him from his stalled car near the end of Fourteenth Street. The storm surge had sent a fast-moving stream of seawater over the road, and Raymond's car had not made it through. Now he was trapped inside as the water rose almost to the car's windows. The doctor stopped at the edge of the stream. "I can't swim," Raymond yelled in desperation. "And I ain't sure I'm strong enough to wade through water that fast and deep."

The doctor dug around in the trunk of his old Ford until he found the rope he kept there for towing. It took three throws before the doctor landed the rope close enough for Raymond to grab on to. Then he told him to tie the rope around his waist and climb out the open window. Raymond did as he was told and staggered through the stream as the doctor pulled him to safety.

It was sometime after midnight before the doctor finally got home and back in bed. He and Gator slept late that Sunday morning. While Gator snored in the other bedroom, the doctor took his morning dose of morphine, showered, dressed, and went downstairs to prepare breakfast. After he had put on a pot of coffee, he fried some bacon in his big cast-iron skillet and sliced some potatoes and onions. When the bacon was brown and crispy, he removed it from the pan and let it drain on an old dish towel. Then he dropped the potatoes and onions into the skillet with the bacon grease. When they were crispy on the outside, he removed them and drained them on another dish towel. By then the smell had reached Gator's room, and he was soon in the kitchen with the doctor, picking at the bacon strips.

"How do you like your eggs, Gator?" the doctor asked as he pulled the egg carton from the icebox.

"Over easy be fine," he said.

"Gator, I do believe you've got not one but two pretty, purple shiners this morning."

"Yeah, I saw that in the mirror. I'm a sight, ain't I? Looks like you got a jaw that's bigger than the other yourself. Not to mention a nasty gash on your forehead."

"Yeah, and a few loose teeth to boot. Sorry I don't have any clothes that fit you."

"Yeah, well, I guess I better get back over to Apalachicola to get some clean things."

"I'll drive you over later," the doctor said as he served Gator his breakfast. "Sorry this won't be as good as Louisa Randolph's, but you'll just have to suffer."

"Sure smells good."

"So how long were you there in her house?"

"At Louisa's? Oh, just a couple of days."

"Did she spoil you?"

"Better than that."

"Sounds serious."

"Oh, hell," Gator said as he chewed a bite of potatoes. "I don't know. All I know is I never felt so easy around someone in my life. She don't bother me 'bout nothin', and she was always feedin' me and makin' sure I was okay. I ain't never had nobody take care of me like that, even when I was a kid. My daddy was too bitter about how he'd been treated by the white man to take much notice of me, and Mama was even madder about their situation than Daddy hisself was, so I got out of there as fast as I could."

"Damn, Gator, this thing with Louisa sounds pretty good then. If I was you, I'd try to hold on to that."

"Maybe I will," Gator said with a crooked smile. "Maybe I will."

The doctor called Bob Huggins and arranged to meet with him that evening at the doctor's house. Then he called Jewel to see how everyone was doing at her house. Jewel said they were all okay, but the doctor heard a strange hesitancy in her voice so he told her he wanted to come over and check on them. Then he and Gator put the dishes in the sink for Vivian to wash and drove over to North Port St. Joe.

The storm, which had raged most of the night, had made a mess of their little town. Trees were down everywhere. A few power lines were draped low over the streets. Some awnings were ripped off the stores downtown. The big Gulf sign at Little's Service Station had been uprooted. And there were pieces of a boat on the beach and an engine peeking out of the water at Eagle's Bay.

But this morning the sun was shining brightly and a cool breeze was

blowing in off the bay from the south. The unpaved streets in North Port
St. Joe were still muddy but not as messy as the previous night. Django
was sitting in his rocker on the front porch as they pulled up, "looking
none the worse for wear," as Jewel would say. The doctor asked him how
he was feeling. Django told him he was fine but he was worried about
Jewel and Marcus. Then Jewel joined them on the porch, looking fresh
and clean and a lot better than the night before. She hugged the doctor
and held him tightly. The doctor never wanted her to leave his arms. But
she did, with a dab of moisture in her eyes. Probably in his too, the doctor
knew.

"How are you?" he asked her.

"I'm okay," she said, "I think."

"And Marcus?"

"He's still asleep. Do you want some coffee?"

"Sure," the doctor said.

"How 'bout you, Gator?" Jewel asked.

"I'm fine," he said. "If it's all the same to you, I'll just sit out here on
the porch with Django and try to get some fresh air."

"Okay, let's go to the kitchen," Jewel said to the doctor.

They walked down the long hall that went from the front of the
house straight to its back. On the left, just before the back door, was the
kitchen. Jewel's mother was there at the sink, drying dishes and putting
them away.

"Good morning, Doc," she said. "Thanks for bringin' me my babies
back. I was fit to be tied, I tell you. Ain't never been so scared in my life."

"It's my pleasure, Mrs. Jackson. I'm sorry about Gabriel."

"Me too," she said, drying her hands and shaking her head. "I've
done called the Royal undertakers and they's takin' care of everything.
Now, if y'all don't mind, I'm gonna go and tend to my garden and do a
little prayin'. I been so nervous the last couple of days, I ain't been able

to set a foot in it, though God knows I been doin' some mighty powerful prayin', that's for sure."

"Please, Mrs. Jackson."

Jewel poured them both a cup of black coffee from the pot sitting on the stove, and they sat across from each other at the kitchen table.

"This has been hard on Mama," Jewel said. "She started cryin' last night and couldn't stop. She even got on about the night I was born thirty-seven years ago and how her and me perty near died. And how she couldn't have no more babies after that. She said she thought I was gonna die for sure this time."

"I didn't know that."

"Mama ain't mentioned it for years. It's our family secret. But, of course, it's always there."

"Do you feel responsible?"

"Yes," she cried.

"It's not your fault."

"I know," she whimpered.

The doctor stood up and went to her and wrapped his arms around her shoulders and held her while she sobbed. When she finally stopped, he asked her, "Do you want to talk about it?"

"I'm not sure I can," she said, wiping her eyes on the hem of her apron. "He wasn't mean to us most of the time. I mean he locked us in that filthy barn, but there was a little room in the back with a couple of cots and a bathroom. He came to check on us every few hours, but that was about it. But he had this look about him. You know. You saw him: crazy, out of whack."

"What about Marcus?"

"That was the bad part," she whispered. "At first, I told Lucilla that I didn't know anything about him or Sally Martin. That you hadn't told me anything. But he didn't believe me. So he put Marcus up on the table next to the saw and then turned it on. You can bet I told him everything then."

"I'm so sorry," the doctor said, "about getting you and Marcus involved in all this."

"It's not your fault, Doc. You know I would have gotten it out of you one way or another. Ain't nothing about you I don't know."

"So now what?" the doctor asked.

"Well, I'm gonna let Mama take care of the arrangements for Gabriel and I'm gonna tend to Marcus. I don't know what this is gonna do to him."

"Me either," the doctor said. "About the only thing you can do is love him and hold him and listen to him. Kids are resilient. They can take more than you think, but it may take some time to get the old Marcus back."

"I know. And then I guess I need to call Gabriel's boss and tell him what happened. And Reggie in Eatonville. I hope he can keep his job on the radio show without Gabriel."

"What a goddamn mess."

"Yeah," Jewel said. "But what about you, Doc? Your jaw and head don't look too good."

"I'll live at least long enough to see if we can get Gator off. Then I need to go to Charleston."

"Charleston? Why?"

"When I was looking for you, I went to see Sally Martin. She actually told me where you were, but she made me promise not to call in the police or talk about her involvement in all this stuff. I think she was just tired of dealing with Lucky's craziness and thought I might be able to get rid of him for her. I'm not sure."

"But Charleston?"

"Oh yeah, she told me, sort of as an afterthought, that when Sheriff Batson was checking into my background, he found out that I'd been married a few times. So he tracked down Annie. You remember . . . my first wife."

"The love of your life."

"Yeah," the doctor said. "Sally said that she was in Charleston at the Florence Crittenden Home. I don't know if that's true, but I'm going there to find out."

"Why don't you just phone her there?"

"It's too important to trust to a phone call. If she hasn't contacted me in twelve years, apparently she doesn't want to talk to me. It would be too easy for her to hang up on me."

"I see," Jewel said, "but what's this Florence Critter Home?"

"It's a home for unwed mothers. I've sent a few girls there. It's supposed to be very good."

"But . . ."

"I know. I don't get it either. That's why I need to go there. Sally didn't tell me any more."

The doctor told Gator to drop him off at his house and to take his car to Apalachicola to pick up his gear. He was too tired to do anything but take a nap. And so he did.

Bob Huggins was right on time that evening for his meeting with Gator and the doctor. They sat out on the back porch, sipped sweet tea, and talked.

"You're doing the right thing, turning yourself in, Gator," Huggins began.

"How do you figure?" Gator asked.

"Well, Sheriff Duffield believes you murdered Dr. Price because he found evidence in your closet that led him to believe that, and presumably you had a motive since you inherited the island upon Price's death."

"But that's not true. I didn't kill him, and I didn't even know he had willed the island to me," Gator protested.

"Who killed him then?" Huggins asked.

The doctor had promised Sally Martin that he would not tell anyone any more about her involvement with Lucky Lucilla and his trail of terror, but faced with the decision to help her or help Gator, he realized that he no longer cared all that much about protecting her. He had to admit to himself that he still did care for her but not enough to hang his best friend. Besides, how much concern could you have for someone who allowed a man like Lucky Lucilla to do the things he had done? But now Lucky Lucilla was dead. Without him, he doubted she could muster the fire power to mount another vendetta against him and his friends. The doctor felt more than a little foolish for clinging to his infatuation with her for as long as he had. He was such a hopeless romantic.

"Lucky Lucilla did," the doctor said.

"But why?"

"Wood," the doctor said and then told them about Sally Martin's trying to snare the timber rights to St. Vincent Island.

"I think Duffield and Denton will find your story interesting," Huggins said, "but I expect Sally Martin will deny ever telling it."

"So where does that leave us?" the doctor asked.

"I'm not sure," the lawyer said. "I'm inclined to think that Judge Denton will give us the benefit of the doubt in all this, but I'm not sure about Duffield. He wants to pin the murder on someone, and he's still mad about Gator slugging him and stealing the evidence and his gun. Let me set up a meeting with them, at which point we'll deliver Gator. That will reinforce the fact that he has nothing to hide and is innocent."

"Will they put me in jail?" Gator asked.

"I don't know," Huggins said. "It depends on how upset Duffield is. If he insists, then Denton may be hard put to set you free. At any rate, I think I know Denton well enough that he'll set reasonable bail so you won't have to be locked up for long."

"What is it exactly that you have on the judge?" the doctor asked.

"That's between me and him," the lawyer said as got up to leave.

Chapter 32

Gator wanted to go back to Louisa Randolph's house until he turned himself in at the meeting with the judge and sheriff, but Bob Huggins advised him to stay out of Sheriff Duffield's jurisdiction for the time being. If Duffield happened to find him there, he would toss him in jail for sure, Huggins figured. So Gator stayed with the doctor until Tuesday at four when the meeting was scheduled.

That morning, the doctor walked to his office and reviewed the day with Nadyne. She reminded him that it was the day he had been dreading, the day of Millie Williams' abortion.

At a little after nine o'clock, Nadyne led her and her mother into the emergency room. The doctor explained the procedure to them. He would have Millie lie on the examination table. Nadyne would undress her below the waist and put her feet in stirrups. He would then insert a syringe filled with something called Leunbach's paste, a potassium soap solution, into the girl's cervix and then inject the paste into her uterus. It would be a bit uncomfortable but not painful. He would then pack her vagina with sterile gauze. The procedure would take only about ten minutes and then she could go home. In eighteen hours she was to remove the gauze. By then a miscarriage with a little cramping would have occurred. She should take two aspirin about an hour before removing the gauze, the doctor instructed. If any continuous bleeding or unusual pain occurred, she was to call the doctor immediately.

"Do you understand?" the doctor asked her.

"Yes," she whimpered.

"Then Nadyne will help you get ready," he said to the girl, and then to her mother, "May I see you outside for a moment?"

She followed him into the hall.

"Have you done anything to keep this from happening again?" he asked her.

"Not yet," she whispered.

"Chief Lane cannot do anything unless you or your daughter tells him what happened."

"I know."

"So?"

"I'll take care of it," she said.

"Please do, for your daughter's sake."

"Okay," she said.

"Also, please do not tell anyone about this. It's illegal for me to perform this procedure unless the mother's health is endangered."

"I understand," the woman said as she began to cry, "and thank you, Doctor."

That afternoon, after he had finished his house calls, the doctor drove over to the Jacksons' house. Django was sitting on the porch swing with his wife, watching the few cars passing by on Avenue C.

"How are y'all feeling?" the doctor asked as he climbed the porch steps.

"Okay," Django said, "we're doin' okay."

"How about the rest of your family?"

"Jewel's in the kitchen with Marcus," Mrs. Jackson said. "Why don't you go on back? The funeral's gonna be on Sunday at New Bethel. Please come."

The doctor nodded and walked back to find Jewel and Marcus at the kitchen sink, Jewel washing and Marcus drying dishes. Jewel, in a black skirt, white blouse, and apron, turned and smiled weakly at the doctor.

"How are y'all?" the doctor asked them.

"I'm survivin'," Jewel said

"How about you, Marcus?"

"I'm okay," he answered.

"You know, I've been craving a big bowl of strawberry ice cream and a cherry phosphate all day. Since I've finished my house calls, I was wondering if maybe Marcus could come down to LeHardy's Pharmacy with me to keep me company."

"Could I?" Marcus asked his mother.

"Of course," she said, "but don't eat too much and spoil your supper."

The boy didn't say a word all the way to LeHardy's. Once there, the doctor decided it was not the time to risk a confrontation by sitting with Marcus in the white section of the soda fountain area and instead led Marcus to a seat at one of the two little tables in the back by the storeroom reserved for colored folks. He ordered a scoop of strawberry ice cream and a cherry phosphate, and Marcus asked for a root beer float.

"So how are you, really?" the doctor asked.

"I'm sad."

"Because of your daddy?"

"Yeah."

"We're all gonna miss him. How are you with all the scary stuff you've been through in the last few days?"

"Yeah," the boy whispered. "I never been so scared in my life. I thought that man was gonna kill Mama and me."

"I know, but you're safe now."

"I know," Marcus said, sipping his drink, "but I'm still havin' some bad dreams. Mama calls 'em night mirrors."

"Well, I have those sometimes too, but they'll stop soon enough. Meanwhile, anytime you get thirsty for a root beer float, just have your mama bring you around to my office. I'm always looking for a good excuse to come over here and have some strawberry ice cream and a cherry phosphate."

"Okay," Marcus said. "Thanks for askin' me, Dr. Berber."

It would take some time, the doctor told himself. Time, patience, and love.

Since Judge Denton's office was in Wewahitchka and Sheriff Duffield's was in Apalachicola, they decided to meet in the middle in Port St. Joe. The judge had arranged for them to use a room at City Hall. It was a cramped, windowless conference room with a long oak table with six chairs around it. Judge Denton and Bob Huggins were already there, on either side of the table, facing each other. Gator sat down next to the lawyer and the doctor sat next to the judge, as Chief Lane marched in and joined them.

"Where's Duffield?" Huggins asked.

"Well," Judge Denton said, looking from man to man, "I hate to be the bearer of bad news, but Sunday night the sheriff was working with a couple of his men to clear some of the storm damage down by the docks, under the John Gorrie Bridge, and a power line dropped on him. I'm afraid it was live."

"What?" the doctor said.

"The power line was live," the judge repeated, "but Duffield's dead. Killed him instantly."

"Jesus!" Huggins said.

"Did he have a family?" the doctor asked.

"No," the judge said. "He had a wife once, but she left him while he was overseas during the Great War. The man was crushed. Never remarried. To top it off, his folks died in a car accident while he was in the Army. So he really didn't have anybody. The only thing he seemed to care about was his job, and sometimes I wondered about that."

"It's a damn shame," Huggins said.

"So, Gator," Denton continued, "if he were here, Sheriff Duffield would want to prosecute you for the murder of Dr. Elmer Price. Your attorney and friend here contend that you're not the murderer and that perhaps Lucky Lucilla was responsible. But now Lucilla is dead, I understand, and we've established no motive for his taking Price's life."

"Wood," the doctor said.

"What?" the judge asked.

"Tell him," Huggins said to the doctor And so he did—everything Sally had admitted to him about her trying to acquire the rights to the timber on St. Vincent Island.

"That's a pretty serious charge," the judge said. "Do you expect me to believe this pretty, young widow, with four little children, killed an old man to get the timber rights to St. Vincent Island and then blamed it on Gator? Why Gator?"

"That's a long story," the doctor answered.

"Let's hear it," the judge ordered.

"Well, Chief," the doctor began, "the confession that Lucky Lucilla made to you out at Indian Pass was not entirely true."

"No?" Chief Lane said.

"No. It's true that Sheriff Batson hired Lucilla to kill Sally's husband. But that was because Sally and the sheriff had been seeing each other, and they wanted to get rid of her husband, who was a drunk and a gambler and had gambled the family deep into debt. So Sally, without her husband's knowledge, raised his life insurance policy from three to twenty thousand dollars. Then she and the sheriff hired Lucilla to kill him."

"So you're saying Sally Martin was responsible for the murders of both Dr. Price and her husband? So what has this got to do with Gator?" the judge asked.

"Yeah, that's right, but that's not all," the doctor continued.

"I can hardly wait," the judge said.

"Sally also had Lucilla kill the sheriff."

"Why? I thought you said they were lovers."

"They were until Sally found out that the sheriff liked to beat up on colored prostitutes. So she decided she didn't want to share the insurance money with him as they had originally planned."

"So she cut his head off?"

"Well, Lucilla did, just as Sally requested."

"Damn," the judge said, "that's pretty drastic. But I still don't see what any of this has to do with Gator?"

"Sally figured that I had told Gator and Jewel about her involvement in all of this mayhem so she told Lucilla to kill us, and he almost did."

"Well," the judge said, scratching his balding head. "Why didn't you tell me or Chief Lane about all this before? It's been over a year now since Martin and Batson were killed."

The doctor looked at Bob Huggins for help, but the lawyer just shrugged and said, "Well?"

"Both Sally's husband and Sheriff Batson were scum. They deserved what they got. Sure, Sally shouldn't have had Lucilla kill them, but the world's no doubt a better place without them. And I thought Sally and her children needed the insurance money to survive. And . . ."

"Yes?"

"I loved her."

"I see," said the judge. "So how do you know all this?"

"Sally confessed it all to me when we broke up last year, and Lucky Lucilla confirmed it when Chief Lane left to radio everyone that we had caught the man out at Indian Pass."

"And you've kept it to yourself all these months?"

"Yes, sir."

"Well, I'll be damned," the judge said. "I'll be goddamned."

Chapter 33

The next Saturday, the doctor boarded a train to Charleston. He took the same 8:00 Apalachicola Northern train to Chattahoochee that he had taken to Tampa a few days before. And he again enjoyed breakfast in the dining car, this time without the unpleasant company of Dr. Price's daughter. Instead, he chatted briefly with an overweight traveling salesman who was returning home to Atlanta after a week working in Florida. He was trying to sell a new type of pen called a Birome that had a tiny ball at the tip instead of a point. The doctor thought it was a good idea but doubted it would ever catch on.

Nevertheless, the doctor bought one of the salesman's pens. He liked the man and felt sorry for him. Then he finished his breakfast and watched the Panhandle pass before him. He thought about Jewel and Marcus and Gabriel's funeral the following day. He had explained to Jewel that he couldn't take any more time off from work and needed to take this trip this weekend. She seemed to understand. The truth was the doctor hated funerals almost as much as he abhorred death itself. He had attended only three funerals in his life: his father's, his mother's and Carrie Jo's. He had had his fill of them. This renunciation had begun a long time before when his childhood friend Rachael Manuelian had died of polio at age twelve. His parents had tried to talk him into going to her funeral, but he had refused. He couldn't bear it. Instead, he stayed in his room and cried and vowed to become a doctor so he could someday save children like Rachael, his first true love.

When he returned to his seat in the Pullman car, the doctor thought about Gator and how Bob Huggins had somehow secured his freedom, at least for the time being. Of course, it didn't hurt Gator's case that Sheriff Duffield had conveniently been electrocuted. That certainly took the pressure off Denton to prosecute Gator to appease the sheriff. None of them—neither Gator nor the doctor nor Bob Huggins—understood what this meant as far as the ownership of St. Vincent went, but Huggins advised Gator to lie low for a while until Judge Denton was ready to rule on the matter. The judge wanted to talk to Sally Martin and hear what she had to say about her involvement with Lucky Lucilla. He told Gator to stay close until he had talked to Sally and decided what to do next, so Gator asked the judge if he could go as far as Apalachicola. Judge Denton consented, so Gator packed his bag and took the opportunity to get a little closer to Louisa Randolph.

The doctor again changed trains in Chattahoochee, transferring to an Atlantic Coast Line train going north. Going into Georgia, the land was greener and not as deforested as it had been in Florida. He tried to get into the new translation of Franz Kafka's *Amerika,* which he had heard about on the radio, but the rhythm of the train and the undulating view lulled him into a daze, sort of the Southern version of a Kafkaesque dream, he thought. Vivian had again made him a lunch, so after morning stops in Thomasville, DuPont, Waycross, and Jessup, the doctor walked to the club car and ordered a beer to have with his lunch. Vivian had given him a bologna sandwich on her homemade wheat bread, some carrot and celery sticks, and a Satsuma orange. He also found a note at the bottom of the brown paper bag.

Dear Dr. Berber,

I hope you are enjoying your trip. Don't worry about anything here. Between Nadyne at your office and me here at home, we will take care of everything. Please have a good time.

Sincerely,
Vivian

P.S.
The Lord shall preserve thee from all evil; he shall preserve thy soul. The Lord shall preserve thy going out and thy coming in from this time forth, and even for evermore.

Psalm 121, 7–8

She was right on both counts. At this point, the doctor was feeling superfluous. Nadyne was just as competent as he was, and Vivian ran his simple household like an army general. And since Jewel was so blasted independent and Gator had found a girlfriend, there wasn't anybody left who really needed him anymore. And God knows someone was watching over him, and he was thinking more and more, as unscientific as it sounded, that it just might be God Himself.

As the doctor read on in *Amerika,* he became more and more fascinated with its young hero and Kafka's take on a country he never set foot in. Maybe when he started receiving Social Security benefits in a couple of years, he could afford to see more of it.

They stopped in Savannah for a long time and finally pulled into the Union Station in Charleston at a little past seven in the evening. The doctor asked for directions in the station and was pleased to find out that the Florence Crittenton Home was not too far away. He thought it was probably too late on a Saturday night to show up there unannounced, however, so he decided to wait until the next day. He was anxious to see Annie again, but he was afraid of what he might find. Perhaps Sally had lied. Maybe Annie was no longer there. And if she was, would she want to see him? It was best, he decided, to do a little sightseeing while it was still light and take his time in the morning to make himself look as presentable as possible.

The Francis Marion Hotel downtown was almost as opulent as the Floridan in Tampa, with its high vaulted ceilings, dark wood, potted palms, and crystal chandeliers. From the window in his room, he could see the harbor and several church steeples. He decided to walk down King Street toward the Battery and find a place to have supper. Shops of all kind lined the busy street, but none were open at this hour. The city smelled wonderful, the doctor thought: an intoxicating brew of pollen, rice, and tidewater. And it was good to walk after being cooped up in a train all day. So he strolled through the open-air market over to East Bay Street and followed his nose south down a little alley to a restaurant called McCrady's. The waiter showed him to a corner table in a comfortable room with brick walls and wide plank floors. He ordered a glass of Sancerre and studied the menu. It was a hard choice, but when the waiter returned he ordered a cup of okra soup with low country rice on the side to start, grilled cobia with country ham broth, collard greens, and ramps and rhubarb for his main course, and an Anson Mills cornmeal cake with Red Bay crème anglaise and sorrel for dessert, as well as another glass of wine.

The meal was delicious. *I must get out more,* the doctor thought as he walked back through a neighborhood of big, beautiful antebellum houses with tall, double porches on their sides. He stopped at the Battery and stood next to a huge cannon and looked out over the wine-dark sea to

Fort Sumter where the Civil War had begun many years before. He felt tired and stuffed and ready for bed. He wondered what tomorrow would bring.

Lots of sunshine and humidity, as it turned out. So the doctor, freshly showered and outfitted in a snug blue surge suit, decided to take a taxi to the Florence Crittenton Home on St. Margaret Street. It was a large, stately brick structure with a small front porch with two simple white columns on either side. The doctor walked up the steps and knocked. An old, gray-haired woman answered the door and invited him into a small foyer.

"How may I help you?" she asked.

"I'm looking for someone. Her name is Annie Berber."

"I'm sorry, sir, but we have no one here by that name. Are you sure you have the right address?"

"This is the Florence Crittenton Home, isn't it?"

"Yes."

"Perhaps she is using her maiden name," the doctor said. "McVey, Annie McVey."

"Why, yes," the woman smiled. "We do have an Annie McVey. She works here, but she's not here right now. This is her day off."

"Could you tell me where she lives then?"

"And who is asking?"

"Van Berber. I'm her husband."

"Her what?"

"Husband."

"Oh, my," she said, "I didn't know she was married. Would you mind if I phone her and ask her if it's okay for you to call on her?"

"No, not at all. Thank you."

The old woman left him standing there alone in the foyer and disappeared into a room down the long hall. When she returned she gave

SECRETS OF ST. JOE

him the address and directions on how to get there. It was several blocks away on a street named San Souci, and he decided to walk there to give himself time to think about what he was going to say. He hadn't really expected to find her so he hadn't planned anything. Now he had to think of something, but nothing appropriate came to mind. When you are about to see your wife for the first time in twelve years, what in the world would be the right thing to say?

It was further than he thought, and even though the sidewalks were mostly shaded by grand live oaks trees with hanging Spanish moss, he was sweating by the time he reached the modest white cottage on San Souci. He knocked on the front door and waited.

And there she was, standing before him, as beautiful as ever. The hair, the eyes, the smile—they were all the same. Maybe a few wrinkles that he didn't remember and a little more weight, but mostly the same.

"Hello, Van," she said. "Please come in."

She led him into a small, sparsely furnished parlor, motioning for him to sit on a couch across from her.

"Can I get you something to drink?" she asked.

"Yes, thank you."

"You still prefer sweet tea?"

"Yes, that would be fine."

She left the room and he wiped the sweat from his face with his handkerchief. She soon returned with a glass of iced tea for each of them. She sat her glass on an end table and sat primly with her hands clasped in her lap.

"Where to begin . . . ," the doctor said.

"Indeed."

"Maybe from the beginning," he suggested. "I last saw you at the train station in Tallahassee."

"I know," she said. "A long time ago.

"Where did you go?"

"Here," she said. "To Charleston."

"But you were supposed to go to Washington to see Alexandria."

"I know, but . . ."

"Why?"

She sat quietly for several seconds as tears welled up in her eyes. The doctor didn't know what to do. Go to her or wait?

"Oh, Van," she finally whispered. "I don't know how to tell you . . . but . . ."

"Yes?"

"You remember your friend in Lynn Haven City, Karl Rossmann?"

"Yes, of course."

"Well . . . he forced me," she whimpered. "I didn't know what to do. I knew how much you liked him, and I didn't know if you would believe me. You always said I was a flirt, and I thought you would blame me. I didn't tell you because I was so embarrassed and ashamed and knew you would hate him and me. So I made sure I was never around him again. But unfortunately it only took that once. . . . I thought I was too old, but I . . . I was pregnant."

"I wish you had told me then," the doctor said.

"Maybe I should have. I don't know. I was very confused at the time. And I wanted to have the baby. You know how much I always wanted to have children. But I thought you wouldn't allow it, especially since it was not yours. So . . ."

"So you came here to have it?"

"Yes, I'd heard you talk about the Florence Crittenton Home so I came here to have her."

"Her?"

"Yes, a beautiful baby girl, but she's almost grown now."

"Where is she?"

"At Sunday School. We were getting ready to go when Nancy called me and said you were here. So I walked her over to the church. It's only a few blocks away. And I came back here to see you."

"Can I meet her?"

"Yes, of course, if you want to."

"I would like that very much," the doctor said, trying not to cry.

"Okay, when she gets back, but let me finish my story, now that I've started it. I was older than the other mothers at the home when I first came here, and they needed help. After I had Sheila, they hired me, at first to just clean up and then to help counsel the girls, and now I'm the assistant director. So now you know. I have a career of my own and a daughter of my own."

"Are you happy?"

"Oh, I don't know. I love my work and I love Sheila, and that should be enough, don't you think? What about you? Are you happy?"

"No," he answered truthfully, "not really. The last year has been a hard one for me, and, if you really want to know, I don't think I've been happy since you left."

"Oh, Van, I'm so sorry. I wish I'd handled it better back then. I've thought of finding you a million times but was always afraid."

"Of what?"

"Of what you would think of me, of what you would say, of losing Sheila. I don't know. I'm sorry."

"Now what?" the doctor asked.

"Do you still love me?"

"Of course. I'll always love you. Do you love me?"

"Yes," she cried, "I do. I've always loved you."

They continued to talk, a little about the past but mostly about the future. The doctor soon met Sheila, who was a freckle-faced, wide-eyed, funny child with whom he fell in love immediately. She looked like her mother and not at all as he remembered Karl Rossmann, but maybe that was just wishful thinking. Annie did not have to explain Van to her daughter because she had already done that. Before the day was over, the doctor was getting to know both women. Annie made them supper and when Sheila went to bed, he kissed and hugged her mother for the first time in twelve years.

He had to admit the whole thing was a little awkward, though. There was a big gap to fill, and it was going to take some time to find a new equilibrium. In the end, he had no idea how he felt about what Annie had done. But he had found her, finally, and that was enough for now.

Chapter 34

The long, hot, humid summer gradually turned into a more bearable fall in little Port St. Joe. The days were growing shorter, and the white-sand beaches on Cape San Blas were quiet and cooler. The St. Joe Paper Company was now operating at full capacity and had hired a doctor to serve its employees, now numbering more than a thousand. Another doctor, a young one fresh out of medical school, had set up shop over on Main Street. And not far from his office, on Avenue B, a young Negro dentist, Dr. Hall, had opened an office that he shared with his wife, Lula, a registered nurse, who began seeing sick and injured colored people.

The doctor and Annie continued to talk on the phone every few days. They had become reacquainted enough that she and Sheila planned to visit Port St. Joe on Labor Day weekend. Maybe, if everything went well, they would move down permanently before school started a couple of weeks later.

The doctor and Gator took Marcus fishing with them on Howard Creek. The boy was still more quiet than usual, but then it was hard "to get a word in edgewise," as Jewel would say, with Gator going on and on about Louisa Randolph. The doctor had never seen Gator in love before and it seemed to agree with him.

Chief Lane dropped by the doctor's office one morning on his way out of town. He was driving with his family to Tampa to attend the funeral of his father, a union organizer in Tampa who had died in a riot at a cigar factory in Ybor City.

The chief updated the doctor on the latest news. Willie Williams, whose daughter, Millie, had had the abortion, had been killed by his brother-in-law in a hunting accident. Mary Morgan, the mother of little Maggie, who had broken her ankle when she had fallen out of a pear tree, had divorced her husband, Eli, and Judge Denton had ruled that the entire orchard go to her. Norman Adams, the man who had been beating his children had lost his right arm in a farming accident. His son Lucas had been driving the tractor that suddenly stopped and sent his father flying off the back of the wagon he was pulling, directly into the mouth of an oncoming corn picker. Norman and his disembodied arm had been taken to the hospital in Panama City, but there was nothing the doctors could do there but clean and dress the wound and throw the offending arm into the trash can.

A few days after the chief returned from his father's funeral, he called the doctor and told him that Judge Denton had talked to Sally Martin and wanted to meet again with the doctor, Bob Huggins, and Gator Mica. So on August 31, they gathered again in the same cramped conference room in Port St. Joe's City Hall.

Judge Denton looked over his hooked nose at the assembled men and said to the doctor, "Chief Lane and I paid a visit to Sally Martin and confronted her with your accusations."

"And?" Huggins asked.

"She denied having anything to do with the murder of her husband, Sheriff Batson, or Dr. Price. And she said she didn't know a man named Lucky Lucilla."

"And when we asked her why she thought you might make such an accusation," Chief Lane said, "she said she didn't know, but maybe it was because you were angry with her for breaking off a romantic relationship you two once had."

"That's preposterous," Huggins said. "People end relationships every day, but they don't accuse each other of murder. Why in God's name would Dr. Berber fabricate something like that?"

"Don't know," Judge Denton said, "but the widow led us to believe that you, Doctor, wanted to discredit her because she had some damaging information about you and Gator Mica."

Uh-oh, here we go, thought the doctor. But when he started to speak, Huggins put a hand on his arm and said, "Okay, Judge, what did she tell you?"

"That Gator Mica had killed a man in a Florida City bar a few years back."

"Yes?"

"And that Dr. Berber was a morphine addict."

Huggins stared at the judge, waited a beat, adjusted his glasses, and looked around the room. "So, let me get this straight," he finally said, peering now at Judge Denton. "Sally Martin tells you Dr. Berber is accusing her of murder because she broke up with him and doesn't want her to divulge these deep, dark secrets to the world. Is that right?"

"Yeah, that's about it," the judge said.

"Wouldn't it have been more to the doctor's advantage to keep his mouth shut about her involvement in these murders rather than to risk her telling these alleged secrets?"

"It would seem so," Denton said, "but at this point I'm not surmising why these people said what they said. I'm just telling you what they said, not why, and letting you know that we have a situation here since the widow has denied Dr. Berber's accusations . . . and has countered with some serious accusations of her own."

Everyone sat silently for a moment, letting the impact of the conflicting incriminations sink in.

"So what next?" Huggins finally asked.

"Aside from your allegation, Doctor, I have no evidence that Sally Martin was involved in the murder of her husband or the sheriff or in any way with Lucky Lucilla, for that matter," the judge said. "Until I receive it—from Chief Lane or Sheriff Roberts or somebody else—we cannot charge her with anything.

"On the other hand, I have no evidence, aside from Sally Martin's claim, that Dr. Berber is lying about this matter so I can't charge him with perjury, especially since he hasn't formally testified to her involvement. If he did have knowledge of Mrs. Martin's involvement, he should have offered it long ago. But I'm not going to charge him with withholding evidence since he's not offered any evidence, only his contention that the widow was involved."

"What about Gator Mica?" Huggins asked.

"Well, apparently he did kill a man in Florida City back in thirty-four," Judge Denton said. "We called down there. He slugged a man in a bar fight and the man died. But the authorities there don't care about him anymore. The statute of limitation for assault in Florida is four years, so it expired last year. And no one seems to care about the man Gator laid out anyway."

"What about Dr. Price?" Huggins asked.

"Well, again," the judge said, "we have the question of who to believe. As in the other murders, we have no hard evidence that Sally Martin did anything wrong, just the doctor's assertions that she had Dr. Price killed to get the timber rights to St. Vincent Island, which she has of course denied. So, once again, we can't charge her until someone comes up with some hard evidence.

"As far as the evidence against Gator, we had a bloody machete and a rifle, according to Sheriff Duffield, but Gator absconded with them so all we have is Duffield's testimony that they once existed. Unfortunately—or perhaps fortunately for you, Gator—we no longer have a Duffield. So, unless someone can find these pieces of evidence or some other evidence, I don't believe we have enough to hold you at this time."

Gator smiled and started to get up, but Judge Denton motioned for him to stay seated. "Not so fast. Sit down," he ordered. "There are still two more issues here. First is the matter of your assaulting an officer of the law. Here again we have only the testimony of a dead man. Unless, of course, the doctor witnessed such an assault, in which case we would have to charge you for it. Doctor?"

The doctor didn't know what to do. He turned to Huggins, who shrugged and said, "Tell him the truth."

"Okay," the doctor said, "Gator decked him . . . but only because he didn't want to go to jail for a crime he didn't commit."

"All right then," the judge said, "guilty as charged."

"Wait a minute," Huggins interrupted. "Is this a trial?"

"Shut up, Bob," Denton said and then turned to Gator. "The court orders you to pay a fine of fifty dollars, payable within thirty days, or thirty days in jail."

"But . . . ," Gator stammered.

"Shut up, Gator," Huggins said.

"What about the morphine addiction?" the doctor asked.

"Again, Dr. Berber, I have no evidence of that either. And even if I did, what you prescribe for yourself is your business and not mine or anybody else's, as far as I'm concerned."

"And the second issue?" Huggins asked.

"I've studied Dr. Price's will," the judge answered, "and everything seems to be in order. And since Gator has been exonerated for beating the man to death in Florida City and killing Dr. Price, he is the rightful owner of St. Vincent Island. Bob, you can deal with the paperwork with the clerk of the court. Any questions?"

Everyone looked stunned.

"Court's adjourned then," Judge Denton barked and dropped his fist emphatically to the tabletop. Then he put on his felt fedora and stalked out.

"What just happened?" the doctor asked.

"Let's go home," Huggins said, rising from his chair with a broad smile.

And so they did.

Chapter 35

Gator moved back to the beautiful, eighteen-square-mile piece of paradise that he now owned and reestablished the oyster business that had been shut down since Price's death. Gator had mixed feelings about his good fortune. On one hand, he was pleased to be able to protect a wilderness that he loved. On the other, he disliked having the added responsibility and leaving the comforts of Louisa Randolph's home in Apalachicola.

The doctor stopped by Bob Huggins' office the next day to thank him for everything he had done for Gator. He asked the lawyer again what it was that he had on Judge Denton.

"Well, you seem pretty good at keeping secrets. You promise you won't breathe a word to anyone?" Huggins asked.

"I promise."

"Well, the judge has a lover."

"A lover? But isn't he married and a deacon in the Presbyterian Church in Wewa?"

"Yep, two kids in high school too."

"Who is she?" the doctor asked.

"Well, that's the thing. She's not a she. He's a he."

"What?"

"A court reporter, with a wife and kids too."

"But . . ."

"I went back to the courthouse one night 'cause I had left my briefcase in the courtroom, which was locked. I talked the sheriff's dispatcher into loaning me the key. When I opened the door and flipped on the lights, I found the judge and the court reporter on the floor . . . trying to cover up and get dressed."

"What did you do?"

"I said, 'Excuse me, gentlemen, but I left my briefcase,' and I got my briefcase, turned off the light, and locked the door behind me.

"And?"

"Never breathed a word of it until now."

"You've never said anything?"

"Nope," Huggins smiled. "He knows I know, but I've never mentioned it to him or anyone else. He's a good man. He and I were football heroes at Port St. Joe High way back when. I turned into a fair-to-middlin' country lawyer and Art turned into the wisest, fairest judge I've ever known. So fair that he calls them the way he sees them, even though he knows I could ruin him anytime I wanted. And when there's some doubt, he usually gives me the benefit of it. I couldn't ask for more."

Reggie Robinson, Gabriel's friend and fellow bluesman, had returned briefly to Port St. Joe for Gabriel's funeral and had then driven the new red Cadillac that Jewel had given him back to New York City to continue performing in the radio show and singing the blues, as a solo act, wherever he could find a gig. When he got back to Harlem, he packed up Jewel's belongings and shipped them back to Jewel in Port St. Joe.

Jewel, ever resourceful, had started her own business. After the doctor went to work each morning, she and Vivian turned his kitchen into an assembly line, constructing sandwiches of various types with Vivian's homemade bread and adding other items, like hard-boiled eggs, pickles, and fresh fruits and vegetables to make sack lunches that they sold at noon to the workers at the St. Joe Paper Company. At a quarter a bag, the workers were able to choose what they wanted instead of eating what their wives gave them, and they also enjoyed the little notes that Jewel and Vivian included: "For thou shalt eat the labor of thine hands; happy shalt thou be, and it shall be well with thee" and "Goodness and hard work are rewarded with respect." Their wives were pleased to have one less chore each morning. Nevertheless, Jewel still had time to organize a little party to celebrate Gator's inheritance and Annie and Sheila's visit.

On September 1, German troops invaded Poland. Two days later, France, Britain, and the Commonwealth declared war on Germany. That evening, on the other side of the Atlantic Ocean, Jewel and Marcus White, Vivian Jackson, Gator Mica, Louisa Randolph, Annie and Sheila McVey, and Dr. Van Berber gathered at the doctor's old Victorian house on Seventh Street.

Annie and Sheila had arrived the night before and the doctor had been showing them around the area all day, while Jewel and Vivian had been preparing all kinds of delicacies for the party: a baked ham, red rice, butter beans, corn relish, cracklin's, and cornbread. Louisa, not to be outdone and by previous arrangement with Jewel, had been baking all day and brought along peach and blackberry cobbler, pumpkin cheesecake, and the lemon chess pie that the doctor and Django had enjoyed in her Apalachicola kitchen a few weeks before.

Gator brought a gallon jug of moonshine and wasted no time filling everyone's glass. Marcus went straight to the doctor's Gramophone in the parlor and put on Fats Waller's *Your Feets Too Big*, which he loved to play over and over again. Jewel had borrowed another table and some mismatched chairs from Miss Shriver next door, and she placed them next to the usual setup in the kitchen. There was a lot of chatter going on, but with the music playing, the doctor's high-frequency hearing loss wouldn't allow him to distinguish one conversation from another. So he just sat there and drank, deaf to the chatter, enjoying having the people he loved around him.

When the food was laid out, Jewel told Marcus to turn off the music and call everyone to the kitchen for supper. The tables were so covered with bowls that there was hardly room for the plates and utensils, but Jewel and Vivian had somehow managed to squeeze everyone in.

As Jewel started passing bowls and Vivian began carving the ham, the doctor said, "Thank y'all for coming tonight. And even though a war's started overseas, we still have a lot to celebrate. First, I'm celebrating finding Annie and Sheila, whom I'm doing my best to talk into moving down here from Charleston. What do y'all think of our little town so far?"

"Very beautiful," Annie said. "Not as much character as Charleston, I'm afraid, but it does have its charm."

"Yeah," Jewel said, "about as charming as dirt."

"Now, now, Jewel," the doctor said. "Don't be bad-mouthing our little slice of paradise."

"A mighty slim slice, if you ask me," Jewel said.

"Speaking of which," the doctor said, "how's your luncheon business going?"

"Oh, my," Jewel said with a laugh, "it's goin' gangbusters. If we keep growin' like we've been, we're gonna have to find a bigger kitchen."

"Well, more power to y'all," the doctor said. "Just don't you be moving Vivian out of my kitchen, that's all."

Vivian smiled and blushed. "Don't worry," she said.

"We're also celebratin' Gator's ownership of St. Vincent Island," Jewel said. "What are you gonna do now that you own a whole island?"

"Well, I'm gonna keep harvesting oysters, I guess. I got about a dozen people workin' for me right now, and they all need the jobs. I'd just as soon hunt and fish out there on St. Vincent and nothin' else, but now I got these folks and their families dependin' on me."

"What about Louisa?" Jewel asked. "Are you gonna take her out there with you?"

Louisa laughed, and Gator just said, "I'm workin' on it."

"Marcus," the doctor asked, "What about you? You glad to be back in Port St. Joe? You ready for third grade?"

"I reckon," Marcus said. "I like it here."

Everyone ate and drank too much. Marcus continued to put records on the doctor's Gramophone. Gator danced with Louisa, and the doctor danced with Annie, and then Sheila, and then Jewel. It was late by the time they had dessert and cleaned up.

Finally, when everyone had left and Sheila had gone upstairs to bed, the doctor sat with Annie on the wicker love seat on the back porch and listened to tree frogs croon in the dark night.

"What do you think?" the doctor asked her.

"About what?"

"About tonight?"

"You're a lucky man," she answered, "to have such good friends."

"I suppose," he said. "They're sort of an odd lot."

"Yes but still good people."

"What about the town?" the doctor asked. "Are you ready to move down here with me?"

"Well," she whispered, "I don't think so, Van."

"Why not?"

"Because you're in love with Jewel. It's plain to see."

"It is?"

"Yes," she said.

So he drove Annie and Sheila to the depot the next morning and watched them board the train back to Charleston. He didn't want to see them go, but what could he do? Annie had made herself a home in Charleston, and he had made himself a home in Port St. Joe, such as it was. And she had recognized something that the doctor had hardly admitted to himself.

Gator finally talked Louisa Randolph into moving to St. Vincent Island with him, but the doctor wondered how long she would last in such a remote wilderness without all her friends and relations in Apalachicola. Who, besides Gator and the few remaining families, was she going to cook for out there?

The following week, Marcus started third grade at the little colored schoolhouse in North Port St. Joe. He was still quiet but just as smart as ever. He no longer had nightmares, and it became gradually easier for the doctor and Gator to coax a smile from him as they continued to include him in their occasional fishing and hunting expeditions.

Django Jackson continued to improve, and the doctor stopped whenever he was in that part of town to check on him. He usually found him with his wife or some of his old cronies out on his front porch, breathing in the smoke from the mill and watching the world go by. The doctor didn't know how many days Django had left, but he seemed to be enjoying them.

Vivian and Jewel's lunch business continued to thrive. Vivian made the sandwiches and kept the books. She was earning enough now to move out of her strict Baptist parents' shotgun shack in North Port St. Joe to a new apartment on Avenue F. Since then she was beginning "to come out of her shell," as Jewel reported, being more vocal and less introverted. She had even started dating Robert, Gabriel's best man.

Jewel selected and prepared the other lunch items and played the charming "front man." The doctor had to admit that he enjoyed having Jewel drop by every morning before he left for work and having breakfast with her and Vivian before they started preparing their lunches for the day.

*****

Then, as they moved deeper into autumn, Jewel began stopping by to see the doctor after supper as well. Three or four times a week she would drop in after she had put Marcus to bed, and they would sit on the back porch and sip a little moonshine together and talk about what had happened that day, how Marcus and Django and her mama were doing, the war in Europe.

With the new doctor at the mill and another one on Main Street, as well as the new Negro nurse, Dr. Berber's workload decreased. He had more time to hunt and fish with Marcus and Gator, who had now fully trained his employees so he could do what he really wanted to do. As Django grew stronger, he too would join them occasionally.

One night in October, when it was finally starting to cool down in the evening and the harvest moon was blazing golden through the live oak limbs, Jewel nestled against the doctor in the wicker love seat. He put his arm around her as naturally as leaves to a tree. They sat silently for a while.

"I got some news for you, Doc," Jewel whispered.

"Yeah, what's that?"

"You remember my friend Lily Kate Williamson? Her husband works at the paper mill, cleanin' bathrooms and such."

"Vaguely."

"Well, she told me yesterday that the mill had hired Sally Martin away from the Kenney Mill. Accordin' to Lily Kate's husband, who's as handy as a pocket in a shirt, they hired her to buy up timber rights all over north Florida. They gonna move her and her family to Jacksonville, where the company's headquarters is at."

"Really?"

"That's what Lily Kate said. You still got a thing for the widow?"

The doctor had to think for a minute. He hadn't thought of Sally Martin for a while, and he wasn't sure how he felt about her now. Finally, he said, "No, not anymore. Not after what she and Lucky Lucilla did to us. I was silly to protect her for so long. I'm glad to be rid of her."

"Even if she did save our lives?"

"What do you mean?"

"Who else knew we were at the Kenney Mill that night?"

The doctor thought for a moment.

"You're right," he said.

"And so?"

"It's still over."

"Okay, just checking," Jewel said as she rested her head on the doctor's shoulder. "I knew you was perty stuck on her."

"I was—foolishly—but, really, it's over."

"What about Annie? She's not coming down here to live with you?"

"No. She has a life of her own now in Charleston. Besides, she told me she could tell that I was in love with you."

Jewel was silent, but the doctor felt her breathing quicken. He waited for her to speak, and when she didn't, he whispered in her ear, "Jewel, I can't tell you how much you mean to me. Annie's right. I . . . I do . . ."

"Oh, shut up, Doc," Jewel interrupted, "and kiss me."

And so he did.

Here are some other books from Pineapple Press on related topics. For a complete catalog, write to Pineapple Press, P.O. Box 3889, Sarasota, Florida 34230-3889, or call (800) 746-3275. Or visit our website at www.pineapplepress.com.

Secrets of San Blas by Charles Farley. Most towns have their secrets. In the 1930s, Port St. Joe on the Gulf in Florida's Panhandle has more than its share. Old Doc Berber, the town's only general practitioner, thought he knew all of the secrets, but a grisly murder out at the Cape San Blas Lighthouse drags him into a series of intrigues that even he can't diagnose.

Secrets of St. Vincent by Charles Farley. Things are not always as serene as they seem in the little Florida Panhandle village of Port St. Joe. Bluesman Reggie Robinson has been wrongly arrested for the gruesome murder of Sheriff Byrd "Dog" Batson. Doc Berber and his best friend, Gator Mica, mount a quixotic search for the sheriff's savage killer on equally savage St. Vincent Island. If they survive the adventure, they'll return with the shocking secrets that will shatter the town's tranquility forever.

Conflict of Interest by Terry Lewis. Trial lawyer Ted Stevens fights his own battles, including his alcoholism and his pending divorce, as he fights for his client in a murder case. But it's the other suspect in the case who causes the conflict of interest. Ted must choose between concealing evidence that would be helpful to his client and revealing it, thereby becoming a suspect himself.

Privileged Information by Terry Lewis. Ted Stevens' partner, Paul Morganstein, is defending his late brother's best friend on a murder charge when he obtains privileged information leading him to conclude that his client committed another murder thirty years earlier. The victim? Paul's brother. Faced with numerous difficulties, Paul must decide if he will divulge privileged information.

Delusional by Terry Lewis. Ted Stevens' new client is a mental patient who is either a delusional, psychotic killer or an innocent man framed for the murder of his psychologist—or maybe both. Nathan Hart hears voices and believes that a secret organization known only as the Unit is out to get him. Is the Unit responsible for the murder of Dr. Aaron Rosenberg? Or is something more sinister afoot?

Doctored Evidence by Michael Biehl. A medical device fails and the patient dies on the operating table. Was it an accident—or murder? Smart and courageous hospital attorney Karen Hayes must find out: Her job and her life depend on it.

Lawyered to Death by Michael Biehl. Hospital attorney Karen Hayes is called to defend the hospital CEO against a claim of sexual harassment but soon finds she must also defend him against a murder charge. The trail of clues leads her into a further fight for her own life and that of her infant son.

Nursing a Grudge by Michael Biehl. An elderly nursing home resident, who was once an Olympic champion swimmer with a murky background in the German army, drowns in a lake behind the home. Does anyone know how it happened? Does anyone care? Hospital attorney Karen Hayes battles bureaucracy, listens to the geriatric residents ignored by the authorities, and risks her own life to find the truth.

Seven Mile Bridge by Michael Biehl. Florida Keys dive shop owner Jonathan Bruckner returns home to Wisconsin after his mother's death, searching for clues to his father's death years before. He is stunned by what he discovers about his father's life and comes to know his parents in a way he never did as a child. Mostly, he's surprised by what he learns about himself. Fluidly moving between past and present, between hope and despair, *Seven Mile Bridge* is a story about one man's obsession for the truth and how much can depend on finding it.

Death in Bloodhound Red by Virginia Lanier. Jo Beth Sidden is a Georgia peach with an iron pit. She raises and trains bloodhounds for search-and-rescue missions in the Okefenokee Swamp. In an attempt to save a friend from ruin, she organizes an illegal operation that makes a credible alibi impossible just when she needs one most: She's indicted for attempted murder. If the victim dies, the charge will be murder one.

Mystery in the Sunshine State edited by Stuart Kaminsky. Offers a selection of Florida mysteries from many of Florida's notable writers, including Edna Buchanan, Jeremiah Healy, Stuart McIver, and Les Standiford. Follow professional investigators and amateur sleuths alike as they patiently uncover clues to finally reveal the identity of a killer or the answer to a riddle.

CPSIA information can be obtained at www.ICGtesting.com
Printed in the USA
BVOW07s1746090814

362289BV00003B/5/P